Tease

Amanda Maciel

Hodder
Children's
Books

A division of Hachette Children's Books

A Catalogue record for this book is available from the British Library

ISBN 978 1 444 91871 7

Typeset in Berkeley by Avon DataSet Ltd, Bidford-on-Avon, Warwickshire

Printed and bound by CPI Group (UK) Ltd, Croydon, CR0 4YY

The paper and board used in this paperback by Hodder Children's Books
are natural recyclable products made from wood grown in sustainable forests.
The manufacturing processes conform to the environmental regulations
of the country of origin.

Hodder Children's Books
a division of Hachette Children's Books
338 Euston Road, London NW1 3BH
An Hachette UK company

www.hachette.co.uk

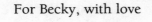
For Becky, with love

July

'Did you ever have a physical confrontation with Miss Putnam?'

'Did what?'

'Did you ever have a—'

'Oh. Yeah. Um, yeah, I guess there was the one time in the locker room.'

The lawyer writes this down, even though the tape recorder is on, has been on the whole time. Also, she already knows the answer to the question. Also, the law firm's intern is taking notes, too. I shouldn't notice how hot he is, but he's the only good thing to look at in here. He's also the only other person anywhere near my age – the lawyers are fortyish and the stenographer lady looks like she's 105 – plus he's new, probably since it's summer now and law school is out for break or whatever. Must be nice. Since the whole . . . *thing* happened, I missed a bunch of junior year, so now I'm in summer school.

And here.

'This was the incident of January the twenty-third?'

This lawyer is all cold and matter-of-fact and wasting everyone's time. She's the head of the firm or something, I don't know. Usually I just meet with Natalie. Who isn't much better, but at least she looks me in the face when we talk. Except today she's *also* taking notes, and somehow barely paying attention at the same time. Maybe they're all just writing their grocery lists or something.

Natalie suddenly looks up at me, raising her eyebrows. Like, *Answer the question*.

'Yeah. I guess so. Was that a Tuesday? You know, because we have gym on Tuesdays and Thursdays, so I think it was a Tuesday.'

The no-eye-contact lawyer nods and then, of course, writes that down. Or she writes down, *toilet paper*, *orange juice*, I don't know. Jesus, this is boring.

Like everything else, this whole process is not at all like it is on TV. I mean, I'm wearing jean shorts right now. There's no dramatic courtroom scene or anything – like, with the afternoon sunlight streaming through big windows while I cry and confess everything on the witness stand or whatever. Apparently you're not even supposed to want to go court at all, though it's gotta beat this, even if it's not pretty or cinematic. We're all sitting in a windowless room with a peeling fake-wood table (which I guess doesn't matter, except I've been staring at it for three hours), and the lights are too bright and the AC is on so high I don't even feel cold anymore, just numb.

I guess I've been numb for a while now.

But I didn't kill anybody.

I sneak another glance at the intern. He's black, with short hair and the smoothest skin ever. It's very dark, and it looks nice against his shirt, which is a bright lilac colour. It reminds me of one of the nail polishes I used to always pick for pedicures, back when going to the salon was no big deal. Before everything was in the newspaper every other day and people at the grocery store started calling me names. Even when I'm just picking up stupid chips and salsa for my little brothers. They've yelled at me in the aisles, said the meanest things.

I never really understood *irony* when Mrs Thale tried to teach us about it in English, but I sure get it now. Now that I get bullied for being a bully. I haven't tried explaining it to the people at the grocery store, though. Mom says that they're morons and I should ignore them, and for once I agree with her.

'Tell us what happened that day.'

Great. Natalie has been making me go through everything all summer, but I still don't like to. Hot Intern is looking at me now, all professional and stone-faced, but I bet if he saw me at the grocery store he'd yell too.

You worthless piece of trash. It should have been you and your friends.

'Um, okay.'

Everyone stops taking notes for a second, and my mouth dries right up. I look down at my feet, my favourite red flip-flops and the stupid silver polish on my toes, and remember how this used to happen in junior high. The year I became friends with Brielle Greggs, eighth grade, I was hopeless. We got paired up in Speech and I was sure she'd hate me when she saw how jittery I got during presentations. I don't like to be the centre of attention.

But Brielle was – still is – fearless. She'd smirk at the whole class and start blabbing on and on about the death penalty or leash laws or whatever random topic we were supposed to give a speech on, and I'd stand there, her mute sidekick. Mr Needy (really, that was his name) would say, 'And Sara, what do you think?' all pointedly. I'd open my desert-dry mouth and nothing would come out, but Brielle would chirp, 'She agrees with me, obviously. She did all the research.' And we'd get an A.

Anyway, now I'm back to dry-mouth-land. And Brielle isn't here. She's doing her own interviews, I guess, somewhere else. With her own lawyers. We're not supposed to talk to each other. And we haven't, not in more than two months.

So here I am, expected to tell the lawyers more bad stuff about Brielle. Because basically, that's what this is all about. Like that stupid day in the locker room . . . that was really Brielle. Everything about what happened to Emma – it wasn't me. I mean, actually, it wasn't any of us. It was Emma. No one hung the rope for her. And even before that, it's not like Emma was innocent. At all. She was the one who—

'Miss Wharton?'

I keep taking these long pauses, I guess. The AC should be keeping us all awake, but it's been at least an hour since I finished the Diet Dr Pepper they gave me and I just feel zonked. I'm still turning the empty bottle over and over in my hands. The wrapper is all loose and saggy and I start to tug it down, like I'm taking off the bottle's clothes. I want to curl up into a ball and sleep for a million years. I sleep a lot these days. It's the easiest way to keep my mom off my case, and to keep from having to explain all of this to my brothers. Like there's any way to explain it to anyone.

I take a deep breath. 'Okay, yeah, so it was a Tuesday. Emma was getting changed. I mean, we were all changing clothes; it was the locker room, we had to get ready for gym.'

Everyone has started scribbling again. I feel itchy, like my skin is too tight. I throw my weight to one side, trying to make the cheap office chair I've been sitting in for all this time more comfortable. No dice. I wonder if the intern thinks I'm pretty, but then I remember that no one does, not anymore. He thinks I'm a monster, just like everyone else. Besides, I'm sure I don't look pretty – in my dumb cutoffs, with my hair pulled back messily, wearing a smidge of mascara. It's been hard to eat much lately so I feel sort of thin, but not in a good way.

I glance at Natalie and go on. 'Brielle asked Emma why she, you know – why she was talking to Dylan so much.'

'Mr Howe?'

5

I carefully don't roll my eyes. 'Yeah, Dylan Howe. My boyfriend. At the time.'

And now, my ex-boyfriend. Mostly. Or something.

'And what did Miss Putnam say?'

I shift to the other side of the chair. 'She didn't say anything. I mean, by that point she knew Brielle was mad at her.'

'And why do you say that?' The lawyer I don't really know isn't even looking up while she talks to me. I scowl at her hair; it's that shade of blonde that older women think is young-looking but actually just makes them look even older and more out of date than being, like, grey-haired would.

'*Every*one was mad at her. Everyone knew she was texting all these boys all the time and that she was totally obsessed with Dylan. Brielle thought she was a psycho, and so did everyone else.'

My voice goes up and Hot Intern is looking at me kind of sharply. It's been a long time since I talked to new people about all this, and I kind of forgot how much people hate me. Even Natalie gives this little sigh, like she's sick of my crap.

But it's *not* crap. Everyone thought Emma Putnam was a pain in the ass. We didn't kill her, but I'm sorry, that doesn't mean we liked her. And now that everyone's decided we *did* kill her, or at least sort of, I think I like her even less than I did when she was alive.

'And what did you and Miss Greggs do?'

6

I don't answer right away, but she still doesn't look at me. 'Brielle called her a bitch,' I say. 'And I guess I sort of shoved her. A little.'

'You pushed her up against the lockers, is that right?'

'I guess.'

'And what did Miss Putnam do?'

'Nothing.'

'Nothing?'

'I mean, I guess she was crying.' *She was* always *crying*, I want to add, but Natalie told me not to 'embellish', to just answer the questions as simply as possible.

'You guess?'

'She was crying, okay?'

'And what did you say to her?'

Sigh. 'I told her to stay away from my boyfriend.'

'Did you say anything else?'

'What?'

'We have testimony that you . . .' The crappy-shade-of-blonde head turns toward Hot Intern and he hands her a piece of paper with a bunch of writing on it. 'Yes, here. You called her a slut?'

'Okay.'

'Did you call Miss Putnam a slut?'

'Um, I guess so.'

'You don't remember?'

'I mean, I don't remember calling her a slut *that day*.' I do remember pushing Emma against the lockers. Her dark-red hair wasn't pulled back yet and it settled in those

7

annoyingly pretty curls around her shoulders as she sort of scrunched up defensively, wincing and crying in that helpless-little-girl way that just made me angrier. She whimpered a little, I remember that. She held up her hands slightly, either like she was surrendering or finally starting to protect herself – I don't know which. Or maybe I do. I guess it was surrender.

This would all be *embellishing*, though, so I don't say it.

'Do you mean you called her a slut on another occasion?'

'I mean, I thought she was a slut. I'm sure I called her a slut. I don't know if I called her a slut on *January the twenty-third*.'

Everyone stops writing and looks at me, stunned and silent. My heart is pounding. I can't meet anyone's eye. I just stare at the table, wishing I could disappear.

'We need a break,' Natalie says. The first helpful thing she's said all morning. 'Let's take ten.'

The blonde lawyer nods, looking like she'd love to be anywhere but stuck in an ugly conference room with me. Maybe she won't come back – maybe I'll be able to go home.

Instead, I walk stiffly into the slightly less cold hallway, waiting for the feeling to come back to my toes. There are chairs out here, set up in a waiting area, but no one is waiting for me. I drove myself.

'Sara,' Natalie hisses. 'You need to calm down in there. It's just a few more questions, and it's *important*.'

I nod automatically and pace over to the window. It

overlooks the office park parking lot. The sun glares off the windshields of row after row of nondescript four-doors. You can tell how hot it is just by looking, but I have gooseflesh on my arms.

I start silently counting all the white cars while my lawyer keeps talking at me. There are a ton, including mine, which I can't see from here because I parked on the other side. I see a silver Mercedes just like Brielle's and remember how her tyres got slashed, back when we were all first on the news. Maybe she has a new car now. I shove my hands into my shorts pockets. There's a gum wrapper on the right side and I knead it into a little ball.

Natalie finally shuts up for a minute, just as I get to sixteen white cars. When she speaks again, I hear her. I mean, I forget to block out her voice out, so it gets in.

'We're trying to get you out of this. A girl is dead, and everyone wants to hold you and your friends accountable for what happened.'

'But we're *not*,' I blurt out. 'We didn't *do* anything.'

'It's not that simple.'

'It should be.'

Natalie heaves a big sigh. 'I know, but it's just not. People are sad and angry and they just want to see how sorry you are.'

But that's the thing right there.

I'm *not* sorry.

Emma was a boyfriend-stealing bitch right up until the day in March when she killed herself.

I didn't do anything wrong, but she totally ruined my life.

By the time I get back to my old Honda Accord, it's basically an oven inside. The dark upholstery soaked up every minute of sunshine, so even though I'm finally free from the damn interrogation room, I can't leave yet – I have to stand around with the doors open and the fans turned on full blast, waiting for the seats to cool down enough to just sit. I lean carefully against the back door, making sure none of my skin touches the metal, and check my phone. All I have is a text from my mom about picking up milk and an unfinished game on my Free Cell app.

I'm supposed to go to the therapist now, and then home to do summer schoolwork. This is seriously the funnest summer *ever*. And people wonder why I'm not crying about Emma all the time.

I wonder what Brielle told her lawyers about the locker room thing. Everyone seems to know a version of something by now. Most of the school has been interviewed by *someone*, and there were a lot of people in that locker room, and at school with us, and at the other schools Emma went to. Well, maybe not a *lot* in the locker room. Not a teacher, anyway. Not the one girl Emma had been sort of friends with, Megan Corley. Megan is kind of slutty too, and they didn't always get along. Since March Megan's been everywhere, including on a trip to New York to be on the *Today* show with her mom. I guess Brielle and I weren't very nice to Megan, either, because she's basically called us murderers on national television.

And now the whole world thinks Emma Putnam killed herself because we called her a slut – not because she *was* a slut. That makes sense.

Waving my hand around in the car, I decide it's safe to at least sit on the edge of the front seat. Sweat is starting to make my shirt stick to my back and I aim one of the vents toward it, but there's not much point.

The real mistake I'm making, at least according to Natalie, is acting like I don't care that we were mean to Emma. No matter how much I try to explain that Emma did her share of crap to us, that it wasn't this big conspiracy like the papers keep saying, it doesn't matter. So now I have a lawyer, Brielle has a lawyer, the guys have their lawyers. We're all blaming each other. No one's blaming Emma for anything.

My chances of graduating on time are slim to none. I might never get into college. But if I'm more careful, if I work hard and do what Natalie says and *be sorry*, things might be okay, even if we go to trial.

That's what they all say. But it's not like I was ever getting into Harvard or anything. I wasn't such a great student before all this. And I'm not saying I was a great person, either. It's just – it's like Brielle said, after it happened: Emma got off easy. Everyone keeps saying she's not here to defend herself – but I'm here, and it seriously sucks. It's like, someone dies, so everyone left alive is automatically guilty.

Except, in this case, only five of us are. And with all the separate lawyers and charges, my best hope is to just avoid taking *all* the blame.

After another minute of the car not cooling down, I sigh and pull my red-flip-flopped feet in, yank the door shut, and try to steer out of the parking space with my fingertips. Muttering every curse word I know, I almost don't see the person walking up to the passenger-side window until she's tapping on it.

'Gah!' I scream, slamming on the brakes and accidentally grabbing the wheel. My hands are instantly scorched and I curse again.

Outside the car I hear, 'God, you skank, you almost ran me over!'

Brielle.

I put the car back into park right where it is, halfway out of the space, and jump out again. Sweat is pouring down my back and my neck now, but Brielle looks fresh as a daisy. She's actually wearing a loose white tank top with daisy cutouts around the hem.

'Hey,' she says easily, like we haven't just spent a solid ten weeks not speaking. I haven't even been able to Facebook-stalk her – Natalie made my mom shut down my account. Which was just as well; if I thought the people at the grocery store were mean, I was completely unprepared for what they'd be like online. I probably should've closed the account myself, instead of staying up

12

until two a.m. Every night, looking at how many insanely mean comments people posted under any and all photos I was tagged in. Hundreds of mean things, millions. A lot of dislike out there.

'Hi,' I say lamely. I must look like a nutjob, almost driving into her and then jumping out of my car like it's on fire. Pulling my shirt out a little, to let some air in between it and my back, I try to smile at my (former?) BFF and say something normal. 'Your, um – your lawyer's office is here, too?' I guess I was right; that must've been her SUV I saw.

'Uch, yeah,' she says. She tilts her head to the side and shrugs, her perfect beach hair falling over her shoulders in its perfectly highlighted, slight messy waves. I resist the urge to touch my unintentionally messy ponytail.

She looks like maybe she's put on a little weight, though, and she isn't as tan as I would've expected for this far into the summer. The Greggses have a huge pool in their backyard, so usually Brielle and I are both pretty dark by the time school starts in the fall. Maybe I'm not the only one who's been spending all her time inside, watching TV or sleeping.

'This whole thing is such bullshit,' she says. She doesn't actually sound worried. Just tired. Or maybe . . . Is she stoned? I actually open my mouth to ask before thinking better of it. 'Oh,' she goes on, waving her hand like she's daintily chasing away a fly, 'I guess we're not supposed to talk.'

When she says that her voice gets an edge to it, like it

13

was my idea not to talk and she's mad at me. 'I—' I start to say, then stop. Suddenly I miss my best friend so much – so much it feels like a physical pain, like the heat that's still trapped in my hands after grabbing the sunbaked steering wheel. 'How are you?' I finally manage.

'Well, I'm *fat*,' she says with a dry laugh. She's not fat, of course. I'm shaking my head and she adds, 'No, I totally am. I can't, like, go to the gym any more, my parents are being total Hitlers. God, Emma really fucked everything up, right?'

She rolls her eyes in that dramatic way she always has and I nod, totally agreeing. God, what a relief, after all this time, to know she's still there, she still gets how hard this is, she doesn't hate me—

I want to walk around the car, to reach out and just hug her – even though we never really do that – but I haven't moved an inch before her face changes completely, goes totally back to that casual, not-a-care-in-the-world expression.

'Blah blah blah,' she says, shaking out her hands at her sides, shaking it all off. She's definitely stoned. '*You* look skinny, you whore.'

I look down, trying not to smile or be too flattered. 'Thanks,' I say, but my voice is too quiet. A little louder I add, 'You look great, really. It's nice to see you.'

'Yeah, right – so nice you almost hit me with your car!' she says with a laugh. The edge is back in her voice, and I don't know what I said wrong. 'Anyway, you're leaving,

I just wanted to say hi. So, you know, hi. And bye! Ha!'

And just like that, before I can even say 'Hi' – or 'Bye' – back, Brielle has disappeared into the rows of cars.

When I get back into my car, I just turn the AC off. It feels better to be too hot. I feel like I'm suffocating, anyway, and what difference does it make if it's hard to breathe? It's always hard to breathe now. I haven't had a good, deep breath in months.

January

'I'm telling you – she must've gotten his number from someone else's phone. Like probably Tyler—'

'Bullshit. Jesus, Sara, you are so naive when you want to be.'

I pull up my chemistry book protectively, as if covering my boobs will make what Brielle is saying not true. As if I could just curl up and pretend that my boyfriend, Dylan, who is the best thing that's ever happened to me, isn't getting texts from another girl. And that I don't know this because I didn't find one.

'You don't have to whip out the vocab words,' I tell my alleged best friend, but she's rolling her eyes at me.

'Okay, fine, you're a dumb bitch – is that better?' She starts walking toward Chem and I trail after her. She struts past a group of senior guys and they all nod hello, turning to keep watching even after she's nodded back. 'You know they're in Language Arts together,' she's saying to me, 'And you know she keeps hooking up with Jacob *and* Tyler, and you know she's a dirty skank. Don't assume she's not creeping up on your man.'

'But he doesn't even know her!' I hate the squeak in my voice. I hate the tears that choke up behind my eyes. I already cried about this last night; I don't need Brielle and the whole world to see me break down now, in the middle of the hallway.

But suddenly Brielle turns and looks so sorry for me that I really do almost cry again.

'Oh, honey,' she says kindly. 'It's not Dylan's fault, I know that! He's just a stupid boy. Of course he loves you. But boys don't know how to deal with sluts like Emma Putnam. He's used to nice girls like you!'

She gives me a lightning-quick hug, crushing my textbook to my chest, then holds my shoulders for a second before letting go. I give her a little smile, trying to seem like I'm not falling apart over this.

'It's Emma,' she goes on, leading the way into Chem lab. 'Trash needs to be taken *out*, for *reals*. Who knew a sophomore could be such a freaking pain in my ass?'

I grunt in agreement as we sit down at our table. Our lab partners, Jeff Marsh and Seamus O'Leary (Brielle calls him Irish O'Irish), are already perched on the stools across from us, and we smirk at them. They aren't exactly the coolest guys in school, but they usually do most of the work in this class and let us copy their answers. I'm actually better at chemistry than either one of them – or I was at the beginning of the year, anyway. I only have two classes with

17

Brielle this semester, so we *need* to spend the whole time talking. I don't think my grades are gonna be so hot in Chem or PE this term, but at least Jeff and Seamus will keep me from failing this class.

I have two classes with Emma, too – American History and PE – even though she's a year younger. For some reason the school she transferred from back in October has American History as a sophomore class. So Elmwood decided she should keep taking it, which messed up her schedule for gym, blah blah blah. She's already dated a bunch of juniors and she's always trying to suck up to the girls in our class too. Everyone knows she's a head case, always starting pointless drama. Brielle pretty much hated her at first sight.

'So. Irish,' Brielle says, pointing a beaker at Seamus. 'Is your brother getting us that keg this weekend?'

This is the first I've heard of Seamus having a connection, and I raise my eyebrows at him hopefully. The party is going to be at Brielle's house while her parents are on a cruise to Bermuda. As far as I knew we were just going to steal what we could from their liquor cabinet, and maybe some beer from Alison Stipe's dad's basement fridge. And I didn't think Seamus or Jeff were even invited.

'Aye, me lassie,' Seamus says in a thick brogue. He loves that Brielle gave him a nickname and he always plays along. Boys love Brielle in general – she's got that rich-girl shine, with the superlong hair and the Abercrombie wardrobe, but she's also so ballsy and bossy that boys never get bored around her. She laughs at their jokes before they even realize they've made any. Because she actually makes the jokes for them.

It's pretty amazing to watch, but basically impossible to imitate. I've tried.

'Groovy,' she says, flashing him what anyone would think was a genuine smile. Then she swings her hair back around, shutting him out.

She looks me in the eye and goes, 'We need to resume our discussion of *the party*.'

Ah, yes. The discussion. The debate, more like, over whether I should lose my virginity to Dylan *at the party* – or, like, *after* the party, I guess, possibly in Brielle's guest room – or not.

I've been kind of leaning toward *not*, but ever since Brielle lost her V-card last summer with a college guy at her swim camp, she only wants to talk about my sex life. Or lack thereof. I never met the guy she was with, but I saw pictures, and now I totally see why she's always complaining about how lame high school boys are.

Still, it's easy for her to say – she's the brave one. And the one who's already had more than one real boyfriend, even if they have been the lame high school variety. Dylan is basically my first, and I kind of feel like I'm still getting the hang of just making out with him. He's older, he knows what he's doing. He'll know that I *don't* know what I'm doing. It sounds like a good idea, and I know everyone does it, but when I'm actually with Dylan and everything,

I don't know. It's freaking scary.

But like I said, Brielle doesn't get scared, and even if she did, I wouldn't know how to explain why I am. And just like in eighth grade, Brielle has a killer argument ready:

'He obviously won't be texting Emma Sluts-a-lot if he's getting the good stuff from *you*,' she whispers, snorting a little at her new nickname creation.

I don't get a chance to come up with a counterpoint for this, because Ms Enman shows up and we have to pretend to pay attention for a few minutes.

As soon as Ms Enman turns back to the dry-erase board, though, I hear Brielle say in a low, singsong voice, 'You know you want to!'

My mom works at a big insurance company and is never around after school, so I'm in charge of making sure my little brothers, who really aren't that little anymore, eat something and do at least enough of their homework to not flunk fifth and sixth grades, respectively. I kind of like that there's a bigger age gap between us – for one thing, I got to enjoy being an only child for a while, and most of that time was before my parents started hating each other. I think they had Tommy (who wants to be called Tom) and Alex (who wants to be called A-rod) to try to feel like a real family again. But it didn't work. About five seconds after Alex was born, Dad moved out and I got promoted to full-time babysitter–slash–co-parent.

But the boys are cool. They love it when I pick them up

from their after-school stuff, which is sometimes a sport and sometimes, like today, just an extra study period at the elementary school. Volunteers from the university come over and help with their homework, so half my job is done by the time I pull around the Pleasant Hill Elementary circular drive.

Tommy, the sixth grader, flops into the backseat after losing a shove-match with fifth grader Alex, who's gotten kind of husky in the last couple of months. Maybe I'm not helping. I mean, like, today, as soon as they're in the car I go, 'Whoever can find some loose change in here gets to pick between Taco Bell and McDonald's!' and then I get practically slammed into the steering wheel as Tommy dives onto the back floor and his head shoves into my seat.

Alex opens the glove compartment and starts tossing out pieces of paper and crap I didn't know was even in there. 'Yeah!' he yells. 'A dollar bill!'

'How the *hell*, Alex?' I say, but I'm smiling.

'Ta-co Bell! How the hell! Ta-co Bell!' he chants triumphantly.

'Dude, language,' I say, but by now we're both laughing. Even Tommy's face is just a big grin in my rearview mirror.

Luckily for the whole childhood-obesity deal, we still only have enough for everyone to get one taco each, so it's not like we're having an extra dinner there. And I make them go into the restaurant, so there's some exercise involved too. If walking across a parking lot counts.

We take our tacos to a booth next to the windows, even

though the winter sun is almost gone and it's cold over here. Alex and I put mild sauce on our food, while Tommy opens about nine packets of the hottest kind and then tries to pour some onto Alex's too.

'Quit it!' Alex cries, shoving Tommy back to his side of the bench seat.

'Wuss!' Tommy yells, shoving back.

'Come on, guys,' I say, licking a stray piece of lettuce off my finger. 'Would you just—' I don't finish because they're still shoving, so instead of trying to reason with them I just get up, grab Tommy's arm, and pull him out of his side of the booth. Pushing him around and onto the bench I was just sitting on, I flop myself down next to Alex and slide my taco across the table. 'Okay?' I ask, a little out of breath from the whole manoeuvre. 'Can we eat?'

Alex smirks at Tommy, but luckily, once he's yanked his food over to his new seat, Tommy just smirks back.

'How's Dylan's fastball?' Alex asks me.

I smile. Alex is obsessed with my boyfriend. I guess I can relate.

Dylan's always been pretty much varsity across the board, but now that he's a senior he's super committed to being really, really good so he can secure some college scholarships. These days all he does is practise for baseball tryouts. He really wants to be a starting pitcher this year. Or is it a closing pitcher? I guess I've only been half listening – I mean, when we're alone, we don't talk that much.

The day after Christmas Dylan came over, and since it

was freakishly warm outside, he took Alex out to the backyard and practised with him. So now my ten-year-old brother always wants to talk about Dylan's pitches. Tommy will be twelve in April, and he usually acts like he's too cool to be impressed by his sister's boyfriend. But he gets pretty interested too.

'I think it's good, bud,' I tell Alex. 'The season starts soon, so you can come to a game with me and see for yourself.'

Alex does a little hop on his seat while Tommy asks, 'I can come too, right?'

'Of course,' I say. I hope Dylan's ready for a tweenage fan club.

I'm still not sure why Dylan Howe wanted to go out with me in the first place. We got thrown together a few times last fall because Brielle was dating another guy on the basketball team, Rob. I'd always thought Dylan was gorgeous – it's more like a fact than an opinion – so at first I had a hard time not acting like a complete idiot around him. If I could talk to boys my own age as easily as I talk to my brothers, things would be so much easier. Well, maybe – Alex and Tommy talk a lot about farting. I've hooked up with guys at parties and stuff, but nothing ever seems to happen, nothing official. For most of sophomore year I thought I was in love with Parker Anderson, and we had this whole texting affair. But it was only the texts. At school Parker totally ignored me, and finally Brielle convinced me that I had to ignore him back.

So anyway, if Brielle hadn't been dating Rob, I wouldn't have gotten anywhere near Dylan Howe.

And then one night over Thanksgiving break, a bunch of us snuck over to the Pleasant Hill playground. Brielle and Alison were drinking peach schnapps and acting all crazy, jumping off the slide and stuff. I was on the swings, which had always been my favourite. Suddenly, Dylan sat down on the swing next to mine. He'd had a couple of the beers the guys brought, and I could smell the hops and sweat and just general boy-scent on him, all mixed in with the cold air and that dead-leaf-autumn smell. Somehow I actually started talking to him, like a semi-normal person. And then out of nowhere he just pulled the chains of my swing over toward his and started kissing me.

It was the most exciting thing that's ever happened to me in my entire life.

Dylan has these really strong hands, like *man* hands, and with one holding my swing and the other wrapped around my waist . . . I can't even think about it now without feeling my heart speed up, my blood pulsing in my ears. That night I even reached up and put one hand on the side of his face. Like we were kissing in a movie or something. I was just so stunned, and I was thinking, *This might be the only time I have a chance to do this*, and suddenly I felt so daring and confident and – God, I don't know, maybe kind of sexy? His face was really soft, with just a little bit of stubble along his jaw. The tips of my fingers brushed against the line of his hair, under his ear.

I wanted it to go on forever. But after a few minutes Rob yelled to him from across the playground and Dylan let go of me. 'See you later,' he said, and left. Just walked away, with me dizzy and swinging sideways, the chains squealing in protest as I tried not to pass out.

Who knows what would have happened after that if Brielle hadn't intervened. She told Rob to tell Dylan to text me, and he did. I started sitting right behind the team with Brielle at every basketball game. And I started making out with him a lot more, mostly in his SUV after those games, his hair still wet from the locker room showers.

Around Christmas, Dylan started pulling at my pants while we kissed. Sometimes he'll bring my hands to his belt, too, but any confidence I might have in kissing him just disappears when he does that. Usually I just kind of kiss him harder and at the same time my hands sort of go limp, like they don't work anymore. He's a gentleman, he's never pushed me. But it's gotten pretty clear what he thinks is going to happen next.

Brielle broke up with Rob right after she caught him flirting with Emma Putnam at the holiday dance. Emma went to the dance without a date and wore this crazy low-cut red dress, so half the room was staring at her already. I mean, everyone knows the holiday dance isn't that formal. It was kind of sad to see her show up like it was the Oscars or something.

Honestly I don't think Brielle minded it *that* much when Rob spent too long at the soda table with overdressed

Emma. It gave her an excuse to dump a cup of Coke on Rob and call Emma a whore, loudly, and that's the kind of scene Brielle lives for.

'Can we get another taco?' Alex whines. I realize I've been staring out the window, watching the sky get dark and completely ignoring my brothers.

'Sorry, little dude,' I say, standing up and grabbing my coat. 'All out of cash. But it's cream-of-mushroom chicken night at home!' I say this part as enthusiastically as possible, but both boys are groaning as they put their coats back on.

It's fully dark outside and the wind is brutal. For a second I'm too cold to remember what I was worrying about, and then, two cars over, I see a flash of red. Emma Putnam is getting out of the passenger side of a dark SUV. I can't see who the driver is, but I see Emma's hair right away, lit up like a fire under the streetlight.

Suddenly Emma turns and looks over at me. At first I think she's going to wave, but that would be weird, since she knows I'm Brielle's best friend. And, um, Dylan's girlfriend. She doesn't wave, though. She looks confused for a second.

And for no reason I could ever explain in a million years, I flip up my middle finger at her. I've never done that before – not for real, not in a non-joking way – and it feels really strange. And kind of cheesy. But at the same time it feels really, like, *powerful*.

I hold it up so I'm sure she sees, and watch as her mouth

drops open in surprise.

Then I duck into my car and drive my brothers home.

And I can't stop smiling.

'So what was that text about?'

'Mmmph.'

'I just' – pant – 'It's not that' – *oof* – 'I mean, I totally *trust* you—'

'Wait, what? What's going on?'

Dylan pulls away from kissing my neck and looks at me like I have three heads. His lips are red and a little puffy and his eyes are heavy, like he just woke up – or, I guess, like he's been wrestling me in the back of his SUV for twenty minutes, because he has. He's gotten my shirt off and the button of my jeans undone, and I feel ridiculous, sitting there in my bra. But at least we've slowed down for a second.

'What're you talking about?' he says. Not meanly. Just confused. Which makes sense. I mean, what *am* I talking about? Why did I think this would be a good time to get all insecure and bring up the Emma thing?

'I'm sorry,' I say. I sort of pet his forearms in what I hope is a cute, sexy way, and smile. 'I just, you know, I didn't know you and Emma were . . . friends.'

'We're not,' he says simply, and I guess that's all he has to say on the subject, because he lunges at me again, pinning me back onto the seat. For a second I feel warm and fluttery, and then the pulling-at-my-pants action starts

27

again, and I kind of tense up and go limp all at the same time.

Dylan's mouth leaves mine suddenly, because he's looking down, trying to figure out why my favourite pair of jeans, which are bright pink and practically glow-in-the-dark on this cloudy winter afternoon, aren't going where he wants them to go. This makes it possible for me to take another deep breath and say, 'God, she's just the worst. I'm so sorry she's, like, bothering you.'

That's the right thing to say, right? A pathetic girl who gets insecure about every little thing and drives her boyfriend nuts would never say that, would she? I'm not the jealous type. I'm *not*. But Emma Putnam is . . . stunning. There, I said it, whatever. The bitch is freaking gorgeous. She has all this long red hair with the perfect amount of curl; her skin never seems to break out into anything but a pinkish blush when someone is nice to her (which is always a boy, and therefore *never* a girl); her boobs are big but not *too* big. She's always laughing or smiling or flirting with someone. It's not really a surprise that I can't stop thinking about that damn text I found on Dylan's phone. Even if she weren't also a total skank, I'd still be worried.

He'd handed his phone to me so I could write to his friend Kyle that we were on our way to his house last Friday. Dylan is super careful about not texting and driving, partly because he knows it's not safe, but also (probably mostly) because you get suspended from sports if you get caught doing it. And you don't even have to be actually arrested, just get caught by a coach or something.

So anyway, I'd turned on the phone and the last message had popped up and I blurted out before I could think better of it, 'You got a text from Emma? Emma *Putnam*?'

'I guess,' he said, and then he went, 'Oh, dude, call Kyle and put him on speaker, I need to ask him something about practice.' And we'd never gotten around to talking about it for real.

At the top of the screen it just said EMMA. The text was LOL! with one of those dumb laughing emoji faces.

Which meant there was a text before it. But I didn't have time to see the earlier one, and it's not like I could go snooping through Dylan's phone, right there in the car, to look at the rest of the conversation.

And now I've opened my stupid mouth about it again. Twice.

He stops looking at my waistband for a second to smile up at me. 'Ooooh,' he mocks. 'Somebody's jealous!'

'No, I'm not!' I squeal.

'I think it's cute,' he says, and just like that, we're back to kissing.

He thinks it's cute! I'm going to stop worrying now. Besides, my problem is with Emma, not Dylan. Like Brielle said yesterday, it's Emma's fault she's a slut, not my boyfriend's.

But still, Dylan stops trying to get my jeans off after that, and I'm a little worried. Maybe Brielle is right about the

29

party, too . . . Maybe I need to make sure Dylan isn't thinking about anyone but me.

'Emma Putnam called you a tease.'

'*What?*'

Over the phone Brielle almost sounds like she's gloating, like she's just won something. I wish she would've just texted this to me like a normal person. Then I could hyperventilate in private.

'Jacob told me. Apparently she was flirting with him *again*, isn't that pathetic? He was totally laughing about it.' Brielle snorts.

'And?' I press her.

'Oh. So, yeah, Jacob asked her about texting Dylan, because I'd been asking Jacob about it—'

'You *what*?!'

'Yeah, you knew that! Whatever, we sit next to each other in *Español*, it's *muy* boring. So *any*way, Jacob was like, "I heard you're all creeping up on Dylan Howe," and Emma, like, giggled and goes, "He has a girlfriend," and Jacob's like, "yeah, maybe you should back off," and Emma goes – I'm not even kidding – "Maybe he should go out with someone who isn't a total *tease*."'

I just sit there with my mouth hanging open for what feels like an hour.

Jacob had a girlfriend too, before Emma came along. He's also a huge player, but that didn't make it any less crappy for Noelle Reese when he cheated on her and then broke up with her. He didn't even end up going out with Emma for real; it was just a couple of weeks of hooking up. And then, like, one more week. It's weird, but Emma's like that – guys want to hook up with her, but no one really wants to be the official boyfriend of the slutty girl.

I can't believe she's even talking about me. My whole head feels like it's on fire, I'm so mad.

'I. Am. Going. To. *Kill her*.' My voice is very quiet. It even sounds scary to me.

'Lady, I am going to *help you*.'

We spend another hour on the phone and on Facebook at the same time. Brielle makes up a profile for 'Fat Beyotch' and steals one of Emma's photos for it. She gives me the password so we can both go on to Emma's page and tag all the pictures of her with the fake name. Then I start friending everyone we hang out with. Brielle and I are laughing so hard at the image of Jacob, Tyler, and Kyle getting Emma's picture with her new name attached.

'Send it to Dylan!' Brielle cries. 'No, hang on, I've got it—'

'No!' I shout, but she's still howling and I don't think she heard me. 'Brie, *don't*!'

'Why? He'll think it's hilarious. Oh my God, why haven't we done this before?'

But suddenly it's not that funny anymore. Dylan is Facebook friends with basically everyone at school, but I haven't checked to see if Emma is on there too. Up until a couple of days ago it didn't even occur to me to check. And now . . . I don't even want him to be friends with Fake Emma. I don't want him thinking about her at all.

'We're gonna get in trouble for this,' I say quietly, my stomach suddenly tight.

'God, no, we're *not*,' Brielle says. 'The administrator might shut it down or whatever, but no one's gonna know it was us – and who cares? If they do, we'll just tell them to take a stupid *joke*. And she started it, anyway.'

Right. She did. I think about earlier that day, messing around in Dylan's SUV, and cringe. Am I a tease? Is that worse than being a slut? Does *Dylan* think it's worse?

'She totally deserves this,' Brielle goes on, 'And honestly I'm surprised no one's done it before. Or, you know, something like it. She needs to keep her skanky paws off everybody's boyfriends already.'

'Yeah,' I say, but I push away from my computer and flop back on my bed. Revenge is exhausting.

'Huh, I wonder if we should start a fan page, too, like a Boycott Emma Putnam thing . . .' Brielle seems to be talking to herself about this, so I just grunt noncommittally. A group page doesn't seem like as much fun – not that this seems like that much fun any more either. A minute ago I was really into it, but now I just feel kind of nauseous.

'But seriously,' Brielle is saying, 'what's going on with you and the D-Bag?'

'Don't *call* him that!' I wail, but it's never any use – Brielle thinks her nickname for Dylan is extra hilarious. She's laughing about it right now, in fact.

Finally she gets over herself and goes, 'Okay, okay, *Dyyyllllan*. You gonna rock his world tomorrow, or what?'

I haven't told her about that afternoon in the back of Dylan's car, but now I think about that feeling I had. The feeling that it's basically now or never, that I can only keep pushing his hands away for so long. And maybe I'm ready too – I mean, if I don't do it with Dylan, who am I waiting for? He's going to graduate and go to the university an hour away and meet college girls and I'll just . . . I don't know. Be a virgin forever?

'I mean, you don't want Emma to be *right*,' Brielle adds.

I'm used to Brielle being harsh, but this is kind of a lot, even for her. I open my mouth to say something, but nothing comes out.

'Come on,' she says when I've paused a little too long, 'You know what I mean! He is *totally* hot. And he's been super patient with you, right? For like two months! That's like ten million in hot-boy years.'

'Just because I'm not a slut like Emma doesn't make me a *tease*,' I protest, finally.

'Well, I mean, he's your boyfriend . . .' Brielle says. 'So it *kinda* does.'

July

'I don't want to talk about it.'

'You don't want to talk about what?'

'About any of it. No one cares what I think, anyway.'

'They don't?'

Therapist Teresa looks at me over her reading glasses. She has glossy black hair and this ridiculously smooth light-brown skin, and she wears weird, colourful scarves all the time, even when it's blazing hot outside like it is today. She's always very pretty and colourful – but jeez, what a pain in the ass with the questions. I can't say *anything* without it coming back at me with a big question mark tacked on the end.

I sigh loudly to let her know I'm on to her trick. 'It's just – whatever I tell them, whatever I say, it's all, just, like, what's the point, you know?'

'What's the point?'

'Yeah, what's the point, when everyone's decided what happened already?'

'Everyone has decided what happened?'

I throw my arms up in frustration. 'Me and my friends! everyone thinks we're assholes – sorry – and that Emma was all innocent and sweet and shit – *sorry* – and even if I say everything right and it all magically goes away, I still can't pump gas into my f— my *freaking* car without getting *harasse*d or – whatever.'

Teresa doesn't yell at me for cursing or anything, but I don't usually do it in front of grown-ups. It feels weird that she just sits there, nodding, not reacting really at all. And then, of course:

'What would be the right "everything" for you to say?'

I sigh again and put my hands over my face, hiding my eyes. I didn't want to go to a stupid therapist, obviously. And when these sessions started, a few weeks after we had to get a lawyer and the lawyer said we had to get a therapist, I didn't talk at all. Sometimes Teresa actually gets me to start blabbing on and on about the lawyers and my mom and all the crap that is my life now. I mean, there have been a couple of times that I actually talked to her about stuff. But I still hate it. I hate that I have so much *stuff* to talk *about*. And zero people in my life who will listen to me talk. Besides this courtordered therapist.

Or, whatever, lawyer-recommended. Big difference.

Too late, I realize I'm probably smudging the hell out of my mascara, whatever might be left after all the sweating I did on the way here. I lower my hands and carefully run my fingers under my eyes, like you would if you were brushing away tears. Except as usual, my cheeks are perfectly dry.

'I guess, you know, all the stuff they want me to say – that I'm sorry, that we should've been nicer to her.'

'And you can't say that?'

'That it's my fault she killed herself? No.' We've kind of talked about this before, but Teresa always acts like whatever I've said is a brand-new thought.

'But you did call her names,' Teresa says. For once, not a question.

'Yeah, a *couple*. But everyone did that. She called me names too!'

'She called you names?'

I shake my head. This is exactly what I didn't feel like talking about.

'Okay,' she says, settling back in her seat. 'I hear you saying that everyone at school was pretty tough on Emma.'

I nod. Then I add, 'On everyone. I mean, it's high school. You say stuff, people say stuff.'

'It's normal, calling each other *bitch* or *slut*.'

With a shrug I say, 'If someone's acting like one.'

It's Teresa's turn to nod. 'But you and your friends – people think you took it too far.'

'Yeah, I guess,' I say. I stare at my hands, then tuck them under my thighs. It's cold in here. All summer it's been getting colder, the AC cranked up higher all the time. I should bring a sweater. Or at least stop wearing shorts

36

everywhere. I wish I had a tan. I wish I wasn't sitting here.
I wish—

'Why do you think that is?'

I look up at Teresa again and just stare at her. 'Why do
you keep asking me dumb questions?' I snap. 'Do you
think I'm an idiot?'

A little furrow puckers between her eyebrows and
she looks stung, but just for a moment. I wonder, not for
the first time, how old Teresa is. Not old enough to be a
good therapist. Not young enough to remember being in
high school.

She shakes her head just slightly and says, 'I'm trying
to lead you through all of these questions, these things
other people see that you don't seem to see. Does that
make sense?'

'No,' I say flatly. It doesn't.

'I think if you could understand where everyone is
coming from – Emma's parents, the lawyers, the kids at
school . . .' She holds her hands out, gesturing wide as if
she's talking about the whole world. 'You're not alone, you
know. But you're very closed off. You're in your own world,
and no one can understand what that's like unless you let
them in.' She pulls her hands back together, forming a little
space between her palms. My little world.

I shake my head. Then I shake it again. Then I stand up,
grabbing my bag from the couch.

'I have to come here, fine. I talk to you, I talk to Natalie.
But it's not my fault that you don't understand. It's not my

37

fault that the reporters are a bunch of idiots, that Emma's parents were obviously totally crappy. I just want my life back. Maybe it was stupid, but it was mine.' I point to her hands, still cupped together, and add, 'And it was bigger than that.'

We stare at each other silently for a minute. Teresa looks at me steadily, and I bet she thinks this is good, that she's proving some point right now. I want to tell her she's wrong, but I'm tired of talking, of fighting, of defending myself.

So I shake my head one last time, and then I walk right past her chair and out the door.

Alex has been at baseball camp this whole week, and Tommy's at a regular one, so the house is cold and empty when I get home from Therapist Teresa. My car hadn't gotten any cooler during my hour of interrogation, so I'm all sweaty again, and the cool air in the house is a relief. So is the shower; as soon as I'm upstairs I just strip, dump my clothes where I'm walking in the hall, and get right into the water.

It's so embarrassing to be seeing a therapist. A lot of people at school do it, but not very many of them admit it – and only, like, one or two don't seem totally pathetic when they do. When everyone found out that Emma saw one, which was pretty much the same week she started at Elmwood, she was basically crucified. It hadn't taken anyone long to discover that her parents hadn't just moved across town for a bigger house – the internet is nothing if not useful for dirty details on transfer students. Emma had been a slut from way back. Or, as they've been saying on TV, *troubled*. She knew how to *make* trouble, that's for damn sure.

With a sigh, I wrap a towel around my head and walk back to my room naked, reluctantly picking up the clothes I'd tossed. It's a nice break, not to be worrying about the boys. But it's lonely, too. Mom enrolled them in basically every summer activity known to man, just to keep them away from the house and the evening news. At least we don't get so many reporters these days. Nothing much is going on that's newsworthy right now, I guess. Even if we go to trial, it won't be until this fall or even winter. Natalie says that's really fast, but right now it feels like forever. And the fall was supposed to be about other things; it was supposed to be a time I could look forward to. When Brielle and I were supposed to be enjoying our senior year. When Dylan was supposed to be starting at the university. Last I heard, they hadn't decided whether to take away his scholarship, but it's pretty likely they will, especially if all the lawsuits go to trial. All the guys are probably going to defer, Dylan included.

But I'm not supposed to talk to him any more either. I mean, things had gotten so weird even before Emma . . . left. And then the lawyers got called and our parents went crazy and everything fell apart completely. Now, things are . . . still weird. Weirder.

I dump my clothes on my bedroom floor and crawl under the covers on my still-unmade bed. It's a beautiful summer day, the kind I used to spend at Brielle's pool or forcing my brothers to go to the park.

But the only thing I'm good at anymore is sleeping. So I close my eyes.

'Sara!' *Thump thump thump.*

Perfect. What awesome, perfectly perfect timing.

'Sara, your car is blocking my – oh. Are you sleeping?'

'No,' I say, my voice muffled by my pillow. And by a couple thousand layers of sarcasm.

My mom heaves this really big sigh and goes, 'It's the middle of the afternoon.'

I push back the covers and look at her. Work clothes – the kind of Ann Taylor boringness that you wouldn't be able to describe to the cops if someone went missing. Reasonably good hair – on the short side, but still a pretty chestnut brown, and not as short as most moms' (but not *too* long, like Brielle's mom's, who is gorgeous but also trying too hard). Angry face – always, always the angry face.

I close my eyes again. 'My keys are downstairs,' I say.

'Well, good, then you'll know where to find them.' I can hear her picking things up off my floor and I can't even find the energy to tell her to stop.

But after a long pause, I sit up.

There's a semi-clean T-shirt on the foot of my bed and I grab it, pulling it on, which requires taking the towel off my head. Mom hangs my abandoned clothes over the back of my desk chair. Her eyes linger on the stack of summer school books on the desk, but she doesn't say anything. When she turns back to me she holds her hand out, and I silently pass her the towel.

'I wish you'd help out around here,' she says.

'The boys aren't home.'

'There's a lot that needs to be done besides driving the boys around. The kitchen is a mess, there's no food down there but cereal—'

'I'm supposed to do the grocery shopping now?' This is a new one. I mean, run to the store for extra supplies, sure, but—

She sighs again and sits on the foot of my bed, still holding the towel.

'Bear,' she says, the nickname startling me. I haven't heard it in months, and for some reason it makes my chest hurt. 'I know you're going through a rough time. But Natalie says this is all going to blow over, we'll be back to normal soo—'

'When did she say that?' I ask sharply. I never heard her say that.

Mom must interpret my question differently, though, because she says, 'I talk to her on the phone sometimes,' and her voice is angry again. Or defensive, I guess. 'I'm sorry I can't always be there for your meetings, but this affects me, too.'

I shrug. 'It just doesn't seem like it's gonna *blow over*,'

I say. 'I mean, they had some other lawyer there today, and they're still asking me about everything. There's a lot of . . . like, notes and stuff. Everyone was taking notes.'

I don't really feel like talking to her about this, but I figure she should know. About a month ago we sort of silently agreed she didn't have to come with me to Natalie's any more. It's not like there are set appointments, exactly, and when the office does call, Natalie always wants to see us during business hours. It was getting to be too much time away from my mom's job, and all the questions were for me, anyway.

But then we kind of stopped talking about it altogether, I guess. We were never one of those, like, crime-fighting mother-daughter teams on TV who tell each other everything about their days. And now we don't see each other much at all. Even when we're in the same room.

'That's just procedure,' my mom is saying now. 'If they don't write everything down, they can't bill us.' She huffs a little, like she's trying to laugh, but I can see she doesn't really think it's funny. Natalie isn't the fanciest lawyer in town, but that doesn't mean she's working for free.

I look down at the quilt on my bed, pulling at the frayed edge of one of the squares. It's handmade, but not by anyone I know. My parents got it for me at an antiques fair a long time ago. I remember Mom was carrying Tommy in the baby pouch, which is what we always called the little carrier thing, and Dad got all excited about this guy selling old vinyl records. I think they wanted me to feel excited about having a baby brother, so they were redecorating my room. But we only got as far as buying this quilt, cornflower-blue and sunny-yellow squares stitched together to make a big star. On the way home we'd stopped for ice cream and Tommy started crying, so Mom had to sit in the car and nurse him while Dad and I kept eating at the little outdoor table next to the parking lot. Even then, Dad didn't really know how to talk to me, or hadn't wanted to. We'd just eaten in silence, then gotten back in the car to drive home.

'I'm parked on the street,' Mom says, standing up again. 'You just need to get out of the driveway for a second, it won't kill you. Where are your shorts?' She's shaking out my towel and hurrying out of my room.

I guess we're done talking too.

The thing that sucks about summer school is everything. All the things about it suck. The school itself just feels totally sad – the parking lot is practically empty; the halls are only half lit; the grown-ups wear clothes so casual you realize they were actually trying to look professional during the regular year. And the air-conditioning isn't turned on all the way, so the whole place is sort of sticky and smelly all the time.

Brielle's parents worked something out where she doesn't have to be here, but when you can barely afford to pay your lawyer, much less make a donation to the school board or whatever they did, you don't get special tutors. So it's just me and the usual slackers, the kids you don't see

43

during the year because they're skipping to smoke weed or drink or play video games all day at, like, their older brother's apartment.

Dylan and the other guys didn't miss very much school this spring, and Dylan didn't get kicked off the baseball team. The charges were filed in April but things didn't really get going until almost the end of the year, so I guess no one saw the point of derailing the boys' senior year. And anyway, people weren't as mad at them, Dylan especially, as they were – are – at me and Brielle. I don't know why. I'm mad at him. I think. My mom used to say he was just as responsible as anyone; that he and Jacob and Tyler should take more of the blame. But lately I think she blames me and Brielle the most too.

Of course, Tyler is up on his own charges, since Emma was under eighteen and he wasn't. So maybe the guys are getting their share of punishment, I don't know. Natalie says we won't see Tyler even if we go to court.

No one seems to care any more that Emma was messed up. I mean, who starts at a new school and within three months has had that many hookups? Obviously someone who came to that new school because she'd been messed up at her old one – someone who was already in therapy, already on antidepressants, already a head case.

Seriously, if what happened with Emma pushed everyone to suicide, every high school in America would be empty.

'Okay, people, follow the steps on the board. And write

44

down your work. One of you does the work, one of you writes it down, got it?'

I'm sitting in summer school Chem class and wishing Irish O'Irish was here. And I wish I was still good at this class – or that I still cared enough to try to be good again. Ms Enman isn't here; a guy from the university, Mr Rodriguez, is our teacher for the summer version of almost all our classes. He's really young, like just out of college, and always kind of sweaty, like this job is already wearing him out.

Today we're doing a titration experiment – basically just pouring stuff into beakers. Less boring than taking notes, but still pretty freaking boring. My lab partner isn't here half the time – little-known fact: it's just as easy to skip summer school as it is the fall-winter-spring kind – but today he shows up. Carmichael. That's his last name, but no one calls him by his first name, ever. He's like a character from a TV show or a book or something: tattoos even though he's underage, crazy hair, the whole one-name thing. He'd be good-looking if he wasn't trying so hard to look terrifying. He's tall and under his black T-shirt you can see he has decent biceps and probably really flat abs. But the T-shirt itself is black and ripped and says DISCO KILLS ART, whatever that means, and the whole look just screams *I'm too cool to talk to you.*

It's not a look that goes well with safety goggles. But they probably look just as ridiculous on me, so I try to concentrate on the acid and base beakers on the table in

45

front of us. I can see a blurry Carmichael out of the corner of my eye, silently staring at the instructions.

Once I've got the burette set up, Carmichael wordlessly hands over the funnel and waits while I start pouring the acid. Then I turn the knob on the burette, letting the liquids mix, waiting for it to turn pink like it's supposed to. I close the stopper and watch as the acid slows to a drip and the base goes clear again.

'Lot of weird words in this thing,' Carmichael says, almost under his breath. I'm surprised by his voice but I keep my hand steady as I open the stopper again. The mixture turns pink and stays that way. I turn to make sure he's writing down the volume on the assignment sheet.

Then without thinking I say, 'What words?'

He puts his goggles up on his head, pushing his hair back, even though we're not done with the experiment. Then he puts a finger on the instruction page. '*Titration*,' he says, like it's obvious what he means. 'And *meniscus*. And that thing' – he lightly taps the knob on the burette – 'is called a *stopcock*.'

His voice is totally matter-of-fact, but I feel my cheeks go red. I can't tell if he's trying to make me uncomfortable, but I am.

During the school year I wouldn't have talked to Carmichael under any circumstances. Back in junior high I actually had kind of a crush on him – I thought his wild hair was the sign of an artistic soul, and back then I wanted to be an artistic soul too. But Brielle saved me from all that.

Turns out when you actually have fun things to do on the weekends, moping around reading poetry and listening to indie rock totally loses its appeal.

I figure I should probably go back to ignoring Carmichael now. And then at the front of the room Mr Rodriguez says, 'Five minutes,' and there's too much noise to say anything else anyway. Carmichael takes our whole beaker set to the sinks, leaving me at our table to put my book back in my bag.

When he comes back he looks at me and says, 'Good job.'

His eyes are really green. I never notice that kind of thing, but they are, and they're actually really pretty. And I'm so surprised by how serious he is that I say, 'Thanks,' forgetting all about my decision to not talk to him. He shrugs and smiles. 'I like that shirt,' I add. I'm completely lying to him, and I don't even know why. Two seconds ago I thought he was a freak. Maybe I still do. But it feels good to talk to someone. If this counts as talking.

We switch rooms for our next class, but we still have Mr Rodriguez. We just don't need to be in the lab for English. Some of the courses, like Chem, just cover the same stuff from the school year, or mostly the same. And others, like this one, do different stuff, I guess so we can't cheat. So instead of reading *Macbeth* we're doing *Hamlet*. I can barely follow it – I didn't understand a word of *Macbeth*, either, and Mrs Thale was a way better teacher. Mr Rodriguez says we'll watch the movie when we're done, but I have a hard enough time with Shakespeare when I have the book and a dictionary and SparkNotes in front of me. Watching the movie will be either torture or a good chance to nap.

Carmichael sits next to me again, and for a second I wonder if I've made a mistake talking to him. I know what Brielle would say – he's a loser, a slacker. She wouldn't be impressed with the tattoos or almost-bad-boy vibe. She'd call him a Carless, her term for guys who don't have cars and thus are not worth a second look. Or a first one.

But I'm a loser too.

Mr Rodriguez starts talking about how Hamlet is too introspective to get revenge right away, how he has to think about everything before he takes action. I sneak a glance at Carmichael, at the infinity symbol inked on the inside of his right wrist. There's another tattoo just visible under the left sleeve of his T-shirt; looks like a curled snake or something. He's nodding a little, his book open, like he's good at Shakespeare. And he's not actually that bad at Chem. I wonder why he's here – I mean, I know he skips class a lot, even now, but he seems kind of smart.

Suddenly he looks over and I jerk my eyes back to the book in front of me, my cheeks burning again. God, am I really so desperate to hang out with anyone my own age that I'm drooling over Carless Carmichael now?

When we're finally done for the day, I practically sprint to the parking lot. There are two other girls ahead of me already: Beth, who got mono last year (but in one of those sad, non-hookup-related ways), and Cherrie, who's just a

48

slacker. 'Cherrie' is short for something Latina, but we all pronounce it like the fruit. She used to correct everybody, I guess because we were saying it wrong, but the name just stuck. I suddenly wonder if maybe she skips school all the time because it's hard to get picked on every day, or called the wrong name or whatever, like you don't belong. Like I've been feeling. But then she turns to Beth and they start laughing about something. They get into Beth's car together and I remember: even among the outcasts, I'm the biggest loser.

I'm pulling my Honda around the side of the building when I spot Carmichael on his bike. He's standing up on the pedals, jumping the front tyre up and off the curb. He actually looks like he knows what he's doing. I'm already braked at the stop sign, and I pause there for a minute, watching his crazy black hair and the muscles flexing under his T-shirt. He jumps again, turning the front wheel, but he comes down awkwardly and has to jump off the bike and sort of dance away while it crashes to the ground. It's surprisingly goofy and sudden, and I don't realize I'm laughing until he turns – my window is rolled down, trying to cool off the car, so I guess he heard me – and scowls. Like I was laughing *at* him, even though I totally wasn't.

'Sorry, I just—' I start to call out, but he already has the bike back in his hands and he's jumping on and pedalling out of the other end of the lot.

Fine. Who needs these delinquents anyway.

'We haven't really talked about Dylan. Would you want to tell me about that?'

'I don't know,' I say with a shrug. Then I add, cattily, 'Do *you* want to talk about Dylan?'

It seems funny right before it comes out of my mouth, but once it's said I have to look away. I look down at my nails and say, 'I wish I could get a manicure.'

'Why can't you?' Teresa asks.

I pick at a flake of the glittery gold colour I have on now. It's all coming off, like I've been out partying nonstop, instead of the exact opposite.

'It's expensive. And people look at me funny.'

Brielle used to drag me to the salon at the nice strip mall, the one with the Anthropologie and Williams-Sonoma. But I can't really afford that one on my own. After we had to stop hanging out, I tried the cheaper place in the crappy strip mall, next to Taco Bell. That's when I started noticing that going out in public was going to be impossible. Actually, any place where you sit down for more than five minutes is a pretty bad idea – and way worse if they have a bunch of local newspapers.

I can see Teresa nodding out of the corner of my eye. 'It can feel like a pretty small town sometimes,' she says.

'Try *all* the time,' I say. It's psychotic how many pictures of Emma have been plastered everywhere. My mom says the media loves when bad things happen to pretty girls.

You'd really think there weren't any, like, wars or elections or random shootings to talk about, given how much ink has been devoted to printing and reprinting Emma's last school picture.

'And you don't see Dylan any more?' Teresa asks, trying to bring it back to her original question, I guess.

I look up. 'I'm not supposed to, remember?' I say bitterly. 'But whatever. It's really complicated. I mean, it *got* really complicated. I don't think it was Dylan's fault, I just . . . I mean, you had to know Emma. She was such a . . .'

'She was such a . . . what was she, Sara?'

I puff out my cheeks, pushing out a *whoosh* of air. 'She was one of those girls, you know, who are always hanging out with guys, who don't have any friends who aren't guys. Because all the other girls at school knew she'd steal their boyfriends.'

'She stole boyfriends?'

'God, yes. Like, daily.'

'Including Dylan?'

I scrunch my shoulders up to my ears, curling my arms around my chest. I push my breath out in another big sigh and let everything drop and finally say it. 'Yeah. Including Dylan.'

'That must have been hard for you,' Teresa says.

'Uh, yeah,' I say, but then I have to bite my lip. 'I don't really want to talk about this any more.'

'Okay. Why don't we wrap up for the day?' Teresa says,

setting down her notebook.

'Great.' I stand up and take off the cardigan I finally remembered to bring, since it's about fifty degrees warmer outside than it is in here.

I'm stuffing the sweater into my bag when Teresa adds, 'Love is a really complicated thing. I know it must still hurt.'

I look down at her and pause. 'Okay,' I say. I can't think of anything else, so we just stare at each other for another second. And then I leave.

When I pull up to school on Wednesday, Carmichael is riding his bike through the parking lot, his dark hair flying out behind him. He hasn't been to classes in a few days and my stomach knots, remembering how I accidentally laughed at him last week. I pull into an empty space as slowly as possible. I don't know if I'm trying to go slow so I'll run into him, or so I can avoid him. But then I remember: either way, I'm going to see him in class.

Or right now. I'm walking toward the doors just as he's locking his bike, and he looks up.

'Hey,' I say, for lack of anything better.

''Sup,' he says easily, but he goes back to fiddling with the bike. I'm frozen there, pinned to the sidewalk like a weed growing out of it. The clouds overhead are heavy and dark – it's another hot, sticky day, the kind that makes you wish it would just rain already – and I feel pinned down by the humidity, by the fact that any movement will make me even sweatier than I already feel.

'So . . .' I say, staring at his back. There's an old black JanSport at his feet and his copy of *Hamlet* is falling out of it. 'You like the book?'

He turns back around, kind of squinting at me, confused.

I point awkwardly to his feet, the backpack. 'Or, I mean, the play?'

'Oh, right,' he says. He grabs his bag and pulls the zipper closed, hiding the thing I was just pointing at. 'Yeah, it's okay, I guess.'

I nod. God, I haven't talked to anyone in a really long time. Not anyone my own age, anyway. And now I keep talking to Carmichael, of all people, like I can't help myself. He's so weird. And he really does scare me a little bit, with the tattoos and everything.

It's just – he's the only one who doesn't give me that *look*. That *You're the one who killed Emma Putnam* look.

I realize I'm still nodding and standing there, staring at him. Carmichael isn't giving me *the look*, but he's looking right at me, and I let out a short, self-conscious laugh. 'Sorry,' I say. 'I don't know – I mean –' I turn toward the doors to the school, which feel really far away, and hold my hand out, gesturing. 'You going in? I mean, of course you are, I just – should we go?'

'Well, we've already come this far,' he says. 'Why not just enter the mouth of hell?'

I laugh again, almost a snort. 'Yeah,' I say. I feel like I'm just making sounds at this point, not anything even remotely like conversation. I know Brielle would completely

53

lose it if she saw me like this. She'd probably throw me back in the car and drive away, fast, to save us all from the embarrassment. I wish she could.

But Carmichael is still standing there, a little half-smile on his face. Finally, like an act of charity, he says, 'I liked *Catcher in the Rye* better.'

'Oh,' I say. Then, before I can get my spaz under control, I add, 'I hated that one.'

'Seriously?' he says, genuinely startled.

'Sorry,' I say again, wishing I'd just walked past him instead of getting myself into this mess of a conversation. 'I mean, I can see why *you'd* like it – I mean, I can see why *people* like it, not *just* you—'

'But especially me, right?' he says.

'No! Not – I mean – ah, shit.'

I don't realize I've said this last part out loud until Carmichael's face breaks into a smile. A real one.

'You're weird, you know that?' he asks me.

'Easy for you to say,' I reply, but I'm joking, and I'm smiling too. And this time it actually sounds like a joke, the way I mean it to sound.

'Yeah, I'm weird too,' he says. 'That's why they keep us separated from the general population, right?' Carmichael turns and I fall into step beside him, wondering if he even knows why I'm in summer school. Maybe not – maybe he spent last year in another country, and that's why he's here. Or maybe he doesn't watch the news. Carmichael definitely seems too cool to pay attention to gossip. And lawsuits.

We've just stepped inside the half-lit hallway when I see Beth and Cherrie at a locker up ahead. At first glance you'd think they were just standing there, talking, but I know that locker. This whole hallway makes my stomach clench. In fact, the one *not* totally sucktastic thing about summer school has been that I can avoid this hall, and that even if I have to walk down it, I don't have to see flowers and stuffed teddy bears and candles piled up on the floor next to locker 8043. All that stuff got cleaned up at the end of the year. And it's still gone. But here are Beth and Cherrie, their heads bent toward each other, like they're sharing a secret or praying or something. Beth's shoulders rise and shudder in a big, weepy sigh. I'm not surprised, but I have to grind my teeth together to keep from yelling at them.

Beth and Cherrie weren't nice to Emma either. They wanted to be friends with Brielle and me as much as anyone – more, even. They laughed when Brielle made jokes at Emma's expense. They actually sent friend requests to Fat Beyotch before the page got shut down. And the whole thing on Valentine's Day . . . I remember watching Beth roll her eyes that afternoon, when Emma sat down on the floor next to her locker, hugging her knees and crying. Megan Corley got down there with her and put an arm around Emma's shoulders, but Beth had said something bitchy to try to suck up to me and Brielle.

And now she's back at that damn locker, playing the distraught BFF. I watch as Cherrie pats Beth's arm, and a loud snort escapes me despite my locked jaw.

Beside me, Carmichael kind of jumps. And I remember – everyone knows. And at the same time, no one knows anything.

'Sorry,' I say to him, again. 'I just . . . Those girls are such freaking hypocrites.'

Carmichael studies them for a minute. 'Yeah, everyone's a phony,' he finally says, softly.

I look over, surprised he's agreeing with me, but he's just staring at Beth and Cherrie. Or maybe he's staring past them – it's hard to tell.

'The world is full of phonies,' he reiterates, but it doesn't seem like he's talking to me any more. It sounds more like he's reminding himself of something. Something he'd actually rather forget.

January

'Do you have a – thing?'

The floor pounds beneath me as Dylan shifts to the side and reaches for his jeans. He doesn't even answer my question; he just gets his wallet out of his back pocket and I hear the crinkle of foil.

It's happening. It's happening on the floor of Brielle's parents' guest room. The party's still going on – the music is what's pounding through the floor, through the walls. I practically had to yell about the condom, which kind of killed the mood. I think.

Though honestly, there wasn't much mood to begin with. I started drinking around seven, I guess, well before anyone got to the party. Irish came through with the keg, but even before that, Brielle had gotten out the bottle of vodka she has hidden in her room for 'special occasions'.

'Liquid balls,' she'd told me, pouring way more than a shot into a Solo cup. She poured one for herself, too, smiled wickedly, and downed it. I gulped mine. When I almost choked, she laughed and poured some more. 'It's your special night!' she crowed.

Now it's, I dunno, ten? I'm wasted. I feel sleepy and wired at the same time. I feel like I love Dylan. I feel like he's kind of crushing me into the carpet in a not completely romantic way. He hasn't said much since we came into the guest room. He pushed a dresser half in front of the door. We were kissing and then we stumbled on our way to the bed, so here we are, on the carpet. Which is light blue. *We should get on the bed*, I think hazily – what if we stain the carpet? With . . . whatever?

Oh my God, he's putting on the condom. I see his hands moving and quickly turn my head away, which makes the room spin. It's dark in here, but not dark enough. Suddenly I feel really nervous and I wonder if I want to stop, if I'm about to throw up, if my life is turning into a crappy made-for-TV movie, if—

He's on top of me again, and my last thought as a virgin is *After this I won't have to worry about it any more.*

It doesn't hurt as much as I was afraid it would, but maybe that's because it doesn't take very long. I think I'm supposed to make sounds or something – like the movies, where it's all screaming and moaning, isn't that the way it goes? – but I'm still thinking about the carpet and then I'm kind of embarrassed for Dylan because he's grunting and then—

That's it.

He rolls off of me, still panting.

My bra is kind of wet from where he was sweating on it. I wonder if we should've taken it off first. It seems weird that he's taken it off other times, while we were just making out, but didn't for this.

The ceiling fan isn't on, but it's vibrating a little from the music, the long tassels swinging gently. I try to think about the song that's playing, the song that played when I lost my virginity, but I can't focus. I felt sober for a second, while everything was happening, but now I feel really drunk again.

'Dude,' Dylan says. He's not talking to me; he's fumbling with the condom. He curses under his breath.

I try to organize my limbs. I want to look sexy, how I'm supposed to look. I want him to want to do this again – not right now, but some day. Wasn't that the whole point? Was this time even okay? My underwear are twisted around one of my ankles and I grab for them.

He's not even looking at me, though. I know guys don't like to cuddle afterward or whatever, but he's already got his jeans back on and he's running his hands through his hair, straightening himself up. Where did the condom go? How did he do that?

I reach out and try to gently pull his face toward mine for a kiss. Instead, I end up sort of lurching at his shoulder, grabbing it for support. I hear myself giggle and don't even realize it's me for a second.

'Hey, babe, steady,' Dylan says. It sounds so sweet I

want to cry. That feeling you get at the back of your throat, right before the tears come. That lump. That happens – a split second after I'm giggling, I think I'm going to start sobbing.

Not a moment too soon, Dylan's hands are around me, pulling me, *holding* me up. It's not quite a hug, but it's enough. It's long enough for me to take a breath.

'You ready?' he asks.

I'm standing there in my underwear – sweaty bra and half-pulled-on panties – and I have to push my hair out of my face. But I nod, and I think I smile.

'Okay,' he says. He gives me a little kiss, softly. Nicely. 'I'm gonna go back out there.'

His face is close to mine and I can just hear him over the music. I want to reach out to him again. I want to cuddle, even though that's probably lame. I feel so close to him, I feel so warm inside, but really cold, too, in all the places he's not holding.

But he's not holding me at all now, he's leaving. He's pushing the dresser away from the door.

There's a blast of light and sound from the hall, and then I'm alone.

'OMG, you're such a slut!' Brielle is practically screaming at me and laughing, and I would be afraid of the rest of the house overhearing, but the music is still on really loud. 'On the *floor*?! God, who knew D-Bag was such an *animal*!' Her plastic cup waves in the air as she half dances, half hugs me. 'Woooo!'

I can't help it – I'm blushing like crazy. I'm embarrassed, but proud, too. *I did it*. I feel like my blood is pumping in double time, like my whole body is thumping along with the music.

Brielle has me sort of pinned in a corner of the living room, which is packed with people, but across the mob I manage to spot Dylan playing flip cup with a bunch of guys from the baseball team. It's the last night they can all drink without really worrying about getting in trouble with the coaches, and it looks like they're going to make sure they have enough beer to last the whole season. Still, when I see Dylan – even just the side of his face, just for a second – my heart sort of convulses. My stomach tenses like I'm going to throw up, but in that good way, like when you're just so excited about everything you can't handle it.

'You need another drink!' Brielle shouts. 'Follow me!'

I kind of always thought that losing my virginity would be a little more . . . private, I guess. Like Dylan and I would go to a rustic little cabin in the woods somewhere, and the room would have a fireplace, and we'd stay up all night talking afterward. Not that my mom would let me go to a hotel with Dylan, obviously. She'd have to pay for a babysitter to watch my brothers while I was gone, for one thing.

Anyway, Brielle is totally taking care of me. We stumble toward the kitchen, and from the flip-cup table, Dylan catches my eye and gives me a little smile. I think I'm going to just melt into a puddle right there on the kitchen floor, but then Brielle's shouting again and putting a plastic cup in my hand.

'This is the best party EVER!' she shouts. She yells it just as there's a little break in the music, but instead of laughing at her, the whole room bursts into wild hoots of agreement.

Just as the music starts up again, Brielle grabs my arm and says, 'Okay, you have to tell me *everything*! Everything everything. Every. Thing.'

I laugh and take a deep breath, wondering where to start, wondering if Brielle is going to think I did it all wrong, wondering if maybe we should talk about this later, after the party, but at the same time wanting so badly to talk about it all right now.

But just when I open my mouth, Brielle's hand grips my arm harder, too hard, and her jaw drops. For a second she seems totally sober. 'Oh. My. Freaking. GOD,' she says. She's staring at something across the kitchen, and I follow her eyes.

It's Emma. She's talking to Jacob Walker, and it looks like she's upset about something. Surprise, surprise. He's got his arm around her all comforting and shit – God, that girl will do anything for attention.

'*Skank*.' I think it's Brielle hissing the word for a minute, and then I realize it was me who just said it. It feels good. I say it again. 'What a total *skank*!'

I must be kind of loud, because a couple of girls I don't know that well turn around and look at us. Brielle shoots them a glare and turns to me, all serious. 'Don *eeeven* worryaboutit,' she slurs. 'God, I mean, who even uses Facebook any more?'

'Shh!' I hiss at her. 'You know we're not—' I don't get to finish my sentence because now she's pulling herself up to sit on the counter, knocking over a stack of plastic cups in the process. I've had too much to drink, definitely, but I know better than to announce to the whole room that we set up the Fat Beyotch page. It's already been taken down by the system administrator, but we heard at school that Emma got pulled into the guidance counsellor's office, and who knows what she said in there.

'WhatEVER,' Brielle is saying now, swinging her legs and kicking the cabinets with the pair of Jimmy Choos that I happen to know are her mom's. 'I'm so sick of talking about that *nutcase*. And now you'n D-Bag are all' – she holds up her hand and crosses her fingers – 'and then' – she wraps her other hand around the first one, intertwining all her fingers, then starts waggling her tongue.

I burst out laughing again, despite myself. 'Stop it!' I squeal. She's, like, making out with her hands now, doing these gross moaning noises. The girls who were staring at us before look like they don't know whether to laugh or run away.

Brielle starts grabbing at me, going, 'Oh, Sara! Oh, Dyyylaaaan!' and I'm trying to push her off, but still laughing, and while we're basically wrestling my eyes move to the other end of the room again.

Emma and Jacob are looking at us, obviously a little stunned that we're acting like such freaks, but whatever.

And then, finally, it occurs to me.

That bitch can't call me a tease anymore.

'C'mon,' Brielle says, clumsily hoisting herself back off the counter. She stalks across the kitchen and plants her hands on the island where Emma and Jacob are standing. I follow her, setting down my plastic cup and tossing my hair over my shoulder. It might not be red, but it's long and curly(ish) and I kind of like how tously it looks after my . . . um . . . *time* with Dylan.

'What are *you* doing here?' Brielle says to Emma.

Emma ignores her, though, and talks to me instead. 'Do you do everything she tells you to do?'

'What did you just say?' I snap back, but at the exact same time Brielle goes, 'What did you say, bitch?' so it actually sounds like I'm parroting her.

Emma cracks up, and so does Jacob, which is totally not fair – he was our friend first – and Brielle takes another step toward the corner of the island, closer to them.

'I don't know who invited you,' she growls at Emma, 'but I know who's gonna kick your ass out of here.'

It's not her best line, but it's effective. Emma gives Jacob this look, like a sad Disney princess. Jacob shakes his head, like we're all so immature and he's just disappointed in us, and puts his arm around Emma again.

He looks back at me and Brielle and says sarcastically, 'Really nice party.'

'Really nice *skank*,' Brielle sneers back, but Jacob is already guiding Emma through the kitchen to the front of the house.

Brielle turns to watch them go, then holds her cup of beer up in the air, as if she's toasting them.

'I hope Jacob likes herpes!' she yells.

Everyone's still laughing as Jacob and Emma walk out the door.

By midnight Brielle is mostly in the bathroom throwing up, so I'm mostly in there with her. I only really see Dylan one more time, just as he's leaving, but he gives me this long kiss and says, 'Talk tomorrow?' and it's enough. In the morning I feel like I've slept maybe five minutes, but I don't care. I pad down to Brielle's giant kitchen and make coffee while she's still asleep.

When I bring it back upstairs, Brielle is propped up on her pillows, but still wearing the eye mask she put on last night. 'That smells ahhhmaaaazing,' she says. She pushes the eye mask up and holds out both hands, and I put one of the mugs into them.

'Two Splendas and cream,' I say, sitting on the other side of the bed with my own one-Splenda cup.

'Bless you, you beautiful slut.' She takes a sip and closes her eyes. 'I might actually be dead right now.'

'Actually, I'm not quite dead yet!' I joke, but when she

doesn't laugh I remember it's my mom and my brothers who like Monty Python, not Brielle.

'Uch, you're shouting,' she whines. 'Are you going home now, or what?'

I open my mouth to make another joke, or argue, or something. But I actually should get home. And Brielle's clearly not in the mood to download my Dylan experience. I press my lips back together and swallow my disappointment.

'Yeah,' I say, standing up. 'Just wanted to make sure you had some caffeine.'

'You're the best. Lock the door when you go.' Brielle's eyes are still closed, so she doesn't see me smile, which is just as well. It's kind of a crappy smile.

But when I'm in my car I think about Dylan again, and I smile for real this time. For the whole drive I'm grinning like an idiot, though it fades again when I pull my Honda into the driveway at home.

My mom isn't one of those parents who goes into the office on the weekends, and sometimes I wish she was. Instead she's always trying to fix something around the house, and my brothers and I get roped into the lamest chores, like cleaning the blades of the ceiling fans (*gross*) or boxing up our old toys or electronics or whatever so she can take them to the Salvation army. Or to the garage, more likely, where they become some other weekend's cleanup/ donation/dump project.

It snowed and then rained last week, but now it's kind

of warm out, so I'm not that surprised when I see Alex and Tommy holding a giant trash bag under a ladder while my mom, big rubber gloves on her hands, scoops gunk out of the gutters and tosses it into the bag. They're all laughing about something, and I pause before I get out of the car, thinking first that I'd rather do anything but help clean the damn gutters, and second how happy they look, like some postmodern Norman Rockwell painting. *The Single Mother*, it would be called. She has her hair up and her big red Huskers sweatshirt on, the one that used to be my dad's, one of the things he left behind when he moved.

Alex is telling some story with lots of goofy faces and hand gestures. But then he lets his side of the bag drop and I hear Tommy squawking, and the moment is over.

'Sara, could you get another bag out of the garage?' my mom calls as I'm finally climbing out and slamming my car door shut.

I hear Tommy ask, 'Hey, can I go watch TV now? You said I could when Sara got home!'

'No, I said you could go inside and *start your homework*,' she corrects him. As I carry the new bag over, flapping it open on my way, I see Tommy frown, obviously trying to decide which option is less awful.

'Can I scoop muck for a while?' he asks. I can tell he's already asked her this at least a million times.

'Tom-Tom, you know that ladder is too high,' I say so my mom doesn't have to. 'But I bet next winter you'll be

67

big enough to crawl all over the roof, fixing tiles and cleaning the gutters and sweeping the chimney—'

'We don't have a chimney!' Alex protests, but he's already in a fit of giggles at the very idea. He turns to Tommy and squeals, 'You'd get all covered in sook!'

'In what?' Tommy asks, with his best I'm-twenty-months-older-and-therefore-*so*-much-smarter-than-you expression.

'*Sook*,' Alex says with a sigh, like he's just *so* tired of explaining everything. 'You know, like Santa. And Mary Poppins?'

Our mom smiles nicely as she sends a gross glob of leaves into the bag I'm holding and says, 'Sweetie, do you mean *soot*?'

'You dumbass!' Tommy yells.

'Hey, don't call your brother that!' I say, and at the same time my mom yells, 'Language!'

Tommy mutters 'Sorry' in Alex's general direction, and looks sheepish for about three seconds before he asks, 'Now can I go inside?'

'Sara and Brielle?' Ms Enman looks up from the note she's holding, the one Jeremy Miner just handed her. He's already disappeared back into the hallway, off to messenger some other note to some other teacher, win Hall Monitor of the year, be the AV club captain, die a virgin, etc.

'Yep,' Brielle says lazily. She rolls her eyes, like she's been expecting her name to be called, but I'm actually dumb enough to feel surprised. When we get to the principal's office Brielle smirks at me. 'What a lame effing job this lady has,' she says. 'You know they've pulled half the girls in our class in here already. God, it's like, just hire a stupid IT person, figure it out already.'

And that's when I finally get it: the Facebook page.

My heart drops to my shoes, but two seconds in Principal Schoen's office and I realize Brielle was right. The woman has no idea who set up the Fat Beyotch account. She's just rounding up the possible suspects, two by two. Including the two who yelled at Emma Putnam on Friday night.

So I can't really focus on what's going on, can't figure out if I'm in trouble or annoyed or what. I'm in this, like, free-floating panic about what this might mean, and I don't really hear what the principal says at first. Mostly I'm staring at her shapeless grey hair and wondering whether this would go on my permanent record. Could we even try to explain how much Emma *asks* for it? She acts so pathetic all the time, and then she goes off and starts texting your boyfriend or calls you a tease or crashes your party, and no one calls *her* to Schoen's office.

'Girls, I know Emma has had a hard time making friends,' the principal's saying. In my shock I've just been watching her face, but so far it's been totally calm, almost ridiculously nonthreatening. Finally some of her words start to sink in, and I start to feel like this is all going to blow over. 'And I'm not accusing you of anything,' she says. 'If you could just make more of an effort, you know the school has a strict policy against bullying—'

I jump a little at that word, but Brielle already interrupting. 'Principal Schoen,' she says carefully, her voice dripping with sincerity, 'we've really been trying to reach out to Emma. And I'm sure whoever did this Facebook thing was just trying to joke around, you know? I mean, Sara and I tease each other all the time, right?'

She looks at me and it's eighth grade speech class all over again – I nod vigorously, but I can't think of anything to say, can't force any words out of my mouth.

'So I just know that whoever did this,' Brielle goes on, 'probably thought it was a way to make Emma part of the group, right? We all do that stuff to each other. I know it sounds crazy, but it's just funny – I'm sure it was only meant to be funny.'

Principal Schoen looks like she really wants to believe what Brielle is saying. Hell, *I* want to believe it, and I know better than anyone what a truckload of bullshit it is. I almost wonder if Brielle believes it herself – though I guess the fact that she definitely believes, or maybe somehow *knows* that Schoen and the rest of them can't actually catch us, is more than enough to give her voice that confident tone.

But when we leave the office – after the principal asks us again to befriend Emma and report any bullying we see at school – Brielle is pissed.

'I bet that little tramp stamp gave Schoen a list of names,' she says, storming down the hall toward her locker. The bell hasn't rung yet so the hallways are still empty, and when Brielle spins her lock and yanks the door open so hard it bangs into the one next to it, the sound echoes. 'This stupid school is so scared of my parents they wouldn't *dare* pull me in for *questioning* unless she told them to. I am *so* gonna get her for this.'

'Yeah, well, unfortunately I don't think we're playing dodgeball today,' I say, in a weak attempt at a joke. We'll see Emma next period, in gym, but this week has been the badminton unit. Like any of us – or anyone at all, for that matter – needs to know how to play freaking badminton.

'Holy schnitzel, you're right!' Brielle turns to me with her mouth open in a surprised grin. 'Why didn't I think of that? Jeez, girl, you are a genius.'

'What? I said we're *not* playing dodgeball.'

Brielle leans in and says in her movie-announcer voice, 'Baby, where we're going, we don't *need* balls.'

The tension of the trip to Schoen's office finally breaks, and I start giggling like an idiot. Brielle grabs my arm and practically carries me to the locker rooms, like I wasn't going there, anyway. She flings her purse onto one of the benches and paces up and down – the bell rang on our way here, but we're still the first ones to arrive. It gives Brielle time to rant some more. Her brief moment of humour is already long gone, so when another fit of laughter rises up in my throat I swallow it back down.

71

'First she comes to this school and acts like a total spaz skank, steals everyone's boyfriends, cries like a baby when people tell her to back off, flirts with *your* boyfriend, shows up at *my party* totally and completely *uninvited*, and then tattles to the principal about a stupid *joke* that she totally *deserved*?'

Brielle doesn't stop moving while she talks, and her face is all pink from anger. It's all the stuff about Emma that I hate too, but I just let her talk. I lean against a locker with my arms crossed, remembering how I hung out with Dylan a little bit last night and I feel like we're even closer now – added to being *close*-close at Brielle's party – but the whole Emma text thing still bothers me. It bothers me more, actually. Every time I think of being with Dylan, I get this feeling in my chest, cold and hot at the same time. Like I'm going to explode, literally. And when I think of someone *else* being with Dylan . . . just the idea makes me want to throw up. The cold and the hot and the exploding all mix together, and it's like I can't breathe. It's really intense. It kind of scares me, actually.

Girls start coming into the locker room and there's suddenly lots of noise. When Brielle sees Emma walking in, alone, she stops pacing and comes to stand next to me. We wait quietly while Emma walks over to her locker, and just as she passes by us, Brielle goes, 'Nice *shirt*.'

Emma's just wearing a pink tank top, nothing special, though it is a little tight, I guess. Whatever, everyone knows what Brielle means. Just the way she says the word *shirt* somehow says everything.

But just in case it wasn't already clear, Brielle adds, 'Was the slut store having a sale? Oh, wait, I guess everything there is already cheap.'

Emma has made it to her locker, but she's gone all stiff, and she won't look at Brielle. Everyone else is looking, though.

'Hey, Emma, I'm talking to you,' Brielle says. She puts her arm around me and goes on. 'Done anything fun on *Facebook* lately? Or, wait, you're too busy banging other people's boyfriends, aren't you?'

Emma's head jerks around, finally, and she looks genuinely confused. Or maybe it's just a scared look.

I feel a weird rush of power. The opposite of eighth grade speech, the opposite of sitting in Principal Schoen's office. More like that night in the Taco Bell parking lot. I tilt my chin up at Emma and say, 'Yeah, what *is* it with you? You know Dylan just laughs at you, right?'

'I mean,' Brielle adds, 'who would want to be getting stupid *texts* from a bitch like you when they already had a girlfriend like Sara?'

Emma's eyebrows are kind of furrowed, and for a second it looks like she's going to cry. But she then looks away from Brielle right at me and says, 'Wow, you keep track of who your boyfriend texts? Sounds like a nice relationship.'

In a flash I find myself in front of Emma, too close, the hot-cold-vomit feeling rising up in my throat. I don't even know what I'm about to do until it's already done and I've pushed her. It's just a few inches, but the lockers make a loud banging noise, and I hear every girl behind me gasp.

'Listen, slut,' I hiss, right in her face, 'just stay the hell out of my life, got it?' It's like my voice is coming from someone else.

But I'm the one who sees Emma's eyes up close. At first she shrinks, doing that poor-little-girl thing she practically has down to a science. Then I see her narrow her eyes at me, just for a second. She gives me this look that clearly says, *Yeah, we'll see.*

And then out loud, softly but loud enough for everyone to hear, she whines, 'Okay, I'm sorry. I'm sorry, okay?'

Her eyes are big again, and tears are coming down her face, and she raises her hands up a little, like she's giving up, like I won. I wonder if I really saw that look she gave me a second ago. I can still *feel* it, like a punch to the gut, but she looks so sad now, anyone looking at her would swear I was crazy . . .

Brielle grabs my arm again, pulling me away.

'Whatever, Sara, like she's even a problem,' she says. 'Dylan doesn't want any of that.'

And then Coach Jenks walks in and blows her whistle, and everyone scrambles to finish getting dressed for badminton. Except Emma, of course. She sneaks out with her bag and no one sees her for the rest of the day.

And I finally get some peace. If you don't count the part where everyone else goes into the gym and I go into the last locker room bathroom stall and burst out crying for five solid minutes. My whole body shakes and snot runs down my face and even in the middle of it I know I'm going to have a hell of a time redoing my makeup, but when it's over I do – I put myself back together and go to the gym.

But except for that part, the rest of the day is fine.

August

'And this other guy? Henry? Not Henry Cable but Henry Lehman?'

'Um . . . yeah?'

'He got a home run! Off of *Owen*!'

'Wait, which one is Owen?'

'Owen *Beehner*! My *best friend*!'

I hold up my hands defensively. I've been trying to follow Alex's baseball camp stories, but sheesh, the kid must've met fifty new friends, and his stories are both endless and endlessly complicated. His eleventh birthday is in two weeks and when he's not describing some ridiculously intricate game they played, he's trying to convince my mom that all fifty boys should be invited to the party she's throwing him at the batting cages.

In fact, just as I'm apologizing for forgetting best-friend Owen, Alex whips his head around and starts to ask about the party again. 'Owen lives in Lincoln, Mom! That's only an hour away!'

'I know, I know,' she says. I don't think she's heard a word he's said all morning – it's dangerously close to eight, so I know she's just desperate to get to work. I've poured the cereal for Alex and Tommy, who isn't nearly as chatty. In fact, I've had a hard time even meeting his eye. I guess regular camp wasn't as awesome as baseball camp. Canoeing and archery clearly don't match the magic that is Owen Beehner's curveball.

'So can we invite him? Can we? Can we?'

Mom doesn't even answer him this time. She looks at me and asks wearily, 'You have them until Maggie gets here, right?'

I nod. Maggie's the babysitter, the one who watches the boys when they're not in camp. It should be me; I've been on duty for most of the other summers since the divorce. But this time I have school. And Natalie. And Teresa. Every time Mom says Maggie's name she looks kind of angry, and I know she's thinking that it's just another thing we can't afford.

I think Mom believes that I didn't do anything wrong in this whole Emma thing. Or not wrong enough for criminal prosecution, anyway. But costing us money we don't have, messing up my college admissions, not being around for the boys? Wrong enough.

Yet another reason I just can't feel that bad about Emma. If she'd just sucked it up – or, whatever, gotten help, taken her meds, done *anything else* besides what she did – everything would be normal now. And anyway, if what we all did was so horrible, why didn't we get sued when Emma was still alive?

Tommy picks up his bowl and drops it into the kitchen sink with a clatter, then runs back upstairs to his room without a word. Alex and I raise our eyebrows at each other, but Mom's already gone, so she misses the whole thing. I hear the garage door rolling up and, with a sigh, I grab my own bowl, washing it along with my brother's. Alex starts talking about another baseball game, a professional one, I think. I try to pretend I'm listening while I gather up my summer school books and stuff them into my bag.

The day turns out to be one of those pointless-at-every-turn ones. Carmichael hasn't shown up for classes, which isn't a surprise (though I'm a little surprised that I seem to care whether or not he's here). I get to Natalie's office for our appointment at three but she's not there, some emergency or something, her assistant won't tell me anything more than that the appointment's cancelled and they're sorry they didn't call me. So I have forty-five minutes to kill before my appointment with Therapist Teresa. I could go to Starbucks and spend my last five dollars on some coffee. Or I could do something really stupid.

I pick stupid.

The aisles at the Albertsons supermarket are so cold that goose pimples spring up on my arms the second I walk through the door. At the entrance there are mountains of

78

flower displays. There aren't any holidays coming up, so all the balloons are variations on either HAPPY BIRTHDAY or CONGRATULATIONS. Past that is the produce, regular and organic. Or if you turn left, like I'm doing now, you get to the cash registers.

I just make eye contact with him for a second – he looks up as I'm walking by the express register at the end, where he's checking out an old woman with what look like lemons. I don't glance over long enough to see more than a flash of yellow and that he's seen me, he's looking back at me. There's a nod.

I keep walking, all the way down to register fifteen, the ATMs, and the start of the bakery section. I turn again, right this time, down the coldest aisle of all, the one with the ice cream and frozen pizza. At the fish I turn left. There's a little hallway that leads to a door. The EMERGENCY ONLY sign is just a sign – there's no alarm. I push through and find myself at the back corner of the building, near some Dumpsters but not so close that you can smell them. A few milk crates sit around, cigarette butts fanned out on the ground beneath them. I'm alone. I find a spot along the concrete-brick wall and lean back and wait.

Maybe three minutes later, not even long enough for the chill of the store to fade from my arms, Dylan is there, pushing the door open and striding over to me. We don't say anything. I know he's taken his ten-minute break, I know we aren't going to talk. He presses me closer to the wall, so close I can feel the clip on his name tag digging into my chest a little, like a pinch, and we kiss, and the frozen-food-aisle chill melts from my limbs.

It hangs on in my heart, though. I kiss and kiss him, and he holds me, and it feels good. But it doesn't sink in.

'Okay. We have a solid argument that the antidepressants Miss Putnam was taking have been linked to other suicides. We have the doctor who can testify to that. But what's still killing us is the stalking charge. We just don't have a good plan for that.'

'Yeah, I'm not sure about the online stuff, I still have more research to do there. But for the rest – Miss Putnam lived down the street from Mr Chang, right? So an argument could be made—'

'I thought of that. But Miss Wharton here and Mr Chang weren't really that close. Isn't that right?'

Natalie and the hot law student intern turn to me, eyebrows raised. I shrug in answer to Natalie's question. No, 'Mr Chang' and I weren't that close. I always thought Tyler Chang was kind of a tool, even before Emma's parents filed charges against him, even before we found out what happened that last weekend. He was always partying with Emma like it was no big deal, because he could; she was convenient, too – they were three houses away from each other. He'd hang out with her and post it all online like it was something to be proud of, even while he made fun of her behind her back with the rest of us.

Of course, now things are really bad for Tyler. He's

80

actually in the most trouble of all of us. But that is completely not my problem.

'We've established that Sara's boyfriend was very close to Mr Chang,' Natalie's saying now, 'which I think gives us plenty of access to that neighbourhood for other reasons. If Miss Putnam saw Miss Wharton or Miss Greggs in either the white Honda or the silver . . .' Natalie shuffles through some papers, searching for the word.

'Mercedes,' I supply. Natalie looks up and flashes me the briefest of smiles, then turns back to Hot Intern. Who has a real name, too. David.

'Mercedes,' Natalie repeats. 'If the girls were spotted, they certainly had cause to be on that block. And it's not a big city, after all. Several Elmwood students live in that area.'

'But it was Emma's mom who saw us,' I can't help but point out. 'I mean, that time we – you're talking about the Valentine's Day thing, right?'

Natalie and David look back at me, surprised that I'm actually being helpful. Or maybe not helpful, I don't know – I'm not even sure why I'm here today, since so far they've just been talking to each other. I came in half an hour ago and all I've done is drink another Diet Dr Pepper and try to stay out of the way of the piles and piles and piles of papers everywhere. Natalie's office is huge, with a couch and chairs and a table and everything, but there's not even a place to sit any more – I'm leaning against the wall, trying to not knock over the plant next to me or the diploma hanging behind my head.

'Yes, that's what we're talking about,' she says, crossing to the other side of the table to find another stack of papers. She riffles through them before pulling one out, squinting at it, and saying, 'February tenth?'

I shrug again, but then I nod, too. I know just what they mean, and they know I know. And I'm bored, and I just don't see the point of standing here like an idiot anymore. Maybe if I just talk to them, they'll finally tell me what I'm supposed to do about all this.

I've done one other thing since getting to Natalie's office – I've found out that we're definitely going to trial. Natalie said she'd be discussing 'our options' with my mom, who of course isn't here, but that for now they're expecting a trial date to be set in the next few days.

The guys, including Dylan, have all deferred their real colleges for a year; Dylan and Tyler are going to community college in the meantime, I heard. All of our lives are on hold. Or I don't know, I guess all of our lives might be over. Mine feels like it already is – just when I think it's over, it's *more* over. My mom is sleepwalking through all of this and my brothers are home with the babysitter and my best friend isn't allowed to call me and my boyfriend isn't my boyfriend. I spend my days with delinquents and lawyers, and I'm so. Freaking. *Tired.* Everyone thinks I'm a terrible person, and I guess they're right. I mean, everyone spends every day talking, in detail, about what an awful person I was, and it's too late to change anything, or anyone's mind. Or anyone's life.

And any way you spin it, February tenth wasn't my best day. Or February fourteenth, or basically any other day that week. Month. Year.

Plus all that stuff is already on the record, thanks to Emma's mom. I mean, thanks to both of Emma's parents, I *have* a record.

Natalie's squinting at the paper again. She has reading glasses on top of her head, but I guess she's forgotten about them. Before I can make another helpful observation, she says, 'You're right, Mrs Putnam did see you. She said you and Miss Greggs placed a large heart-shaped sign in the Putnams' front yard. And this was . . .' More page flipping. '. . . A school tradition?'

'Yeah,' I say. 'For the Valentine's dance. I mean, usually a couple weeks before the dance. The guys were supposed to ask the girls by doing something big, you know, like wearing a tux to school or putting a sign up on the Douglas Street overpass or whatever. And then sometimes they'd make another sign or something that week.'

'But this sign wasn't from a boy, it was from you and Miss Greggs?' Natalie turns her squinty stare toward me.

'Allegedly,' I say.

David laughs suddenly, like a bark, and Natalie cracks another *very* quick smile, but she's looking back at her papers. 'Allegedly . . .' she murmurs, flipping another page in her hands. 'And the sign did not say something nice.'

'No,' I admit. Finally, David grabs a box from the chair

83

next to his and moves it to the floor, pointing at the seat. I take it, sinking down a little bit. 'We just . . . It was Brielle's idea, you know. Seriously, Emma was hooking up with *everyone*. We just wanted her to stay away from Dylan. It was a *joke*.'

Natalie looks up again, and this time she really does seem surprised.

'I mean. Not, like, funny, just . . .' I trail off. Maybe I should've kept my mouth shut.

'Okay,' Natalie says, and she finally sits down at the table too, though she has to shove another box aside to be able to see me and David. 'But this sign was still pretty bad, and it was on her property – not at school. We're lucky that only Mrs Putnam can testify to it, and that Emma apparently destroyed it. The stuff online and at school will be harder to deny, since we have more witnesses to that. And you were reprimanded.'

'Sort of,' I mutter.

'And there was another incident at Miss Putnam's home—' David starts saying.

Natalie holds up a hand, stopping him. 'Let's just deal with Valentine's Day first.'

When Natalie found out about the Valentine's Day stuff, back at our first meeting in May, I thought she was going to turn and walk out of the room, not take my case at all. She's really composed most of the time, and all these weeks later I know how unusual that reaction was, when we were just going over the major points of the lawsuits Emma's family filed against me, Brielle, Tyler, Jacob, and Dylan. Natalie's face had gone several shades paler when we got to the number of roses Brielle and I had sent to Emma.

'*Fifty?*' she'd said, like she was sure she hadn't heard me right. Next to me, my mom had gone really quiet and still. Before that part she'd been sitting beside me on the couch in our living room, her hand on my back, very alert. But as I looked at my new lawyer's dropped jaw I realized my mom wasn't touching me anymore. She had moved a little farther down on the couch. Putting about a million miles of cushions between us.

'It was just . . .' at the time I'd tried to explain. It was a lot, okay? But it's not like we beat her up in the school parking lot or something.

And now, Therapist Teresa is making me talk about it too. It's fresh in my mind, since I just got here from Natalie's office, where we'd gone through everything about Valentine's week.

Something about Teresa's room brings back that pit in my stomach I'd had during the whole thing. I tell her how I'd been sort of excited about the flowers until I'd seen Emma's locker, and then I'd gotten dizzy.

'You felt good at first?'

'Well, yeah,' I say. 'It was funny. It was just *so many* roses, you know? It looked ridiculous.'

'You wanted Emma to look ridiculous?'

'She'd been making *me* look stupid,' I point out.

85

'How so?'

'With *Dylan*.' God, Teresa can be stubborn.

'Mmm,' she says.

'But we didn't do the thing to her locker,' I say. 'They freaked out about the sign, because Mrs Putnam *allegedly* saw us in their yard or whatever, and they started blaming us for everything.'

Emma's mom hadn't called the cops about the sign; she'd called the school. Natalie thought that could work to our advantage, because if you saw some kids in your yard and thought they were vandalizing or stalking, why would you wait until the next day and call the school?

But of course, calling our school that week was the worst possible timing for me and Brielle. By Wednesday, you really couldn't ignore that *some*one was hassling Emma. The sign, the locker, the roses – Emma was only too happy to help the principal decide who was responsible for her shitty Valentine's Day.

Teresa gives me a look. 'And you say you're definitely going to trial?'

I nod.

I shift on the couch, pulling my sweater around me.

'You must be worried,' she says.

'Who, me? Nah,' I say.

Teresa's serious look turns into a smile. 'You can be very charming when you want to be,' she says, and I think it's supposed to be a compliment. 'But this must all be incredibly stressful, despite your jokes.'

'Well, I guess some people just deal with stress better than others,' I snap. Teresa stops smiling and I look down at my hands, my face suddenly hot. After a long pause, I hear her writing something on her notepad. It probably says *Shows no remorse. Is terrible person.* No one would disagree with that. Not even me.

February

I guess it's weird, but we never get in trouble – for the Facebook thing or the locker room. No follow-up from Schoen, no phone call to our parents, nothing. I don't realize until a week later that that was Brielle's whole plan, to show Emma what happens when she tries to fight back. Emma couldn't get us in trouble for making the Facebook page, so she didn't even try after the locker room. Neither did anyone else. Coach Jenks didn't see it, and the other girls are acting like they didn't see it either. Of course, I happen to know that most of them hate Emma too. There were a lot of people friending Fat Beyotch before it was deleted.

I start making sure I meet Dylan between classes. I've had his schedule memorized all year, but now I'm not shy at all about being at each door, holding his hand as we walk to his locker. I get to my own classes later and later, but it's worth it for the jealous but defeated look Emma gives us when we walk by. And by the end of the week,

I stop worrying about her so much. I have other things on my mind – the Valentine's dance, mostly, and whether Dylan is going to want to have sex again afterward. When he tells me he got a hotel room for an after-dance party and only a few other people are invited, I figure that means he does.

That's how he asks me to the dance, in fact. We're making out in his car, again, but he has to run to practice in ten minutes, so I know we can't take things very far. And then with five whole minutes to go he pulls back and says, 'I got a room at the Hyatt. After the dance. Tell Brielle to bring somebody cool.' He goes right back to kissing me and my mind spins out, thinking about the dress I'm planning to wear, and whether I can wear it to an after-party, or if I now have to worry about another outfit, and sexy underwear too, and what my mom's gonna say, and . . . And, you know, what the hell this all means.

Maybe it's stupid, but I hadn't really thought past the part where I slept with him the first time. Having sex almost seems scarier now, like I'm definitely going to get pregnant, or he's definitely going to stop liking me if we only do it, like, once a month. There hasn't been a good time or place to hook up since Brielle's party, but it has to happen eventually, right?

I have to pick up the boys from school, but as soon as Mom gets home I go over to Brielle's. Her parents are out at some fund-raiser thing, as usual. She always calls herself Poor Little Rich Girl – she has a tank top with that bedazzled on it – and everyone knows she's bragging. Once my mom said she felt sorry for Brie, that she seemed lonely. But she never seems lonely to me. Besides, I'm almost always here. Tonight we sit at the counter in her kitchen, putting maraschino cherries in our Diet Cokes.

'How often are you actually supposed to . . . do it?' I ask, stuffing three cherries in my mouth as soon as the words are out.

Brielle pushes a cherry off its stem, into the fizz of her soda. 'Don't you *want* to all the time?' she asks. There's a teasing ring to her voice, like she's suddenly my much older, much wiser sister. 'I mean, it's D-Licious! How can you keep your hands off him?'

I roll my eyes at the new nickname, but otherwise I'm not sure how to respond to this. I use a trick I've seen my mom use on my little brothers and turn it around, saying, 'Did you want to all the time with Diver?'

That's the guy she slept with last summer. We never use his real name, for some reason. It's a cool one, too – Kiefer, like the actor – but Brielle came home from swim camp just calling him Diver. He was the diving coach at camp, going to the university on a diving scholarship, apparently. So it stuck as a nickname at camp and beyond, between us.

'Oh, totally,' she says, but she's kind of just staring at her soda, not really looking at me. She never really talks much about Diver. Back when it happened, while she was still at camp, she'd used some of her online minutes to email me that she'd lost her V-card to this cool older guy.

90

And since she's been home she's mentioned it casually, sounding very nonchalant and mature about it. I wasn't even sure if they'd done it more than once. Something about the way she's concentrating on pulling another cherry out of the jar, though, keeps me from asking her to go into more detail now.

I know she hooked up with Rob a lot last fall, but I'm pretty sure they never *did* it, did it. Now she's not really dating anyone. For a second I wonder why I don't know more about my BFF's love life. I used to know everything – when a boy would so much as brush his hand across hers in class, or like when Chris Simmons kissed her at that party in ninth grade, right before he asked Tiffany Martin to go out with him. When Rob first started flirting with her I was there – last semester we all took the Visual art elective together – but now—

'Dude, don't stress about it,' she says. She pushes off her stool, twisting the cap onto the maraschino jar and putting it back in the fridge. I wasn't done with them, but Brielle's mom has weird rules about food, so I guess we ate all the ones we were allowed to already. 'Dylan's a nice guy, he's into you. You're not gonna get pregnant.'

'I'm not gonna have an AIDS baby?' I ask. It's this dumb joke we have, that the worst possible thing will happen to us if we're not careful. Usually the worst thing we can imagine is having a baby with some terrible disease.

'Oh, no, you totally will,' she says, turning around and leaning on the fridge door. 'But it'll be cured, and Dylan will play for the NFL, and he'll have to marry you forever because you had his magically cured AIDS baby.'

'That sounds nice,' I say, even though of course it sounds ridiculous.

'As long as you take me with you to all those NFL parties so I can marry Tom Brady, I promise to help with your sick baby,' she says.

'Okay. I think he's married, though.'

'Whatever. I'll be the hot young second wife.' She comes back to the counter and points at my Coke. 'Are you done? Let's go find Valentine's dresses in my closet. Or better yet, my mom's closet.'

Upstairs, we spend at least an hour inside her parent's crazy room-sized closet, but in the end everything looks too old or is way too fancy for a school dance. Brielle already has a dress, anyway, and technically I do too. By ten thirty I've gotten, like, four *Where are you* texts from my mom, so I finally go home.

I text with Dylan a little. He doesn't have much to say – he never does, especially on days he has practice. It's always about his coach, like *Briggs killed us*, or just *Dead*, but then he adds *Ur cute* or *Sweet dreams*. Tonight he writes *Take that sexy ass to bed* followed by *xo*, and I'm smiling as I go to the bathroom to brush my teeth.

But once I've gotten cleaned up, I don't go to bed. Instead I open up my laptop and check Facebook one last time, scanning the new posts on my wall. I go over to Dylan's page and can't help smiling at his photos. I'm sure

I've looked at them all, but he's so cute, and soon I find myself in his older albums, the ones from last year. There are a lot of shots of him with this girl Caysie he was dating then, and I swallow back a lump of jealousy as I flip through. I wish he'd take these down, but I know I can't ask him to; that would be pathetic. Caysie goes to a different school, the Catholic all-girls' academy, so I don't see her in real life. In photos she seems really happy, one of those girls with shiny hair and an easy smile – like she's really smiling at you, even if she's looking at a camera. Like she means it.

I scan forward again, trying to find pictures with me in them. I have a few on my wall, but the only one Dylan has is a group shot, and that's only because someone else tagged him in it. I'm not tagged, even though I'm standing next to him, up on my toes to see over Jacob's big shoulder. It was after a game and the guys are all wet-haired from the showers. It's not, like, a couple's shot – it's just a bunch of people who happened to be outside the school, on our way to a party at Kyle's house.

My fingers hover over the scroll pad. Do I click on it, add my name to the tags? Will that show up in the feed and make me look like a loser? It will. 'Sara Wharton tagged herself in Tyler Chang's photo because she is an insecure lame-o and she needs you to know that she's totally dating Dylan Howe, so back off.' *Shudder*. I click back to the Photos of Dylan page quickly.

And then I see it. Another group picture, but with fewer

people. Three, actually – Dylan, Tyler. And Emma in between them. Sitting together on a bench. A bench that's in Tyler's backyard. At night. Each of them is holding a plastic cup. It's definitely a party – besides the cups, all three of them are a little glassy-eyed. And it must've been not too long ago, because they're all wearing winter coats. I've seen Emma in that pea coat, in fact. The first time I saw it I couldn't help but feel jealous, because it's this really pretty aqua colour that looks amazing with her hair.

It looks amazing in this photo, too. This photo where Dylan is leaning his head close to that hair of hers, so close you can't tell if they're touching. Tyler is laughing, but Emma and Dylan just look happy. Comfortable.

I was definitely not at that party. I have to take a deep breath before I look down, at the date on the photo. It's another one of Tyler's, so maybe he's just loaded some new ones or something. Because it *must* have been taken earlier in the winter, before Dylan and I started going out officially in early December.

And maybe it was. But the date on it is January 20.

The day after Brielle's party.

Brielle doesn't know about the photo I found on Dylan's page, but it's like she does, because suddenly we're practically on a mission to Get Emma. Every day Brielle finds a way to say something mean to her, at least in gym – though after the locker room thing, Emma isn't around for gym very often.

But Brielle is like the late-winter weather outside, cold and relentless. She makes us go out of our way to walk down the hall where Emma's locker is. She finds Emma in the library. She never says much, but that's almost scarier – just hissing 'Slut' at someone as you walk past, so quietly they're not even sure they heard it, is like a poison dart in the forest. Emma's head always jerks up, and she always knows it was us, but she never really knows for sure. She just feels the sting.

It's just, I don't know, a hobby. There's nothing to do at school these days. I want to try out for the spring musical, but that's not for another three weeks. Brielle used to play basketball, but she dropped it this year. I guess everyone's bored, because Brielle seems to be gathering recruits to our anti-Emma campaign. Alison Stipe and Jacob aren't even a little bit friendly to her now.

Emma's helping the cause, of course. Kyle asked her to the Valentine's dance, so now she's on to Boyfriend #256 or whatever.

'She's always *around*,' Tyler complains when we're all having lunch off campus one day. It's, like, two degrees outside and I'm sunk down in my puffy coat, not concerned that I must look like a turtle squished down in its shell. I can't help it, though. Even now that we're inside Burger King I can't get warm.

'Well, dude, I mean, they're "*dating*",' Jacob says, making air quotes with two french fries.

Tyler laughs, but Brielle wrinkles her nose. 'Are they,

95

though?' she says. 'I mean, Kyle keeps texting me. I think she's just stalking him, like she did with all of you.'

The guys act like they haven't really heard this; they all seem to be very interested in their food suddenly. I shoot Brielle a look, but I don't think she sees it. To be fair, only a small part of my face is visible right now.

'Whatever, you know, she's just gross,' Brielle goes on nonchalantly. 'I just hope Kyle's being super careful, because we *seriously* don't know where that thing has been.'

Now everyone laughs. I feel a little confused – isn't this more insulting to Jacob and Tyler than the stalking thing? – but I'm relieved that the tension is gone. The boys go back to talking about baseball and I come out of my coat long enough to eat a few chicken nuggets. But Brielle is still kind of frowning, like she's trying to figure something out. I try to catch her eye again, but when I finally do, she looks right through me.

Dylan and I walk back to his car together, and he puts his arm around me on the way. 'Are you always this cold?' he asks.

'Yes! It's ninety billion degrees below zero!' I say, and I wiggle my arm under his open coat, around his waist. 'You're so warm.'

He just laughs and lets me into the SUV, where I sit and shiver until he comes around to the driver's side and turns on the heat. 'Sorry,' he says, 'I should've started it from inside.'

'That's okay.'

He's backing out of the parking lot, craning his head over his shoulder to see behind him, when he adds, 'Why's Brielle such a bitch about Emma, anyway?'

I look over at him, startled. The car jerks as he shifts from reverse to drive, and underneath me I feel the heated seat kick in, starting to burn the backs of my legs.

'Brielle's not a bitch,' I protest, but he laughs.

'Um, yeah, she is,' Dylan says. 'She's, like, the Original Bitch. The O.B.'

My mouth is hanging open, waiting for some words to come out. But I don't know what to say. I never know what to say. Is my boyfriend really being mean about my best friend?

'She's cool, though,' he says. 'I just think you guys don't need to get so mad at Emma. She's a cool girl.'

'To you, maybe,' I mutter.

'Come on, you know what I mean,' Dylan says. He reaches across the car and grabs for my hand. I have it tucked under my legs for warmth, but I let him take it. 'And really, Emma's totally fun when you get to know her. And she's nice, like you. I think you guys could chill, you know?'

I *don't* know. I don't want to know. What is *once you get to know her* supposed to mean, anyway? What does Dylan know about Emma being *fun*? Not just fun – *totally* fun.

I stare out the front window, blinking fast so I don't cry.

I'm holding Dylan's hand, I remind myself. *I'm his girlfriend. He just said I'm nice and fun.*

Just like Emma.

After school I drive to the fancy mall with Brielle in the passenger seat. We're going lingerie shopping for the dance. It might be fun, or I think it's supposed to be fun. But Brielle hates my car, which I know because every time I drive she complains nonstop, like she's doing now.

'What is this?' Brielle asks, not kindly, grabbing my iPod and turning on the screen. Just as I'm opening my mouth she says, 'Who are the *National*? That's a stupid name.'

'C'mon, they're my favourite, you should just listen,' I protest. Lately I feel like I'm always playing defence around Brielle, always explaining something. But the explanation is never good enough.

'Whatever,' she says, throwing the iPod back down on the console. 'You and your deep thoughts. Blech, I hope you don't go all emo on me again.'

It's been forever since my emo phase, but I don't say that – and I also don't point out that it seems like *she's* the one being all moody. She stares out the window sulkily for a while, then turns back to crank up the heat. 'God, it's like a freaking freezer in here. We should've taken my car.'

I swear I'm the only one in our group of friends who doesn't drive a big SUV. Brielle's 'car' is a silver Mercedes M-Class that probably cost more than my house, and we almost always do take it. But I really like to drive. And I really like to be able to listen to my own music. I mean, singing along to Beyoncé is fun and everything, but sometimes I like to be the one in control for a change.

'Sorry,' I say. 'You'll drive next time. And we're almost there, anyway.'

We're pulling into the parking lot, actually, and I don't even bother to find a spot close to the door; I just pull in at the first open space on the side with the Nordstrom. And for some reason, after we're parked, I reach over and grab Brielle's hand. We're not affectionate like this – there are girls at school who walk around with their arms linked or do each other's hair all the time or whatever, but we don't really touch besides the times Brielle does my nails. But right now I take her hand in both of mine, and it is cold, and I give it a friendly little shake. It's something I'd do with my little brothers to snap them out of a bad mood, and I guess the instinct just takes over.

'Hey,' I say brightly, 'let's go buy some sexy-time underwear!' I grin like an idiot and wait for her to laugh.

Instead, Brielle bursts into tears. Her head falls to her chest and she's shaking, sobbing.

My heart stops. I've never seen this. Brielle is not a crier. Not even when her parents separated for a month back in ninth grade and she thought they were going to get divorced. She's barely a talker, even – she's always got a plan, a joke, a designer suit of armour to throw on in any situation. But now she's full-on ugly crying, her mouth open and turned down like a sad clown doll, snot already starting to come out of her nose.

I reach into the back seat and grab a couple of tissues, grateful that I always keep a box in here and even more grateful that Alex hasn't used them all. Brielle takes the whole handful and covers her face, then folds herself over, face down on her knees. She's shaking, and all I can do from here is rub her back. The car is still on, so with my other hand I reach over and turn the heat up full-blast, hoping that will help a little. She's wearing her puffy white down coat – I have no idea how her hands could even be that cold. I'm also not sure she can feel my hand through the layers of down, but I keep circling it on her back, just quietly waiting for her to sit back up and – I hope – tell me what the hell is going on.

After what feels like an hour, Brielle throws herself back up into a sitting position. I jerk my hand away in surprise and try not to gasp when I see that she's got mascara all down her cheeks, like the cartoon version of a girl crying. She's even a little puffy. I cannot stop being shocked by seeing her so upset. And I completely don't know what to say.

'It's so *stupid*,' Brielle wails, letting out another sob. 'I don't even know why I'm making such a big *deal* about it.'

'About what?' I manage to ask. 'What's going on?'

Her head drops down and she stares at the tissues, suddenly going still. Taking a big, shuddery breath, she says, 'Diver. Stupid . . . fucking . . . *camp* guy.'

I don't know what I'd been expecting her to say, but it

wasn't this. Has she been in touch with Diver again? Is this another thing I didn't know about, another thing she didn't feel like telling me? But she's so upset, it's not like I'm mad – I just want her to keep talking. I reach over and turn the heat down – the vents are blasting, too loud and way too hot – and put the box of tissues up on the dashboard.

'What about him?' I finally manage to ask.

'He didn't . . . We didn't . . . you know, I mean, he had a girlfriend. He didn't even seem to *like* her and we were hanging out all the time and then that night, he just . . . It was just making out, but he just . . .'

She waves her hand across her body, like she's pointing something out. I look but it's just her puffy coat, the pile of tissues.

'I thought you guys––' I start to say, but she's shaking her head fast.

'No. He did. He did it. He just *did it*. Like, *on* me. Like, just––'

And then she has the box of tissues and she's beating it against the dashboard, the window, her knees. She's pulling it apart and throwing her weight back and forth in her seat, throwing a fit, a tantrum. I'm so scared I can't breathe or move. I'm pretty sure she's going to hit me next, or hurt herself, or hurt the car – and then she's doubled over again, crying even more.

This time I fall on top of her, hugging her as best as I can in the confines of the car. 'It's okay,' I'm saying, 'it's going to be okay,' but I don't know if that's at all true. I'm not even sure what she just told me – that Diver hurt her? That he . . . raped her? That . . . what? Girls like us don't get raped. Girls like Brielle don't get in trouble at all. Girls like Brielle get roses on Valentine's Day from half the damn school. Girls like Brielle get whatever they want.

Gradually, her crying slows down. She stays bent over, but I see her gather a handful of tissues to her face and hold them there, and suddenly she's quiet. From the crumple her voice comes out, very small, muffled. 'God, this is pathetic.'

'No, it's not,' I say. 'I'm glad you told me,' I add, though I'm still not sure *what* she's told me.

'I just thought it would be romantic, you know? I thought it'd be like how it was for you and Dylan.'

I still have my hand on Brielle's back, and I have to stop myself from flinching, moving away. How *was* it for me and Dylan? I'd thought it'd be romantic too. But maybe it was? Maybe that's as romantic as it could be?

And I'm shocked to realize that Brielle never talks like this – she never *confides* stuff. She's never unguarded, never unsure. I feel closer to her, but I'm scared, too; is she going to just pull away? In a minute, will she fix her mascara and pretend this never happened?

Do I want her to?

I sit there, frozen, waiting for what will happen next. But it's not that dramatic after all. Brielle sits up and gives me a sloppy smile, her eyebrows raised in an *Isn't this ridiculous* expression. Her eye makeup is smudged but she mostly just looks tired and sad. 'Seriously, it's not that big a deal,' she says quietly. 'I wanted to . . . you know. I wanted to be with him. I wanted to do it.'

I nod. Of course she did.

'I just . . .' She trails off with a shrug, looking out the front window at the parking lot like there are some answers there.

'It could have been more romantic,' I say, trying to finish her sentence.

She snorts. 'Yeah,' she says, her voice hard and sarcastic, the wall going back up. 'More romantic. More consensual. All that good stuff.'

I hesitate, wondering if I should just drive us home now. But Brielle pulls down the passenger-side visor and fixes her makeup in the mirror. 'So where do you think, Victoria's Secret?' she asks.

'Uh – yeah, sure,' I say, trying to not sound surprised.

She raises an eyebrow at me. 'Oh, don't be like that. You're not getting out of this just because I'm all PMS-y.'

She opens her side of the car and jumps out, leaving a blast of freezing wind in her place. I give my head a little shake, trying to make these new things fit. Brielle being hurt by someone is just so . . . foreign. And the fact that she's still thinking about it, still *crying* about it, all these months later . . .

For a second I wonder if it could be because of me and Dylan, if she's jealous. But Brielle has never been jealous of me, not even for a second. I'm jealous of her; that's the whole deal. She's the confident one, the one who knows all the seniors, the one who pays when I run out of my measly allowance. She knows where to buy fancy underwear. Well, I mean, I know *where* to buy it, but the last time I went to VS I just got some of those cotton Pink ones. Brielle knows how to take the lacy black bras up to the cash register without dying of embarrassment.

'Hey!' she yells. She pounds on the roof of the car, making me jump. 'It's the effing tundra out here! Let's go!'

I yank my keys out of the ignition and jump out of the car, feeling the wind again. It stings my eyes and clears everything away with one violent *whoosh*, leaving nothing but two regular girls, running across a grey parking lot, puffy coats flapping behind us, laughing at how stupid we probably look, but not caring. Not a care in the world.

August

Carmichael slides into the desk next to mine on Friday, waving his copy of *Hamlet* at me like he's saying hello with it.

'Did you finish?' I ask him.

'Yeah, of course,' he says. 'Why, you?'

I shake my head. I finally got the hang of the language, even got into the story a little bit, thanks to the internet's help. But Hamlet is so depressed all the time, and everyone keeps dying in these awful ways. And then Ophelia drowns in the river, and Hamlet says he loved her the whole time, even though he treated her like crap when she was alive, and I just . . . it was just too freaking awful.

I don't say all that to Carmichael – for once I seem able to actually choose what comes out of my mouth around him. I just shake my head again and say, 'It's too sad.'

He raises his eyebrows at me. Then he holds his copy up again and points to the word *tragedy* on the cover.

'Shut up,' I say, and I reach out to slap his arm. It's

playful – maybe even flirty – and to my shock he jumps back, like I've actually hurt him. But he's just playing along. Maybe even flirting.

'I could help you study,' he says. 'If you want.'

Just then Mr Rodriguez walks in, right as Carmichael accidentally knocks his book off his desk, onto the floor between us. The *slap* it makes on the linoleum isn't even that noticeable amid all the paper-shuffling and bag-zipping in the room, but Mr Rodriguez shouts, 'Everyone please get your books off the floor and start taking notes!' I roll my eyes at Carmichael, but he's facing the front of the room, all model-student mode. I don't get him at all.

I try to concentrate on the *Hamlet* review, because I actually am worried about the test on Monday, but I keep thinking about what Carmichael said. Does he mean it? I really am starved for male attention, I guess, or just a friend. Or just something to do besides going to Natalie's or Teresa's.

It isn't a lab day in Chem and we only have one other section, foreign language; I'm in French while Carmichael's in Spanish. By the end of the day I figure I should get in my car and leave before I do or say anything else idiotic, but just when I've made it to the trunk of my Honda, there he is again, standing on his bike pedals and coasting over slowly.

'So I'll see you tomorrow, then,' he says.

'That's gonna be quite a trick, since tomorrow is Saturday,' I say.

He just nods, acknowledging my stupid joke without laughing at it. 'Right, that's why I'll meet you at your house. You live on Grandview, right?'

I have no idea how he knows this, but I nod.

'So, seven?'

'Are you sure?' I say, and quickly add, 'Because I really suck at Shakespeare. Really. I keep getting Polonius and Claudius mixed up.'

Carmichael has been riding his bike in a circle this whole time, looking down at the pavement, his face mostly hidden by his hair. But when I finish talking, he stops and sets his feet on the ground, looking up at me.

'Well, then you really do need my help. You have something we can stream one of the movies on? Or Netflix?'

I nod.

'Great. We'll watch it, and we'll figure out how you can keep two totally different characters straight, okay?'

'Okay,' I say, embarrassed but inexplicably happy. It's a strange kind of relief to have someone be bossy with me – someone who isn't a lawyer, I mean.

He nods again and then pedals away, and I stand there, watching him go, wondering why the hell he's bothering with all this. But then I shake off the thought and get in my car. I can't worry about that. I have to just enjoy having someone to talk to. While it lasts.

'Alex! Where are you?' I shout when I walk in the door. Mom's not home yet, I can tell – no other car in the garage

– but there are boy socks all over the first floor. Seriously, I think my brothers have some kind of sock-generating machine in their rooms. And another machine that makes them all dirty and throws them all over the house. Two boys could not possibly produce that many dirty socks *and* distribute them so widely in the course of just a few days. I'm not as good at math as I used to be, but I know that doesn't add up.

'Tommy?' I call, less certainly. Tommy's been over at his friends' houses a lot lately. I think. He's just never around, as if he's the world's first twelve-year-old emancipated minor. On the one hand, it's good – only one brother to feed and yell at about socks. On the other, I kind of miss him. Because whenever I do see him, Tommy's always really quiet. Like he's not there, even when he is.

I pause for a second, throwing my bag on the floor next to the stairs, and consider my middle sibling. He's been quiet since . . . since he got back from that last camp. Maybe he didn't like it?

I hear laughter from the kitchen, so I kick off my flip-flops next to my bag and make my way back there. There's no actual kitchen door, but you can't see the little nook table from the front hall, so when I get to the kitchen I'm completely unprepared for what I find. Or *who* I find, more accurately.

At the table, sitting around a big tub of ice cream, are Alex, Tommy, and our dad.

The boys are lit up like it's Christmas morning – which

is appropriate, since visits from our father are about as frequent as ones from Santa Claus. Dad's in a suit, as always, and it's kind of wrinkled and messed up, like he's been driving in it all day. He probably has. He lives in Chicago, which is about eight or nine hours away, with his other family. Technically Chicago is pretty drivable to here, especially when he needs to stop for work somewhere in between – in Des Moines or wherever – but the new kids are really young, and somehow Dad just never seems to make it all the way out here to see his old ones.

But then once in a blue moon, these surprise visits. It's been a while, but the guy definitely likes to be Mr Hey, I Brought Ice Cream. The boys love it, but I know better. Or maybe it's just that I'm not the one he brings the ice cream for.

'Where's your mom?' Those are the first words he says to me. Tommy and Alex are still shovelling Neapolitan into their mouths, oblivious that our dad didn't even say hi to me first.

'Um,' I say, not moving any farther into the room. It's like we're two magnets facing each other the wrong way – I feel physically repulsed by him, like even if I tried to move closer, I just couldn't. 'It's four thirty on a Friday, so I'm going to take a wild guess and say . . . work?'

'Sara,' he says. Sharp, short. In his voice, my name is a knife. But as much as I can't come into the kitchen and sit down with them, I can't leave, either, and he knows I won't. So he goes on. 'There's no need for that tone. I came a long way, I'm tired, I'd just like to have one peaceful minute before I have to get back in the car and drive another five hours.'

I don't know if I'm supposed to respond to this, or to point out that I wasn't trying to ruin his *peaceful minute*, or if I'm only here to play substitute punching bag. But Alex, innocent as ever, is already jumping in, saying, 'Wait, Dad, you're not leaving yet, are you? You just got here! You have to see my pitching! I'm gonna be as good as Dylan by the time I'm in high school.'

Right after he's said it I can tell Alex knows he's made a mistake. Dad's face is a thundercloud. I think my knees might buckle underneath me.

We're all silent for a minute. I don't move, and Dad doesn't look at me, he just stares over toward the sink, fuming. It amazes me that he can be so far away – geographically, emotionally, everything – and still know exactly who Alex is talking about when he says 'Dylan'. My dad never even met Dylan, never saw one of his games, never talked to me about him. I know he talks to my mom about everything that's been happening, and I know my lawyer's always trying to get both my parents in a room. But Dad doesn't want to talk about it. As far as he's concerned, it's all going to blow over and we can all 'move on'. That's what he says to my mom when they talk – 'let's just all *move on*.' Like that's not what we all want.

Alex is looking back and forth from my dad's face to

mine, trying to figure out what's going on and, more importantly, what's going to happen next. But Tommy seems to know the drill this time – he's practically facedown in his bowl, shovelling ice cream, refusing to even come up for air.

And then, like nothing happened, Dad whips his head back around to his beloved (for the next few hours, at least) youngest son and says, too cheerfully, 'So where's your glove? Let's go outside!'

Alex jumps out of his chair and goes galloping upstairs like his life depends on it. Tommy's scraping the bottom of his bowl and Dad says to him, 'You sure you got enough there? Need you ready for high school sports a lot sooner than your brother.'

Tommy pushes his bowl away and wipes his mouth on his wrist, still not saying anything but giving a little shrug.

'Huh,' Dad goes on. 'They teach you anything at that camp I sent you to? Cost a fortune, could've been an all-star retreat.'

Dad is smiling as he says this part, like it's a joke, but I hear the edge creeping back into his voice. I guess I'm not the only one disappointing our father these days.

Tommy is still looking down at his spoon, and from across the room I can see his jaw clenching. It's the thing he does when he's trying not to cry – and he never cries, he's the toughest kid I know.

Seeing my little brother's moment of weakness breaks

the spell I'm under, and I practically lunge through the kitchen door and over to the table, grabbing the empty dessert bowls and opening my mouth to let a stream of nonsense cover up this crappy moment.

'It was a really, like, all-around camp,' I say, my words a little too fast and too loud. 'You know, boating and horses and hiking and stuff? Tommy got really tan, he said he had fun, didn't you, TomTom? They had campfires and everything. S'mores. Wasn't there a talent show at the end? Didn't you win a ribbon for something?'

Tommy finally looks up at us and says quietly, 'For archery. But it was just a finisher ribbon, not a real one.'

Dad snorts. 'These places with their self-esteem crap.'

'Yeah,' Tommy says. 'It was pretty dumb.'

'Well, I'll save my money next year,' Dad says. 'Get you to a football programme.'

Tommy hates football, but our dad is the world's biggest Huskers fan, so there's no way either of us is bringing that up.

'Football can be really dangerous,' I say. I have no idea why I'm opening this argument – the words just pop out, and immediately I wish I could shut up again. I don't say anything when Dad's talking to me, or *about* me. But when it comes to the boys I can't keep quiet, even though I should. It's not like we get to see him so often that we have the luxury of fighting.

But Dad's mood has shifted again. 'You're a strong guy,' he says to Tommy, patting his shoulder. 'You can take it.'

112

Tommy doesn't look strong. He looks sad. I'm standing there, still holding the bowls and halfway to the sink, when Alex comes tearing back into the room, holding two baseball gloves.

'I found one of your old ones!' he tells Dad breathlessly.

'Okay, then.' Our dad gets up and takes off his wrinkled suit jacket. He rolls up his sleeves and Alex bolts to the back door, sliding it open. He looks like an eager puppy, and Tommy looks like a wounded one, though he's getting up to go outside too.

As they all troop out the door, I wonder what I look like.

The cleaning lady, I guess.

'He's so mean to her,' I say, almost to myself. Mel Gibson is yelling at Helena Bonham-Carter – or Hamlet is yelling at Ophelia, I guess – and even though I really only understand the gist of the dialogue, I can tell he's being cruel.

'He's just pushing her away,' Carmichael says. He takes a sip of his Coke and then points it at the screen. 'He has a lot going on, right? His dad was murdered.'

'But she can't help it if she likes him,' I say.

Carmichael doesn't respond, and we watch in silence for a while. When Carmichael got here we ordered a pizza. Actually, we talked to my mom and my brothers and ordered two pizzas, but they ate theirs upstairs. My mom didn't even blink when she saw Carmichael's all-black ensemble. I don't know if she saw the tattoos, but she said, 'I like your T-shirt,' which today has a screen print of John Lennon. He smiled and said, 'Thanks,' and I noticed Tommy looking at our mom, obviously waiting until we were gone to ask her who the guy on the T-shirt was.

I grab another slice of pizza, willing myself to eat even though it feels wrong to stuff my face in front of a boy. Carmichael already had three slices and this is only my second, but still. Around Dylan I couldn't eat more than a couple of french fries or I'd feel fat and self-conscious.

But this isn't Dylan. This isn't a date. Even if I did spend an hour trying on every tank top in my wardrobe. I finally settled for a pair of shorts and my favourite grey V-neck T-shirt, the one that's so old it'll probably fall apart at the seams the next time I wash it. But it's super soft and it definitely doesn't look like I'm trying too hard.

And Carmichael's not acting like this is a date. He's acting like we're just friends, or at least study partners, and I know that should be good enough for me. I shouldn't be so lonely and desperate.

But still. I put my plate back on the table and wipe my mouth with a napkin. I fuss with my hair a little, wishing I hadn't decided that chin-length was a good choice for summer. I tug at my T-shirt and make sure it's not covered in crumbs.

And then, finally, I just settle back on the couch and watch the movie. For a while I actually relax. But by the time Ophelia is found floating in the river, I'm curled into a tense ball in the corner of the couch, biting my thumbnail, feeling like I might throw up all the pizza.

Carmichael looks over at me and says, 'You okay?'

'Yeah,' I say, more defensively than I mean to. 'Why wouldn't I be?'

'No reason,' he says easily. 'I just thought, you know. It's kind of tough, watching all this stuff about death and suicide and everything.'

I glance at him, but he's still facing the TV. 'Is it tough for you?' I ask.

'Yeah, of course.'

I don't know what to say.

'I didn't really know Emma,' he adds softly. 'But it's hard not to think about it. And she seemed like a good kid.'

I don't want to talk about this. I jump off the couch, grabbing my empty Coke can. 'Do you want more?' I ask. 'I'm getting more.'

I don't wait for him to answer, I just hurry upstairs. We've been using the basement TV while my brothers are playing Wii in the living room. I keep trying to get my mom to move the console downstairs. She says it's easier to keep an eye on the boys this way, and she's right, but it's loud and obnoxious with them jumping around in there all the time. And it leaves me no choice but to invite a totally random guy from summer school down to my basement, which seems kind of desperate.

But when I reach the top of the stairs, it's actually pretty quiet. Mom and the boys already had dinner, so I guess she went up to her room. Alex is still playing Wii in the living room but Tommy's in the kitchen, sitting at the counter with his DS.

'Hey, bud, what's up?' I ask him, dropping my can into the recycling bin and crossing over to the fridge. We got a bunch of free cans of soda with the pizza because they were out of litre bottles, so there are still a few left. I grab two and slam the door shut, realizing that Tommy still hasn't said anything back.

I sit down next to him at the counter and take a deep breath, steadying my nerves before looking over at his game. He's not playing very enthusiastically, and I know from one look that his score is really low. Kinda matches his mood, I'm guessing.

'You excited about school next week?' I ask more quietly. 'Junior high already. You're such a grown-up.'

He shrugs, still focused on the little screen.

'Do you have an outfit picked out?' I ask, trying to draw him out.

'Ew, gross,' he says. I knew that would get him – picking out clothes is something girls do, according to my brothers. Not manly enough for them.

'Right, I forgot,' I say. 'Well, are you and Daniel in the same class?' Daniel was his best friend last year, though I'm suddenly pretty sure I haven't seen him in a while. I don't even know if they're still tight – things like that change a lot between elementary school and junior high. And

Tommy's been busy with camps half the summer.

Sure enough, Tommy flinches when he hears Daniel's name. 'Yeah,' he says, but he sounds anything but happy about it. 'Do you guys still hang out?'

Another shrug.

'That's okay, you know,' I say, pulling out my well-worn Big Sister Wisdom Card. 'I made a lot of new friends in junior high, and only kept a couple people from grade school. Like Brielle – that's when we started being friends. Well, eighth grade. But still. You get older, you meet people more like you, people you have more in common with.'

'Brielle isn't like you,' Tommy says in a low voice. I'm almost not sure I heard him right, but then he adds, 'She's a bitch.'

'Tom!' I say, stunned. 'That's not a nice thing to say!'

Finally he looks up at me. 'But it's true,' he says. 'She got you in all this trouble. She's the reason nothing's good any more.'

I open my mouth and hesitate, totally lost for words. Usually, Tommy and Alex are the two boys I can always talk to. But I guess this one is growing up, already learning how to stump me, even before he officially starts seventh grade. Suddenly I remember that day in Dylan's car, when he said the same thing. I didn't know what to say then, either. I never thought Brielle was a bitch. I thought she was strong. She stood up to people; she fixed things. Like my life.

Tommy and I look at each other for a long minute, and I think about everything he just said. Finally I ask, 'What's not good? I mean, I know things are messed up right now, but it's my mess, right?'

He looks back at his DS, then sets it down on the kitchen counter and puts his hands in his lap. 'It's my problem too,' he says. His voice is almost a whisper.

I think about yesterday, with our dad, how Tommy wouldn't look any of us in the eye. 'Is this about Dad?' I ask, still struggling to understand.

'Why does everyone keep *asking* me that?' he yells. 'It's not about Dad! God!'

'Okay, okay!' I throw up my hands, trying to call a truce, calm him back down. 'I just thought – I mean, you didn't seem that happy to see him.'

'Like you were?'

This is true. But I try to not show the boys how I really feel. He's their dad, too, and they don't deserve to hate him. At least, not until they're older. And he's usually good to them, aside from the fact that he's almost never around. Like yesterday, coming over with ice cream and then spending a few hours playing ball with them both before Mom got home. Of course, then he yelled at her for a while and left. Like usual. But the ice cream and game of catch – those were pretty nice, weren't they?

Maybe *pretty nice* isn't enough for Tommy any more, like it stopped being enough for me.

'Everyone at camp knew about – you know,' Tommy

says. 'Emma. I tried to tell them that it wasn't your fault, but some of them were saying that you and Brielle and them, like, beat her up, which you *didn't*, and that you made her . . . you know. Really sad. So no one would believe me. They said I was a bully too. No one would talk to me.'

I feel like I can't breathe. I put a hand on Tommy's shoulder and give him a little rub, but inside I feel like I'm dying.

'That's . . . that's really unfair,' I say. 'You didn't do anything wrong. You've never bullied anyone.'

'Neither did you!' he insists. Then he pauses, and looks me right in the eye. 'Right?'

In that instant, tears pop into my eyes. It stings like hell and it happens so fast I nearly choke. All I can do to answer Tommy is shrug a little. I keep my hand on his bony little shoulder blade, holding his gaze. His big brown eyes look at me steadily, but even through my tears I can see them change. Like, one instant he trusts me, he's a kid – and then a second later, I'm looking at older eyes, harder ones. He looks so much like our dad. And suddenly it's like our dad's eyes are looking out of Tommy's face now.

He picks up his game and slides off the kitchen stool without a word. I watch him go, and that's when I see that Carmichael is standing in the doorway, looking at me. The tears have started falling now, so I can't see what his eyes look like. Which is good. I don't want to know.

But when I put my head down on the counter and start

to sob, I hear Carmichael walk across the kitchen and sit down next to me. After a minute, he puts his hand on my back, just like I did for Tommy.

It doesn't help me any more than I helped my brother. But it's not nothing, either. It's not nothing.

February

'See, that's him over there, warming up.' I point, and Alex cranes his neck, as if sitting up straighter will make it easier to see across the indoor field.

'Oh, yeah, I see him,' Tommy says. 'Do you know all those guys?'

'Not really,' I say. Alex is still squirming around, a bundle of excited energy. 'Bud, you wanna go get us some sodas from the machine?' I ask him, hoping that'll burn off some of the wiggles. Or just give me a break from them for three minutes, at least.

'Yeah!' He keeps shifting around as I pull a five-dollar bill out of my purse and hand it over.

I expect Tommy to go with him, but his eyes are glued to the field, and the vending machines are within sight, so I can keep an eye on Alex. He sprints away.

'Dad likes to play catch with us,' Tommy says.

I'm not sure what he's trying to say, but I get that sometimes he just likes to talk about our dad. Even if I don't. So I go, 'Yeah, I know. We have all those gloves in the garage. I bet Dylan will come over again soon, if you want to practise? For the next time Dad comes to visit?'

'Yeah, cool,' Tommy says.

We turn our focus back to Dylan and the rest of the team. It's just a bunch of drills, not a game, but it's sort of more fun this way. The giant indoor facility is on the university campus, and I like the way the white canopy feels like it's a mile over our heads. I texted Dylan that we were coming, mostly so he'd know I couldn't stick around after practice because my brothers would be here. But I don't mind. I feel so grown-up, driving two kids around a college campus, visiting my varsity boyfriend, watching a bunch of senior guys I didn't even know three months ago but who now keep waving hello. I feel like this is what college will be like – though hopefully I can at least get into (and pay for) the bigger university, in Lincoln. If I stay here I bet my mom will want me to live at home.

'They only had Sprite!' Alex is yelling, holding up a plastic bottle to me. The boys aren't allowed to drink anything with caffeine, so I assume this means that they didn't have, like, 7-Up or anything. 'And I only got two, they were two-fifty!'

'Ouch,' I say. I'm talking about the price, but he also accidentally smacks me with one of the bottles. Not on purpose or very hard, but still. I take it and pass it over to Tommy, who opens it without looking at us. 'Hey,' I say, nudging him.

'Thanks,' he says automatically, still not looking over. It occurs to me that he's feeling kind of grown-up, too, and probably doesn't want his big sister bugging him. Or his little brother.

I look around the bleachers, wondering if Brielle is gonna be here. She said she might come, but she's not that into my brothers. I get it. Sometimes it bums me out, of course, but Brielle's an only child, so it's not like she could even understand. Still. She's been hanging out with this guy Marcus a lot, and he's on the team, so I guess there's a chance she might show.

But instead I see Emma. She's just walking in, with Beth. Ugh, I forgot that Kyle's on the team, so I'll probably be seeing even more of her. Whatever.

I try to look away, but it's like my head is stuck. She and Beth are talking in low voices, and Emma looks like she's been crying or something. She always looks that way – when she's not flirting with some guy or whatever. Or even when she is, sometimes. She's this permanent bruise, always getting her feelings hurt, always *injured*. Everyone at school knows she sees a therapist, and I wonder why they haven't just put her on antidepressants already. Or ones that actually work.

Beth looks up and sees me and waves. I don't really like her, but I nod a little. Emma looks over and I glare at her, but I don't know if she sees it. She has on that pretty coat again, and everything about her looks, I don't know, *vivid*. But fragile at the same time. Like when Mom took us to see

123

Finding Nemo in 3-D and the fish looked like they were real, they were so bright – but then you reached out your hand and it would pass right through them.

Finally I manage to stop staring at stupid Emma Putnam and turn myself back toward the field.

'Are you friends with them?' Alex asks. 'Why aren't they coming to sit with us?'

'Probably because you're such a tool,' Tommy says.

'Am not!' Alex protests.

'See, that's just what a tool would say.'

'Tommy, how do you even know that word?' I ask, torn between wanting to yell at him to be nicer to Alex and wanting to laugh at him saying *tool*.

'Everyone knows it,' he says with a shrug.

I manage to keep a straight face when I add, 'Well, it's not okay to call your brother.'

'Yeah,' Alex says, sucking on the lip of his Sprite bottle. He's chewing it like he's a puppy or something, and I can't help but wrinkle my nose.

'But Alex, come on, you could stop being *gross*.'

Then Tommy lets out a burp and I shake my head, wishing I'd thought harder before bringing them here. I'm positive that Emma is staring at us – we're in the front, so I don't know where exactly she and Beth are sitting without turning around again. And I am *not* turning – but I can feel her stupid eyes on us.

Suddenly Dylan jogs onto the field, up to where the plastic pitcher's mound is set up. He does a bunch of professional-looking stretches, then looks over toward us and smiles, waving. The boys wave back like their lives depend on it. I smile, lifting my hand. But at the last moment I think, *What if he's actually waving at Emma?*

It's a crazy thought. Stupid. But it ruins the rest of the afternoon.

'Oh my God, I'm going to pee my pants!' Brielle squeals, doubling over.

'Shh, shh, shh . . .' I chant, but I'm giggling, too. And shivering, and tiptoeing, and hoping we don't both face-plant on the icy street between Tyler's and Emma's houses. 'Come on,' I say as softly as I can, 'we have to do this fast!'

Brielle stops and takes a bunch of deep, fast breaths, biting her lip to stop herself from smiling. She holds up her end of the giant poster-board heart we just got out of her car and says, 'Okay, okay. I got this. You got that?'

I shake my side of the heart – I'm holding the wooden post it's been staple-gunned to – and a cloud of glitter floats through the night air, shimmering in the glow of the fancy lantern-shaped streetlights. With my other hand I salute Brielle, which is a mistake because then we both start giggling again.

We're only one door down from Emma's house, but we're never going to make it at this rate. We were studying at Tyler's, which was really just an excuse to hang out with him, Dylan, and Marcus, who it turns out is taking Brielle to the dance on Friday. The guys don't know we're doing this – they think we're going home, but really we just stopped at the car to get this thing. It's a secret mission. Secret and *freezing*. Which I guess is why this all seems so hilarious, when actually it might be incredibly stupid. Like, maybe stupider than the fake Facebook page.

But Brielle is determined. I think she spent like forty dollars at Michaels getting the supplies for the sign last weekend. And it looks pretty amazing, I have to say. I went over to her house yesterday and we worked on it for, like, two hours. If we were boys and this was really a sign asking someone to the Valentine's dance, the girl would totally say yes, even though the dance is only three days away.

That girl would be impressed until she actually read the message, I mean. We made a giant, glittery heart that says 'Roses are red, violets are blue, Emma's a slut, and a skanky ho, too.'

So . . . not exactly romantic. But you have to be kinda close to the sign to read it, even with the puffy glitter paint we did the letters with. Brielle says that's the best part, that Emma will think it's a real sign right up until she's standing right in front of it.

Now that I'm looking at it, though, the word *slut* is pretty gigantic. It's bigger than Emma's name, even. And to me, *that's* the best part.

Finally we get our hysterics under control, enough to scurry across the dark, quiet street. We pause again in front of the wide lawn of the Putnam place. Emma's parents – or her stepdad, anyway – are pretty loaded, though tonight their yard looks just as sad as everyone else's, covered in patches of half-melted snow and dirty bits of ice from the last storm. Another fancy lamppost lights up the brick walkway leading to their pillared front door, and a big wreath made of roses hangs there. Totally Martha Stewart.

'I wonder why she never throws parties here,' I murmur.

Brielle yanks the heart poster forward and practically pulls me off my feet. 'Because she's a *loser*, dummy,' she snarls. 'Who would come to her parties?'

Of course she's right. And suddenly I get this flash of Dylan hanging out here, sitting close to Emma and smiling like he is in that photo online, and I yank my end of the poster right back.

'Here,' I say, 'lemme stick it in.'

Brielle lets go of the heart completely and doubles over with giggles. 'That's what *he* said!' she cackles.

I'm pushing the pointed wooden stick into the almost-frozen yard and laughing, when suddenly a much brighter light pops on.

A spotlight, mounted over the Putnams' garage, floods the yard, the sign, *us*.

'Run!' Brielle squeals, and we do, back across the street to her SUV. Of course it's pointed the wrong way, so even when Brielle starts it up and steps on the gas, we have to drive past Emma's house. Out of the corner of my eye I think I see someone standing on the big, ornate porch, the rose-wreathed door flung wide. But then we're gone, down the block, and I don't look back.

The sign wasn't even really stuck in the ground when we ran away, but that's fine, since Brielle and I have already done something epic that's going to happen on Wednesday. But the best – or worst, I guess – thing on Wednesday turns out to be something we hadn't even thought of.

Someone has written *SLUT* in huge red lipstick letters down the door of Emma's locker.

'Amazing,' Brielle breathes when we spot it. 'Maybe everyone at this school *isn't* a total moron.'

My stomach does a little flip. It seems like kind of a scary coincidence, since this is the day that the student council is delivering everyone's Valentine roses. You can pay a dollar to send a rose to anyone you want, and they attach a little note if you fill one out.

Brielle and I didn't write on Emma's locker, but we did send her some roses.

Fifty of them.

We wrote notes for most of the flowers, and some we signed from real guys Emma's already dated, like Kyle and Jacob and Tyler. A lot more of them are 'from', like, the school janitor, or the creepy guy who works at the gas station closest to school.

It's just a *prank*. Obviously we're trying to call Emma out for being a boyfriend-stealing skank, but they're just flowers. The locker thing, though, feels like it's kicking everything up a notch, defacing school property and everything. I mean, the sign in her yard was public, but this is right there, right where *everyone* can see it. Suddenly I'm scared again – terrified, really – of getting into serious trouble. Technically, Elmwood has this big anti-bullying policy. None of us have ever seen it in action, but they like to talk about it at assemblies and stuff, and Principal Schoen's words at our post-Facebook-page meeting ring in my ears again. If anyone figures out that all those roses are from me and Brielle, they'll definitely assume we're the ones who wrote on her locker, too.

Brielle and I keep walking down the hall like we haven't seen anything, though Brielle is smirking. The first bell hasn't even rung yet.

And for the rest of the day, Emma gets roses.

In every class, a student council member comes in at the beginning with everyone's delivery. In a regular class, they have maybe a dozen roses total. But if you're in a classroom with Emma, the student council person comes in with an armload, because she gets almost ten every single time. Deliveries only come to real sit-down classes, not gym or whatever, so Emma's desks are pretty obviously piled high with flowers. I hear people from her first period class talking about how popular she is all of a sudden, but by lunch everyone knows that it's all a big joke. And by lunch, Emma can't even walk down the hall where her locker is. The *SLUT* letters must've been written in permanent ink or something, because they're still on it, and other people have started piling their own roses on the floor in front of it. They're tossing flowers at her in the hallways, too, when there aren't any teachers around.

I only end up really seeing her once, from way down the hall, right after fourth period. She's throwing an armful of flowers away in the big trashcan outside the cafeteria. Jacob and Tyler walk by her, and I see Jacob clutch his chest over his heart, all fake-dramatic wounded. From all the way at my end of the hall I hear him exclaim, 'Don't you *love* me anymore?' and then he and Tyler are cracking up, walking away.

After that, I hear, Emma spends the rest of the day in the nurse's office. I figure that's why I don't see her in History, which is my last class of the day and the only one I have with her besides Gym.

When the last bell rings, Brielle and I walk down the hall past the *SLUT* locker, almost defiantly. That's when we see Emma again.

'God, of course,' Brielle mutters as we spot her sitting down on the floor in front of her locker, huddled in a ball, crying. Megan Corley is kneeling down next to her and holding some tissues. The *SLUT* letters are all smeared from where Emma or the janitor or whoever has obviously tried to wipe them off with bleach or whatever. Now it looks like something out of a horror movie, just a bloody red mess. The whole door is obviously going to need to be repainted.

I hear a snort on my other side and turn to see Beth rolling her eyes and smirking at me and Brielle all confidentially, like we're the Three Musketeers all of a sudden. Didn't I *just* see her hanging out with Emma? I guess they're already not friends any more, because Beth goes, 'What a freaking drama queen.' The words are barely out of her mouth before Brielle snaps, 'You're one to talk.' Beth's face freezes. Brielle has already turned away, pulling me down the rest of the hallway, out into the colourless February afternoon.

'We are not calling your parents – yet. But we are taking this very, very seriously. Girls, I cannot tell you how disappointed I am.'

Principal Schoen is leaning over her desk, trying to look us in the eye and clearly wishing she could scare us. It's working on me – I'm staring at the floor and wishing I was dead.

Brielle, not so much.

'I wish you *would* call our parents,' Brielle says evenly. 'I think you know that my mother is an attorney and that my father has invested heavily in this school. I'm sure they would both find this all very interesting. I don't see how you have any evidence that implicates me or Sara.'

I glance up and see Schoen narrow her eyes at Brielle. Shit. The Greggs family might be rich and powerful and legal-minded, but the Elmwood principal is no fool. Plus she probably knows that Mrs Greggs is an attorney – for an insurance company. Not, like, the take-you-to-court-for-harassing-my-daughter kind. Though it's true that Mr

Greggs is crazy rich.

'Miss Greggs,' Schoen says, her voice just as even as Brielle's, 'this is not the first time you've been in my office this semester. Your name seems to be coming up quite a lot these days, and I am not pleased. The Putnams are also not pleased. And no matter what you think, this is not a court of law. I have complete authority to mete out punishment as I see fit. Therefore, you and Miss Wharton here are banned from attending the Valentine's dance this Friday.'

'What!' Brielle yelps, bolting forward in her chair like she's been electrocuted. 'That's ridiculous! We didn't *do* anything!'

Schoen looks over at me, and I scowl. I can't look her in the face and lie like Brielle can, but I agree that this is completely unfair. Maybe Dylan didn't make a big fancy sign to ask me to the dance, but that doesn't mean we don't have plans – big, after-party hotel room plans – that are now going to be destroyed. My knotty stomach sinks even lower, in an even bigger tangle of knots. Which I didn't even realize was possible until just now.

'Ladies,' the principal says sharply. 'If I have to speak to either of you again, trust me, things will be much worse. I don't want to have to suspend you. I don't want to bring your parents in. I trust that you can correct this destructive behaviour and show me that you embody the inclusiveness and open-mindedness that Elmwood prides itself on. I am holding you both to a higher standard. I expect you to live up to it.'

132

At the end of this speech Schoen abruptly stands up from her desk, gesturing toward the door.

'I believe you have classes to return to,' she says.

Even Brielle doesn't know what to say. But she makes a loud huffing sound as she grabs her bag and pushes out of her chair. She's already throwing open the principal's office door as I get up and collect my things.

'Sara,' Schoen says, more quietly. 'Think about what I've said. You can do better.'

I look at the floor again. I don't know what to say to this. So I just leave.

September

'So, which one did you pick?'

'Pick? What do you mean?'

'You know. To be, or not to be? Wasn't that the question?'

We've just passed our papers forward to Mr Rodriguez and Carmichael is giving me this totally serious look. A second ago I was sweating, not sure I'd finished the last essay question very well, not sure why I care about my summer school pass/fail status at all, and now I'm looking at Carmichael's green eyes. Which have – it has to be said – a *twinkle* in them.

'You're messing with me,' I say, trying to push down the smile at the corners of my mouth. Trying to not look shocked, though I kind of am. 'You're being *funny*.'

'I have my moments,' he says.

For a second we look at each other and we both smile, like we're having a moment. Together.

And I guess we did have a moment – a last one. That was our last test. Carmichael is picking up his bag and getting up now, and I feel my stomach drop. We finished watching the movie on Saturday, but we didn't really talk after the Emma thing, and now he's going to walk out and bike away and I'll be alone again. Or I'll go back to see Dylan, and just end up feeling worse. Something about Carmichael makes me feel . . . not worse.

'Hey, you want to get, um, a drink?' I blurt, grabbing my own bag and sort of stumbling out of my chair, trying to catch up with him before he's gone.

Carmichael turns. He pushes his hair back with one hand and raises an eyebrow, and I realize what I've just said. 'I don't really drink,' he says seriously. 'Not my thing.'

'I didn't mean *drink* drink,' I say quickly. 'I meant, you know, coffee. Or tea. Or iced tea. Or iced coffee.'

'Or one of each,' he says.

'Sure,' I say, wishing I could just talk like a normal person. Brielle would – well, I already know. Brielle would not approve. But Carmichael is smiling at me again, and nodding, and I nod back at him and we walk together to my car.

We don't talk while I drive – the closest Starbucks is only about a block away from school, so it's more like moving the car to another parking lot – and by the time we're sitting down with our drinks I realize I seriously don't know what to say to him. I stare at his Occupy This T-shirt and wonder why I never watch the news; maybe I'd have something interesting to bring up right now if I knew

135

anything besides a few theories on Hamlet's manic-depressive personality.

But of course I don't watch the news. Sometimes I'm *on* the news.

'So,' Carmichael says, finally breaking the silence. He shakes his venti iced green tea, rattling the ice, sighs. 'Real school in a couple days.'

'Go seniors,' I say, with zero enthusiasm in my voice.

'Are you gonna be there?' he asks, and the bluntness of the question takes me by surprise.

Of course I know exactly what he's asking. I look down at the ring of condensation my iced latte is making on the table and shrug. 'Yeah,' I say. 'I mean, I have to go to court in like a month. But for now, yeah, I'll be in school.'

I can't look up at him, but I feel him nodding. 'That's rough,' he says.

'Yeah,' I say again. It *is* rough. I don't know what else to say.

'People judging you . . . I mean, whatever happened, that's hard,' he adds.

Finally I look up at him again. He's staring at me like I might not understand what he means, like I might not believe him. Like I haven't been judging him since the second I laid eyes on him – first as a hot emo guy, then as a pathetic burnout. I didn't even know him that whole time. All I know, even now, is that he's the type of guy who will talk to me – will have coffee with the girl who's been accused of a horrible crime.

And then I realize he's probably talking about ninth grade, when everyone called him Bomb Boy for basically the whole year. I'd forgotten all about that until just this second, but of course, it makes sense. Someone said there'd been a bomb threat at school – turned out that wasn't even true, but Carmichael was already into heavy metal and wearing black all the time, so the name stuck. I try to remember if I called him that. I'm sure I did.

I look toward the window, a few tables away, and notice a woman staring at me. At least, I think she was staring – she sort of glances away when I catch her eye, like she'd been staring right up until then.

Turning back to Carmichael I try to change the subject. 'What's that tattoo about, anyway?' I ask him, pointing to his wrist.

He turns his arm, looking at the infinity symbol like he's just noticing it. 'Oh, yeah,' he says. 'Well, it's an infinity symbol.'

'I know,' I say. 'But . . . why do you have it?' I wonder if this is too personal to ask or something. Too late now, though.

He shrugs. 'I lost someone,' he says. 'And I like to remind myself that forever doesn't always mean forever. Or, you know, forever means different things.'

I nod, though I'm not really sure I know what he's talking about exactly. 'Like, gone but not forgotten?' I guess.

'Kind of, yeah,' he says.

'Was it – was it someone close to you? That you lost?'

'My grandma,' he says. 'She was still pretty young, but she had a good life, you know, all that. But I miss her.'

I nod again. I love my grandmother, my mom's mom, though I don't get to see her very much. I start to tell Carmichael he was lucky to know his grandma so well, but I don't know if that's the wrong thing to say.

He leans back in his chair and gives me a little smile, and suddenly I feel a heat creeping up the back of my neck, like his gaze is a furnace. I grab my drink from the table, hurriedly pulling the rest of the coffee through the straw, making the last few ice cubes rattle. When the slurping sound gets really loud, Carmichael laughs.

'You're weird,' he says.

Despite everything, I smile. 'You're always saying that, but in fact, *you're* weird,' I say.

'Yeah, I know. Remember? That's how I can tell you're weird, too.'

He pushes out his chair and tosses his empty cup in the trash can behind us. As I get up to follow him out, I feel lighter. I'm still smiling a little, wondering if maybe I've found someone who really does understand. I mean, we have this dumb inside joke now, right? Maybe I'm not completely alone.

But just as we're opening the door, I look back over at the woman who was staring at me before – and meet her eyes again. This time she doesn't look away. I do; I swivel my head around and march out the door like nothing happened. But I saw that look. I can still feel it.

Bully.

'When you look back on it now, do you think maybe you and Brielle might have been kind of scary? That Emma might have been afraid of you?'

Therapist Teresa peers at me earnestly over her glasses, and I practically have to close my own eyes to keep from rolling them.

'Um, what?' I ask. 'We didn't scare her.'

'You don't think so? It was kind of two against one, wasn't it?'

'Well, I mean . . .' I pause. 'You make it sound like we were, like, Chris Brown or something.'

She tilts her head to the side, asking a question without saying anything (for once).

'You know, the singer? Beat up Rihanna?'

'I know who you mean,' says Teresa, 'I'm just not sure how that applies here.'

'Whatever, I just mean,' I say with a big sigh, 'we didn't, you know, beat Emma up. She didn't have a black eye or whatever.'

'Yes,' Teresa agrees. 'But you made her afraid, right? To go to her locker? To go to her car?'

'She did that to herself,' I say, crossing my arms. 'And we weren't the only ones! everyone at school said stuff about her – they said stuff about a lot of people.' It's freezing in here again, and I forgot my sweater.

Before coming over here I dropped Carmichael off at his bike and said I'd see him at school next week. But as soon as I was alone in the car, I remembered – Brielle will be at school. I'll have someone to hang out with again. I figure they can't keep us apart when we're at Elmwood, even if we're technically not supposed to talk. And besides, what am I going to do without her there? Where would I sit at lunch? Carmichael has his own friends. Brielle will totally burn me for hanging out with a Carless, and Carmichael's friends would probably think I'm a bitch, just like everyone else.

Teresa is just quietly studying me, and it takes me a second to remember what I was saying.

'Look,' I say. Trying to explain the basic laws of high school to this woman – to any adult – is freaking exhausting. 'Emma transferred to Elmwood two weeks into the year, slept with a bunch of guys before we even had winter break, and was constantly acting like a total freak. If she was worried about walking to her car, it wasn't because of whatever me and Brielle might say. *Everyone* was saying it. Because of how she *was*. Because it was *true*.'

'It was true that Emma was a . . . slut?'

I can tell it hurts Teresa to say the word out loud, but I'm relieved she seems to finally get it. '*Yes*,' I say.

'For having a few different relationships?'

'Pfft,' I sputter. 'A *few*? Yeah, she had a *few*. In the span of a *few* months.'

'But why should that make you angry?'

140

'Because one of them was with my boyfriend!' God, maybe she isn't getting it, after all.

'Weren't you already angry with her before she . . . "hooked up" with Dylan?'

'I already knew she was a slut,' I say, ignoring her awkward use of teen-speak. 'I don't know why you keep saying I was angry.'

'You seem angry now,' Teresa says gently.

'Yeah, well, *now* I am! She completely ruined my life!'

'But her life is over,' Teresa points out. Her voice is very quiet and measured, but she's staring at me like I'm a bug under a microscope. One that's trying to escape.

And I do shift on the couch, suddenly feeling hot instead of cold, wanting to get out of here.

'Emma's life is over because of *Emma*,' I say. 'I didn't kill her. Brielle didn't kill her, the guys didn't kill her. Maybe someone should blame her parents for making her transfer schools a million times. Or just being crappy parents, or whatever, I don't know. I just wanted her to stay away from me and my boyfriend, and she wouldn't.'

I'm panting a little bit, feeling like I just ran around the block at top speed. I can't look Teresa in the eye, though I know she's still giving me that stare, but anywhere I look all I can see is Emma's hair. All that red hair, hanging from the garage ceiling. I wasn't there, of course, and I've tried so hard not to even think about it for a second. And now I feel like I'm standing in that garage, I can't stop seeing that hair, just hanging down, lifeless but bloodred,

141

obliterating her pretty face.

Her stupid, stupid, pretty face. *What the fuck, Emma? I* think. If I had been there, if I had been anywhere – for months, that's all I wanted to say to her. *What the fuck? What is* wrong *with you? What the* fuck *are you* doing?

My breathing is even faster now, and I feel kind of numb. There's a whirring sound coming from somewhere, and the cold garage in my mind shifts into a smooth cold cloud, a white, freezing cloud where my head should be, floating away from the rest of me. It seems like Teresa is beside me on the couch, smoothing her hand on my back, like she's always been there. Through the tunnel of fuzzy noise I hear her say, 'lean over', but her voice is coming from a long time ago. I mean, a long way away. I mean, it's a far sound . . . A long distance . . . A . . .

I think my eyes were closed. I'm not sure, though. All I know is that I'm staring at the ceiling and it's suddenly in focus.

I'm lying down on the couch, but my feet are still on the floor. My hands are folded on my stomach. I feel them out of nowhere, like the view of the ceiling, something that wasn't there a second ago. Teresa is putting something wet on my forehead and talking quietly.

'Don't worry, you're okay, you just fainted for a minute, you're fine now,' she's chanting.

It's a wet cloth on my head, and when I reach up to pull it off, my arm feels heavy and watery.

'Have you eaten anything today?' Teresa asks. 'I think I have some cookies at my desk, stay here . . .'

She moves away and I go to sit up, but the rest of my body is cold and watery too. And heavy. So I stay down. I stare at the line of paint, at the turning point from the wall to the ceiling.

I never faint. I'm not a fainter. I always kind of wanted to – it's such a girly, old-fashioned thing to do. To swoon. Some guy is supposed to catch you. I mean, it would be better if it happened that way. This way is just stupid.

It's the stupid heat, I think vaguely. Or maybe Teresa just said that?

She comes back and I eat one of those Pepperidge Farm fruit cookies, still lying down. I think I must have crumbs all over my face and in my hair, and it kind of tastes like dust, but I eat it fast. When I'm done I'm able to sit up and say, 'Thank you.'

'Of course,' Teresa says. She's back in her chair, but she's leaning over her knees, not holding her pad and pen like always. 'Why don't we call it a day? I'll leave you here to rest for a few more minutes, all right?'

I nod, though I don't feel like staying.

'I'll step out, and I'm going to call your mother,' she says, standing up.

'No,' I say, my voice suddenly loud. 'Don't.'

She looks down at me and I know she wants to ask another damn question. But for once she just nods and says, 'Okay. I'll be back in about five minutes to get you.'

I close my eyes as she shuts the door. For a second the image of Emma flares up again, red and white and cold and hot, and I think I'm going to throw up the cookie.

I open my eyes again and Emma disappears. It's just the old wooden coffee table with the box of tissues. Teresa's worn-out chair. My knees are still pale after this long, long summer spent inside, talking about my feelings, talking about a girl I barely knew who didn't want to live.

Didn't want to live in a world that had me in it.

And I'm still here, in this crappy world. Fighting her ghost.

The thing about having one really good friend, one person you talk to all the time about everything, is that you stop *really* talking to anyone else. You sort of talk to other people, but mostly you have your one person and that's enough.

And then one day, maybe for a good reason or maybe out of nowhere, you can't talk to that friend anymore, and you suddenly realize you *can't* talk to anyone else. Like, it's physically impossible. No one understands you except that person. It's like you speak another language, and the one other person who also speaks it is gone.

That's how I feel, walking into Elmwood the day after Labour Day. All the usual changes from summer vacation – Mayla Stotz's new super-embarrassing haircut, and Wayne Halleck's growing about five inches in all directions, and Ms Hillman wearing a giant engagement ring – make me desperate to turn to Brielle and go, *Did you see that?*

But Brielle isn't here. I mean, she's not with me, of course, as I walk carefully to my locker. She must be here somewhere, but I haven't been able to spot her yet – I was checking for her car in the parking lot, and I look down the hall where her locker is as I pass by, but there's no sign of her. I figure they made sure we don't have any classes together, but I have to see her eventually. Or she'll find me.

Carmichael finds me first, though.

'God, I've missed this place,' he says. He leans against the locker next to mine, like we're totally casual, the oldest of friends. 'You know what I mean? If I'm not here every single day of my life, I just feel . . . *incomplete.*'

I smile at him, but I'm nervous. What do I do when I see Brielle? What if Carmichael is still standing here? Do I pretend I'm annoyed that he's talking to me?

Because actually, I'm really not. I'm so relieved to have someone to talk to, and I'm not at all annoyed that it's Carmichael.

On the first day we only have a half hour of each class, just enough to pick up books and get each syllabus and stuff. The fact that it's a half day is the only reason I'm not already throwing up.

We also have to go to the office to check in, because of summer school. We walk there together, and on the way I can feel people murmuring. I can't believe my mom wouldn't let me transfer. Natalie said it wasn't a good idea, said we should maintain my innocence by not acting guilty,

145

or something. I don't know. I guess transferring doesn't always work out – I mean, Emma tried it a bunch of times. But now that the hallways are crowded and the lights are on full blast, I feel like everyone's looking at me. I feel like I really shouldn't be here.

I see Alison Stipe walk by and I try to wave or at least catch her eye, but she's talking to Beth (that's weird), and they ignore me. Or probably they don't see me. Probably.

'Hi, Mrs Gerald!' Carmichael says brightly as we walk into the main office. I glance over at him, surprised.

'Hello,' the head secretary says sourly, obviously well acquainted with Carmichael already. 'You need your summer transcripts and schedules.' It's not a question, and she doesn't wait for our response before she wheels backward in her chair to a filing cabinet.

Carmichael smiles like he's totally at ease in here. Which he probably is.

'Braden Carmichael and Sara Wharton,' Mrs Gerald says, as she wheels back to the desk.

My eyebrows go up even higher, but Carmichael just shakes his head, like he's heard all the Braden jokes already. Then he goes back to smiling at the secretary and says, 'How'd we do?'

'You passed. Here's your schedules.' She slaps the papers up on the counter, still not getting out of her chair, then wheels back to her computer.

'Congratulations, *Braden*,' I say quietly. I can't help it. I must have known his first name at some point in junior

146

high, but I'd totally forgotten it.

He shakes his head again, but he's still smiling a little.

Mrs Gerald's voice cuts through with an oh-so-cheery 'Get to class!'

We hurry back out of the office.

The hallway is even more crowded than before, everyone hugging and talking so loudly I can't hear anything in particular. I scan the faces, but when people look back at me and frown, I look down again. Turning a little toward the wall so I'm not so noticeable, I ask Carmichael, 'Do you see Brielle anywhere?'

'No, didn't you hear?'

I shake my head. Of course I didn't hear anything. I don't talk to anyone.

I can feel a pit opening up in my stomach. I sort of forgot: Everyone's still talking. Without me. Behind my back.

Everyone knows about me, or thinks they know. But at the same time, I'm invisible. I used to be someone at Elmwood – maybe not the most popular girl, but someone you'd talk to in the halls, at least. Someone you'd see at parties. Someone who at least had a stupid Facebook account. And now I've disappeared. No one wants to even look at me.

'Brielle's not coming back,' Carmichael says. 'Tutors and stuff.'

I stare at him, too shocked to think. 'So she's not . . .'

He just shrugs.

Tyler, Jacob, and Dylan aren't here, because they were seniors. They'd have been gone by now anyway. And now Brielle is gone, too.

So I'm the only Emma Killer left at Elmwood High.

Carmichael walks with me to my homeroom. I don't know whether he can't tell he's with a total outcast, or if he doesn't care. All I can hear are the whispers as we walk by, the weird looks at us. *I'm not alone*, I think. Carmichael's height, his black T-shirt, and black jeans, and dark hair feel like a protective wall beside me.

But I am alone. I am completely alone.

I have Mr Bastow for homeroom. I make a beeline for the back row of desks and end up sitting next to Cherrie. I think she might acknowledge me, at least, as a fellow summer school survivor, but she turns away as soon as I sit down.

Then Mr Bastow gets up at the front of the room, calmly holding up a hand. 'Welcome back, everybody,' he says evenly, and the room gets quieter as everyone stops squealing in delight at seeing each other again.

'We had a tough end to the last year. I know we all want to make this year better, and if anyone can do that, Elmwood High can.'

The one cheerleader in the room, Estrella Santos, lets out a little 'Woo-hoo!' and everyone laughs nervously. Except me, of course.

Mr Bastow picks up a piece of paper, and I think it's finally time for him to go through roll call, or tell us about senior clubs, or whatever.

Instead, he starts reading what sounds like an official statement. 'Elmwood is founded on a long tradition of inclusiveness and acceptance,' he recites. 'We strive to provide a safe space for education and self-discovery for all students. We have a zero-tolerance policy on bullying or intimidation of any kind.'

The class goes absolutely silent. Mr Bastow glances up at us and looks a little bit uncomfortable, but he keeps reading.

'The events of last March were heartbreaking and tragic. We are each responsible for restoring Elmwood High School's stellar reputation to its rightful place. This year will be a time for healing, and we will be instituting new initiatives to promote awareness and a mutual respect among the student body.

'We mourn the loss of one of our own, Emma Putnam, and we move forward with the goal of being a better community in the wake of this terrible tragedy. With education comes knowledge, and with knowledge comes understanding.

'We also have a new school policy: any student caught in an act of bullying or intimidation, online or otherwise, will be immediately suspended. Please report any incidents to Principal Schoen or any of your wonderful teachers.' Mr Bastow says this slightly sarcastically, but he waves his hand a little, as if to volunteer himself as one of those wonderful teachers. 'Let's have a great year.'

He reads the last line fast, then slaps the paper onto his desk, picking up another one. 'Yael Abramowitz?' he calls.

Yael pauses a second before replying uncertainly, 'Here?'

'Christopher Black?' Mr Bastow goes on. The class slowly comes out of the trance the speech cast on us, and roll call goes on.

I'm staring at my desk, but on my left I can feel Cherrie looking over at me – not full-on, but just enough that I can feel the burn of her stare. And in front of me, Adam Levitt and Jamie Huang turn to each other, then glance over their shoulders at me.

Those murmurs in the hallway were nothing. Now I'm trapped, and everyone's just waiting for me to say something, to get kicked out of school for good.

I thought my trial started in four weeks, but obviously it's starting right now.

February

'Dude, are you kidding?' Brielle walks straight into the suite and does a spin in the middle of the floor, her arms flung out and her purse whipping around. 'This is so much better than the stupid gym!'

I follow her inside, my heels sinking into the soft hotel carpet. It *is* nice in here. Dylan got a whole suite at one of the fanciest downtown hotels, and outside the big windows I can see there's a balcony overlooking the glittering city lights. It's not Times Square or anything, but it feels very grown-up, and I get a little dizzy from the sight. I feel the way I did at Dylan's practice the other day: like I'm in college, like I have a real *life*. Or I'm starting to, anyway. It's all out there, out in that glittery night.

Behind me, Dylan and Marcus are lugging in the half-keg of beer. Grunting, they set it down next to the suite's little bar area, where Tyler is breaking open bags of plastic cups.

I wobble on my heels a little walking over to the

windows to get a better look. Brielle joins me, breathing heavily from her one-woman dance routine.

'This town is freaking lame,' she announces. I had just been thinking that it looks really pretty like this – at night, from up high, with the winter air making everything extra sharp and sparkly – but I don't argue with her. Brielle's mood has been especially brittle since our talk with Schoen. I know I'm freaked out by the thought of our parents being hauled in to discuss our 'behaviour', and I think Brielle is too. Even if she'd rather die than admit it.

'I can't wait for college,' I say, figuring that's a safe topic. We've both been planning to go out of state if we can, hopefully to the same place. Brielle likes Marquette, but I think that's just because this hot guy from last year's senior class went there. I want to go to Chicago, maybe. Except I'm not sure how I feel about being that close to my dad and his other family.

'Huh,' Brielle says, tapping a long fingernail on the glass. 'Aren't you mostly just applying to Lincoln, though? Not exactly, like, an enormous change of scenery.'

I can't tell if she's trying to hurt my feelings, but this stings. It's not like I have any idea how many options are going to come through with any financial aid or whatever. I have to apply somewhere local, somewhere cheap. Plus it doesn't seem like such a terrible option to be close to my brothers – without actually living at home. And anyway, I want to point out, Brielle isn't exactly on the road to being valedictorian either – Marquette would probably work, but neither of us is going off to, like, MIT – when behind us the guys suddenly let out a yell.

'Whoa, whoa, watch out!' Tyler shouts – the loudest, as usual. He, Dylan, and Marcus are all holding Solo cups under the keg's faucet thing, trying to catch a fountain of foam that's spilling out of it.

'Amateurs!' Brielle yells, running over to the counter and grabbing a cup. She elbows her way between Tyler and Marcus and goes, 'I told you guys you should get a professional in here!'

I use the distraction to sneak off to the master bedroom part of the suite, where I guess I'm staying with Dylan later. My mom wasn't happy about me 'sleeping over at Brielle's after the dance' – a lie so *close* to being true, if we were just in a very nearby alternate universe – because she has, not surprisingly, stuff for us to do around the house this weekend. But I got all dressed up for the 'dance' and let her take pictures of me and Dylan when he came to pick me up, and by the time I left she seemed kind of happy that I was having a normal teenager night out or whatever.

I don't think she'd be so happy to know where I really am, of course. And I can't get her out of my head as I throw my coat on the chair next to the endless king-size bed. Maybe because I suddenly feel like a kid again, here in this room that is so obviously made for adults. My mom expects me to act like her second-in-command, to do all the stuff she doesn't have time to do. But I'm supposed to be enjoying my high school experience, right? I have an awesome boyfriend. I have a whole fun group of friends. I have other stuff to do – I can't be worrying about Mom and her stupid home-improvement projects all the time.

I hear Brielle and the boys shouting from the living room and realize I can just go in there and drink too much beer with them, forget about everything. I kick off my heels, knowing that Brielle and I will end up jumping on the suite's couch and playing loud music. It'll be fun. It'll be great.

As soon as I shake this feeling that I'm a little kid, but a thousand years old, all at the same time.

I'm fully drunk by the time the party goes off the rails. Brielle has been doing keg stands with Tyler and Marcus holding her, even though Tyler keeps letting the skirt of her strapless red minidress ride up. My plain black number with a little lace overlay seems kind of sad and boring compared to her outfit, but at least I'm wearing my new black bra and underwear set from Victoria's Secret underneath it. Not that anyone knows that yet. Dylan and I are dancing around (well, I'm dancing around him), laughing at nothing, having a great time. Or at least we are when he's not checking texts on his phone.

'Who was that?' I ask. I'm too drunk to care that I sound needy or suspicious or lame or annoying. Or all of the above.

'Kyle's coming. And maybe a couple other guys from the team.'

Across the room, Brielle lets out a loud 'Woo-hoo!' but I don't know why. She didn't hear what Dylan just said, though I'm sure she'll be excited that the party's getting bigger soon. I'm finally starting to feel relaxed, and the thought of more people just makes me nervous again.

And then, maybe ten minutes later, the door opens and a million people come in. Jacob walks in with Noelle Reese – I heard they were back together, and I guess it's true – and Rob's there with a senior girl I don't know very well, Eliana Greene. A couple of guys from the baseball team, like Dylan promised, are followed by more senior girls, and then I see Kyle.

I know I've had way too much beer then, because the next part totally happens in slow motion. Like I'm in a movie.

A horror movie.

Emma Putnam is with Kyle. She's coming, she's here, she's in this suddenly *tiny* hotel suite, she's like a burst of blinding colour in a black-and-white world. A flame of red hair and shiny blue silk and my white-hot fury.

Brielle is still over near the keg, talking loudly with Noelle. Dylan is fist-bumping all the guys, moving away from me toward the door where more people are spilling inside. I have a bubble around me, an invisible buffer. No one approaches, no one looks – the slow-motion nightmare fades but I'm alone, completely alone.

Finally, when I see Tyler and Dylan walk over to Kyle and Emma, and the four of them talking and laughing, I

155

have to move. I force myself over to where Noelle and Alison Stipe are doing shots with Brielle. They seem like they're just fine without me, and I have to kind of shove my way between Alison and the kitchenette counter to join them.

'Hey, did you see Emma's here?' My voice is too loud and I actually hadn't meant to say anything about Emma, but all three girls snap to attention.

'Wow, that ho can*not* take a *hint*,' Brielle says, but her tone is way more mild than I would've expected.

Then I see that Noelle isn't surprised at all, so maybe Brielle's just trying to be cool in front of the senior. Noelle shrugs a shoulder – she has on a strapless dress too, in a deep purple colour that looks amazing with her dark hair, and she looks a little bored with everything. But Alison says, 'Well, I guess Kyle really likes her.'

Brielle and Noelle laugh at this, so I do too.

'I guess he doesn't mind sloppy . . . what are we up to now? Fifths? Tenths?' Brielle sneers.

I think of the other day when Brielle insulted all the guys at Burger King, and I watch Noelle for her reaction to this. I mean, she's back with Jacob, one of the fifths (or tenths). But she just laughs and drinks more beer.

'So, pretty sweet digs for you and D-Bag,' Brielle says to me. 'Big romantic night, huh?'

I glance at Noelle again, but she's just waiting for me to respond. 'Yeah, I guess so,' I say. 'Kind of a rager now, though.' I swing my arm out to indicate the growing

156

crowd and accidentally hit one of Dylan's teammates' shoulders. 'Oops.'

'Already trying to chicken out, huh?' Brielle nudges Noelle with her elbow and adds, 'Sara's having second-time jitters.'

'I am n—' I start to protest.

'Oh, totally,' Noelle says, cutting me off. 'You gotta shake it off. Once the chase is over, you start chasing *him*, keep him interested.'

My mouth is still hanging open from my unfinished sentence, and now it's stuck that way in surprise. Brielle and Noelle look at me sympathetically, like they've been there a hundred times, kept a hundred *hims* interested. Like they just jumped out of the February issue of *Cosmo*. I don't look over at Alison, because I don't need to – she's been dating this guy Asher since freshman year. Brielle calls them Alisher behind Alison's back.

'At least he got you this nice room,' Noelle adds, lifting her plastic cup in a little toast. 'I had to remind Jacob to get me *flowers*.'

Brielle laughs knowingly. I look around the room again, wondering where my wonderful, thoughtful boyfriend is now.

Still talking to Tyler and Emma. Standing really close to Emma, actually. I turn around again.

Brielle's eyes have followed mine and she goes, 'She is so *whatever*. I mean, give it *up* already.'

'He is totally hot,' Noelle says, clearly understanding

157

what Brielle means, even though I don't. 'Seriously, dude, you're really lucky. He's a nice guy, too.'

Oh, that's what she means. My nice, thoughtful, hot boyfriend. Anyone would want to have him. So I shouldn't be surprised that Emma's trying to, like, climb into his back pocket.

'Get over there, dumbass,' Brielle says. She shoves me, harder than I think she means to, away from them and in the general direction of Dylan's little huddle. I'm still barefoot, so I don't completely topple over, but I stumble a few steps before bumping into Kyle's back. He doesn't even notice, just keeps talking to a couple of baseball guys. Still, I'm red-faced with embarrassment by the time I right myself and squeeze through the crowd to Dylan.

I press myself to his side and glare at Emma. Her eyes widen when she sees me, and then narrow a little. Like a challenge.

'So anyway, *Dylan*,' she says, like I've interrupted a big conversation they were having, 'it's too bad you couldn't come to the dance. It was super fun.'

Tyler barks a laugh. 'Oh, man, you know we love hanging out in the gym on Friday nights! What a bummer.'

Emma's eyes dart over to him, wounded. 'I helped decorate,' she says defensively. 'It looked really nice.'

'Yeah, I'm sure it *really* did,' I hear myself say. My sarcasm is so sharp and sudden that everyone flinches, even me. I don't want to act like a bitch in front of Dylan, but I can't stand this girl. Who does she think she is? She gets us kicked out of the dance and then shows up at our party? What the—

'Okay!' Tyler announces. 'Who needs beer? I need beer. Dollface?' He turns to Emma, putting an arm around her. 'You look thirsty!'

For once in his life, Tyler does something useful and steers Emma to the other side of the room, leaving me and Dylan alone. I stare after them, wondering how Tyler could be mean to Emma with the rest of us, or tease her about the roses or whatever, and still want to hang out with her when he's drunk. I'm just about to ask Dylan why guys are so weird when he pulls me a little to the side and leans in close.

'You don't have to be mean to Emma,' he says.

'But—' I stammer. 'She's—'

'She's actually pretty nice,' he goes on, as if I haven't said anything. Which I guess I haven't.

'She got me kicked out of the dance. And Brielle,' I finally manage.

'That wasn't her,' Dylan says. 'I heard that was her mom. And anyway, didn't you guys put, like, a sign in her yard or something? And send her all those roses at school?'

He's really looking at me, and suddenly I feel like I'm back in Schoen's office. I didn't realize Dylan knew everything. I try not to ever talk to him about Emma, not since I acted like a pathetic idiot about the text she sent. I'm not supposed to care if he talks to her. And sometimes, like Tyler and Jacob, he complains about her too, calls her a slut and stuff. But then one of the guys starts seeing her – like Kyle – and everyone goes back to pretending she's cool.

Brielle is the only one who gets it, the only one who knows that Emma's a slut and shouldn't be talking to anyone else's boyfriend, much less hooking up with them. I look back over to where I was standing with her and the other girls before, but I don't see her. No matter what I do, I'm always on the wrong side of the room tonight.

I still haven't been able to say anything back to Dylan, and he sighs really loudly and goes, 'I'm gonna get another beer, okay?'

I open my mouth, but he's already gone.

And then Brielle is there, grabbing my arm and pulling me into the bathroom. Everything is moving too fast, I can't keep track of anyone. She locks the door behind us and laughs at my shocked expression.

'You know this is a *party*, right?' she asks, turning to the mirror and yanking up the sweetheart neckline of her dress. She hops up and down, shifting her boobs higher, and purses her lips at her reflection.

I lean a hip against the sink counter, avoiding my own gaze, my own boring black dress. 'I just don't understand why Emma had to come,' I say, hating the pout in my voice but unable to smother it.

'God, I know,' Brielle says. She's leaning in close to the mirror now, doing something to her mascara. 'She totally needs to leave. I'm pretty much ready to bail myself. Marcus is actually kind of a dweeb. I dunno. I guess he's hot. I just don't think I'm in the mood.' She leans back again, puffs out her chest in the mirror, then lets her breath out in a *whoosh* and kind of deflates, crossing her arms with a sigh. She looks sad and worried.

I start to reach out to her, faltering halfway, so my hands are kind of floating between us. 'He seems really nice, but you know, if you're worried about . . . I mean, it's not like you guys have to be alone, I can totally—'

'Uch, God, *shut up*, Sara,' she says, snapping back to her normal self. 'Don't go all life coach on me, okay?'

I pull my hands back, so now we're both standing with our arms crossed, me facing her but not able to quite look her in the eye, and her glaring back at me.

'I didn't mean . . .' I say, but I can't finish. I don't know what I didn't mean. She told me all that stuff about swim camp, but I guess it wasn't supposed to change anything. I kind of thought it changed *everything*. But I'm still the one who doesn't understand.

Suddenly I feel so angry at Brielle I could scream. I mean, I had sex with Dylan so she'd be nicer to me, so we'd have something in *common*, finally. So she'd, like, respect me. Instead, it turns out she had a whole different experience, and I'm still alone, I still don't have anyone to tell me what to do now.

Wait. Oh my God. I slept with Dylan so Brielle would be *nice* to me? *What?*

'Honey, don't look like that,' Brielle says, and suddenly

she's pulling me into a hug. 'I'm totally fine, don't worry about me. Marcus is just all *smart* and stuff, it's kind of a drag.'

She's holding my shoulders so my face is smooshed into her long hair. It's perfectly straight tonight, soft and smelling like flowers, but I can't breathe. Maybe if we ever hugged this wouldn't feel so awkward. It's a relief when she breaks free, almost pushing me away, giving her dress one more little adjustment.

'C'mon,' she says. 'That skank is slutting up the whole place. I'm sure everyone could use a break from her aura of skankitude.'

'Her slutmosphere,' I say, trying to get into the spirit.

'Ha! Yeah. Her *whorbit*.' Brielle grabs her sparkly clutch from the counter and clacks across the tiles, throwing open the door. An Usher song throbs from somebody's fancy iPod speakers in the kitchenette.

Out of the bathroom, I immediately realize two things: One, this party is completely out of control. We'll be lucky if the hotel doesn't kick us out within the hour. I don't even recognize a bunch of the people here, and I'll be shocked if they leave in time for Dylan and me to have any romantic . . . whatever. Even though I was worried about being alone with him before, now I'm kind of sad that it probably won't happen, that the special romantic room has been taken over by this party.

And the second thing is – I don't see Dylan.

A lot of the guys here came straight from the dance, so

they're still wearing nice button-down shirts and stuff. I made Dylan wear a tie, so it'd be more believable to my mom that we were going to the dance, but he took it off when we got to the hotel. Still, he has on a nice red shirt, and he's tall, and all night it hasn't been hard to spot him. I mean, we're in a freaking hotel room. It's a suite and everything, but it's not *that* big.

So I hurry farther into the room, out where I can see the whole kitchenette . . . not here. Or maybe in the big bedroom . . . not there either, and *gross*, Noelle and Jacob are making out on the bed. Ugh. So, okay, there's a smaller bedroom on the other side . . . more people making out, gross again.

I hurry back to the master bedroom and grab my shoes, just so I have them, careful to not look at the bed, and rush back into the main part of the suite. *Think, think.* I stopped drinking a while ago but I'm still all dizzy and wired, and it feels like I'm just standing there forever, until finally – the *balcony*. Duh. Dylan doesn't smoke, but lots of people have been going out there all night and he must've gone with one of them.

I spin around a little too fast and have to catch myself with one of the curtains, pulling it back. That helps me find the handle to the glass door, and it slides open easily, unlocked already.

The cold smacks me in the face as soon as I step outside, and I still have my shoes in my hand, so my feet go numb almost immediately. And then the wind

163

is in my eyes, which fill with tears before I can even blink. So at first, I'm not actually sure that I'm seeing what I'm seeing.

But I am; I'm seeing it.

At the other end of the balcony, leaning against the wall and totally oblivious that they're not alone, are Dylan and Emma.

I blink. Once, twice, but they don't disappear.

And they don't stop kissing.

One shoe has hit Emma in the back before the words are even out of my mouth.

'You fucking *slut*! What the *fuck* do you think you're *doing*?!'

My shrieks are carried away in the icy air, leaving me breathless. And then I'm shoeless, too, as Emma turns toward me, her eyes wide and horrified. But not wide enough to dodge the second shoe – this one hits her on the shoulder, just glances it, really, but she yelps, both hands flying up to her face, like I have anything else to throw.

'I *knew it*!' I scream. I turn to run back into the hotel suite but the curtain is in my way and I have to shove at it, pull it – I hear a *clang* and realize I've yanked down part of the curtain rod, but it doesn't matter because I'm inside again, I can't see Emma any more. Part of me wants to turn around and pull her hair out like I pulled the curtain, but most of me just wants to get away, far, far away from here.

Everything is a blur – I'm running and crying and my

164

feet hurt and the halls in the hotel all look the same and Jesus, I really did have too much to drink – why can't I find the elevators? – and then Brielle is there, and I'm wearing a coat. I'm in an elevator, holding on to the wall. I'm outside, I'm putting on someone's shoes that're too big for me. I'm waiting in the cold, the front entry lights of the hotel shining down on me, making me visible to everyone who wants to see a pathetic excuse for a girl, a walking mascara stain, a stupid, no-longer-virgin, cheated-on, worthless—

Brielle's SUV bumps onto the curb and I have to jump out of the way. I almost lose my balance, but instead I'm able to reach out and grab the passenger-door handle. And then I'm in, on a heated seat, the same stupid Ellie Goulding song that was playing upstairs blaring from the speakers as the car bounces back off the curb and pulls out into the night.

'Blech, sorry, lemme just—' Brielle reaches over and punches the radio button off, and the car fills with silence.

It's quiet until I choke on another sob and hear myself whispering, over and over, 'I knew it. That slut. That *slut*. I *knew it*.'

'Shh, shh,' Brielle says. She reaches over and pets my hair clumsily, but with just one hand on the wheel the car yanks dangerously to the right, so she pulls her hand away quickly.

She's drunk and she shouldn't be driving, I think. But I don't care.

'Don't worry, babe,' she says. 'We'll fix this. That bitch won't even know what hit her.'

Good, I think. I nod my head, or my head nods itself. I just keep nodding. *Good, good, good, won't know what hit her*. Then she'll know how I feel right now.

September

'It's exactly like we went over last time. You just tell me how the Valentine's Day events were Miss Greggs's idea. We have the Michaels receipt for the sign supplies, paid for on her MasterCard. Unfortunately the roses were bought with cash . . .' Natalie flips open a file and peers at some fine print before looking back up at me and my mom. 'Then we'll move on to March, okay?'

I nod and focus on Natalie, across the table, ignoring Mom's jiggling foot next to me. We're running through the testimony I'll have to give in two weeks. *Two weeks*. We were in court once before, when the charges were filed and everything, but this time I'll be in a courtroom with Emma's parents. I'll be on the witness stand. I'll be talking, answering questions, getting to tell my side of the story. Natalie said it won't be like TV, it's just a bunch of tables and I shouldn't talk too much or anything. I should just answer the questions like she's telling me to. But still.

I think I'm gonna throw up.

Mom's obviously not feeling so great, either. She's just fidgeting, not looking at me. She has to come to the meetings because we're so close to trial. I know she doesn't want to be here, but Jesus, neither do I. I didn't choose this. I didn't even come up with any of the pranks that supposedly pushed Emma to commit suicide.

Or that's what I'm going to testify to, anyway. That it was all Brielle. And Brielle's probably going to testify that it was all me.

When I told Natalie how unfair that is, she shrugged. 'It's a lawsuit. You want to win.'

I guess it's just as well that I don't have Brielle at school any more. I probably should have known that this whole thing wasn't just going to take her away for the summer – I should have known I wasn't ever getting my best friend back. She's gone now, just like Dylan. Just like everyone.

Natalie's running through the same questions about last February, and I'm answering them the way we practised. Mom gets really quiet while I talk.

Then Natalie says, 'Now, on March first you visited Miss Putnam's home, is that right?'

'Yes,' I say. I feel Mom sit up a little straighter. She hasn't heard this before, I don't think.

'With Miss Greggs?'

'Yeah. She drove,' I add, since Natalie likes to point out anything that makes Brielle look more guilty. Obviously I feel like a total bitch doing this, but it's too late now. My whole life depends on how guilty Brielle is. Or anyway,

168

that's what I tell myself. There's got to be someone to blame.

'Okay. And why were you and Miss Greggs visiting the Putnam home?'

'To . . . um.' I clear my throat. 'We wanted to tell Emma's mom, Mrs Putnam, that Emma had been . . . you know, hooking up with, um, some guys who were . . . who were older.'

'You wanted Mrs Putnam to know that her sixteen-year-old daughter was having sex with young men who were over the age of consent?' Natalie says smoothly.

'Yeah. I mean, I guess so.' My mouth feels dry again. I grab the bottle of water on the table in front of me and gulp some down. A little bit spills on my chest, the part that's not covered by my tank top. It's so cold it burns.

'You were concerned about Emma's well-being,' Natalie says. Not a question.

'Definitely,' I lie.

Natalie nods crisply, and from that point on, I don't think either of us says anything that's true. After another hour we're finally done for the day, or I think we are until Natalie looks at my mom all seriously and goes, 'We really should revisit our talk about a settlement.'

'I want Sara's name cleared,' Mom says.

'I understand that,' Natalie replies, and I can hear in both their voices how many times they've already had this conversation. Like, more than I've heard it.

Natalie goes on. 'After she turns eighteen we can work

to have her record expunged. But for now – I am very concerned. These are serious charges, and I'd be very surprised if the other defendants go through with the trial.'

I shake my head. 'I didn't do anything. I mean, we went over this, right?' I look over at Mom. Her face is set, her mouth pinched. She doesn't look so sure any more.

Natalie pushes back in her chair and says, 'Please just keep thinking about it. It's a compromise, but everything could be over. I think we could get a pretty good deal. You could have your lives back.' She looks at me for a second, like she wants to say something else.

But Mom jumps out of her chair like it's got springs, and almost too late I realize we're leaving. I'm surprised I even catch up to her in time to share an elevator ride back downstairs.

We're alone in the elevator, but if anyone was with us they wouldn't even guess we were together. Mom's still in her work clothes and I'm in jean shorts, but it's more than that. She won't look at me. I guess she's scared too. Or probably just freaked out about all the details we just went over. Every time we come here, it seems like there's something she hasn't heard before. Every time she gets a little more distant.

I want to say something to her – or really, I want her to say something to me. I mean, I'm freaked out too. We're supposed to settle? That means I admit to being guilty. Which I am not. Doesn't she still believe that?

'This is a nightmare,' Mom says, but her voice is a

170

whisper. Maybe I didn't hear her right.

But either way, it's true. This is a freaking nightmare.

On Friday afternoon I'm driving really slowly past Albertsons, wondering what I'm doing on this side of town instead of going to see Teresa and then picking up the boys. This is not on the agenda.

But my car almost magically turns itself in to the grocery store parking lot and finds Dylan's SUV in the last row. There's an empty spot next to it, and without really thinking, I pull in, shutting off the car but not taking the keys out, so I can roll my windows down and keep listening to *High Violet*. The song that goes 'Sorrow found me when I was young' starts, and by the time it gets to 'I don't want to get over you,' I've got my head on the steering wheel and I'm crying. The tears just gush out in big, heaving sighs, shaking my whole body but not making much sound.

I don't *have* to be alone right now. There are people I could be with. But I don't want any of them. I want Brielle, I want Dylan. For half a minute there, my life had actually made sense – I had a best friend, and friends, and a real boyfriend. I was pretty, kind of, or at least I knew how to *act* pretty. Being with Brielle made me pretty, made me belong. Made me laugh. Being with Dylan made me a real person – people could see me. I could go to the mall and see a bunch of seniors and, like, hang out with them. Even after Dylan and I broke up, I still had Brielle, and we had fun.

But maybe now that I think about it, no one really saw me that much, even with Dylan. I was never tagged in his Facebook photos. I was the jealous ex-girlfriend for, like, a minute. And then I was the girl who was there when things with Emma got really messy. I mean, at that point, I was kind of the girl who made the mess – but Emma has to take some of that blame. She didn't have to go after my boyfriend. She didn't have to flirt with Brielle's boyfriend last fall, she didn't have to be friends with Tyler and Dylan and Jacob, she didn't have to walk around like a huge victim and sleep with every guy in school at the same time. Most of all, she didn't have to kill herself. I mean, who doesn't feel like killing themselves at least once a week? It's gotta be easier than this, than high school. It's definitely easier than being blamed for someone else's suicide.

Emma got right in the middle of everything. If I was invisible, she was *too* visible; she was ultraviolet. She was a nuclear explosion, detonating and destroying everything and everyone else in the process. Now I'm stuck at a school that's still in mourning, stuck in a whole world of people who think I'm the reason this girl is dead. They act like they want me dead too, like I should just go kill myself because Emma did – and no one even seems to see how that doesn't make any sense at all.

I'm still crying, but the sobs have turned into regular tears, just fat drops rolling down my face without my permission. The next song starts and I turn the keys, cranking the engine back on. As I'm backing out of the

172

parking space I think I see Dylan in my rearview mirror, walking out the back door in his stupid store clerk blue polo shirt and khakis. I blink hard, trying to clear my vision, but I don't look back again. Instead I lower the visor and slide open the little mirror. Carefully smoothing the skin under my eyes to hide that I've been crying, even though the tears are still coming, I take a long breath. Then I snap the visor back up and jerk the car into reverse. There's still time to kill and I need to do it somewhere else.

No one from school goes to the Starbucks at the Barnes & Noble on Seventy-second Street because it's right next to the crappy mall, which is another place no one goes. The bookstore isn't so crappy, though, and it's not too far from Teresa's. It's basically the perfect place. As I walk in I think maybe I should just move in here.

There's no one in line so I get my latte pretty quickly, even though the guy working looks like he's baked and hates everyone. There are a couple of little kids running around the seating area while their moms talk and take up all the armchairs. So I put a Splenda in my coffee and head farther into the store, running a hand over the Staff Recommends and Great Reads for Back-to-School tables. I turn aimlessly down an aisle and practically trip over someone sitting on the floor.

It's Carmichael.

'Oh,' I say, almost falling backward. We haven't talked

much at school since that first day, mostly because I don't know what to say.

I still don't know, and for a second I think I should just run in the other direction, when Carmichael looks up and shakes his hair out of his face.

'Hey,' he says easily. 'What's up?'

I shrug. I think maybe I've been avoiding Carmichael, but I'm not sure if it's been for his sake or mine. His friends are all shaggy-haired bike riders and usually he seems busy with other things at school – and our schedules are just different. And I've gotten really good at not looking anyone in the eye during the school day. It's easier that way.

'Sit?' he asks, sweeping a hand over the patch of floor next to him like he's offering a silk pillow or something.

What the hell. I shrug again and lower myself down, crossing my legs and looking at the book he has open on his lap.

'It's a good one,' he says. 'Have you read the others? *The Walking Dead*?'

'Like the show?' I ask.

'Waaaay better than the show.' He flips the book closed and adds, 'If you haven't read them, I don't wanna give anything away.'

I smile a little and sip my coffee.

'So,' he goes on, 'You following me now? Like you did all summer?'

'What? That's the dumbest – I wasn't *following* you!'

He keeps a totally straight face as he says, 'Well,

whenever I went to school, you were there.'

I roll my eyes. 'That's how it works,' I say, unable to stop explaining the obvious. 'And you were never there!'

'I helped you pass English, though.'

'Yeah,' I agree. This is true. And he helped me to feel sort of normal for a couple weeks. 'You know your Shakespeare. What were you doing in summer school, anyway?' I've been wondering this for a long time, but I want to bite the words back. It's like when I asked about his tattoos – I'm sure it's too personal.

But like with the tattoos, he doesn't seem to mind. 'I tried to transfer,' he says. 'Well, technically, I tried to move away, but it didn't work out. And by the time I came back, I was behind, so, you know.'

'Where'd you go?' I ask.

'My dad's. Kearney.'

I nod. I've never been to Kearney, but I know it's a couple of hours away, kind of in the middle of nowhere.

Carmichael looks back down at his book, at the cover with a bloody guy on it. 'It's that same old story,' he says, lifting his head again but staring at the shelves now. 'Crappy dad, never around, gets back in touch, blah blah blah.'

'So you moved in with him?' I ask. I used to think about going to live with my dad sometimes. In the very beginning, before he had new kids and everything, it was like this perfect fantasy – we'd live in a fancy apartment in Chicago and we'd do stuff together. I'd learn to like baseball or fishing or whatever. I'd be one of those pretty tomboy-type girls, with this cool dad teaching her how to fix cars.

Obviously it was a completely stupid idea.

Carmichael nods and finally looks back at me again. 'He's still a crappy dad, so things didn't work out,' he says. 'Not a very good story, I guess.'

I shake my head. 'No, I know exactly what you mean,' I say. 'I have one of those.'

'Does he live in a trailer?' Carmichael asks. I think he's joking but I just smile a little, I don't laugh.

'No, he lives with the new-and-improved family,' I say.

Carmichael nods again.

I want to ask him something else – I want to stay in this moment, this minute of having a real conversation with somebody. But I'm pretty sure I'm late, and when I check my phone quickly – 'Shit, I have to go.'

'Oh, yeah, sorry,' he says, watching as I scramble to stand back up.

'God, no, I interrupted you,' I say. 'Now you can read about your vampires, I just have to – I have an appointment.'

'Vampires?' Carmichael clutches his chest like I've shot him in the heart. 'A palpable hit!' He falls back on the floor, still clutching, and now rolling around and moaning.

'Zombies, sorry!' I say, laughing. 'Calm down! I know they're zombies!'

'Ohhhh,' Carmichael groans.

'C'mon, get up!' I say. 'I really have to go!'

'Just leave me here . . .' He gasps like it's his dying breath. 'I'll . . . be . . . fine . . .'

I shake my head, even though he's not looking at me. 'Okay,' I say. 'See you later.'

I turn and start hurrying out of the store. Behind me I hear one last wounded cry: '*Vampires!*'

I must look like an idiot, running and laughing all by myself.

'I really don't want to talk about that weekend.'

'I know, Sara. But it's going to come up, right? At your trial?'

'I guess.'

'So you've talked to your lawyer about it?'

'Mmhmm.'

'But did you talk about how you felt?'

'How I felt?'

'Yes, how you felt. How did you feel?'

'That weekend? Or, like, now?'

Teresa spreads her hands wide, like, *Take your pick.*

'I feel like shit.'

'Now?'

'Always. And yes, now.'

'What about that weekend?'

I blink fast, forcing back the tears that I can't seem to completely shut off. 'Well, that Saturday . . .' I sigh heavily. 'That night was great. I felt great, okay? I don't understand what the big deal is. I don't understand what the big deal to *Emma* was. I mean, she had *just* done the *same thing* to me! Like, three weeks before that! And did

177

I turn around and *kill myself*? No.'

'Do you think that's what happened?'

Now I throw my hands up, frustrated again by Teresa's endless Q & A, which never include, of course, any As. 'Does it matter? Obviously *everyone else* thinks that's what happened, or I wouldn't be on freaking trial for it!'

She just looks at me, her eyes narrowed in a thoughtful way. If I didn't know better, I'd say she was considering giving me a hug. But people don't hug me. I don't think anyone has – my little brothers don't count – in months. Years, maybe. Does making out count as hugging? Probably not. Especially if you're making out with Dylan, because his hands are so busy, there's no real *embracing* going on.

In the back of my mind a little image of Carmichael flickers – his arm around me in my kitchen while I cried. I push the picture away.

And Teresa doesn't hug me. She and I are just staring at each other. I used to be unable to look right at her, either out of annoyance or embarrassment. Now I'm too worn out to feel annoyed or embarrassed or . . . anything.

'Fine,' I say. I take a long, shuddery breath. This day is the worst already, but I guess it's not worse than that weekend turned out to be. 'Saturday, right? It was just a hang, you know, not even a real party. I knew Dylan would be there, and I thought Emma would be too.'

'So you were hoping to see her?'

'Yeah, kind of,' I say, surprising myself. Seeing Emma and Dylan together had become like a scab you can't stop picking at – it turned my stomach, but I couldn't do anything else. Plus, getting through a weekend without seeing Dylan was like torture. Seeing him with his new girlfriend was torture too, but at least I was out of the house on a Saturday night, still hanging out with cool people. I remember thinking that Dylan would see me in my new tank top and think I looked cool and relaxed and way easier to be around than slutty Emma who everyone hated.

Which I guess is kind of what happened.

In a way, that weekend was the whole story. Everyone did enough terrible stuff to get sent to jail, or juvie, or whatever. I mean, maybe not technically, but it was a mess.

But Emma's the one who got the last word. She'll always be that face, that pretty school photo in the newspaper. And we'll always be the monsters who pushed her over the edge.

I can talk to Teresa or Natalie or my mom – well, I can try – but no one really gets it, no one hears me. No one understands how, when Emma went over the edge, she pulled all of us down with her.

February

Emma and Dylan. Dylan and Emma. Just like that.

For most of the day at school, they're together. But otherwise, Brielle and I are on a mission to make Emma's life a living hell.

Brielle seems to know exactly what to do. We wait for Emma outside school on Monday morning, even though it's still freezing. When she finally walks by I start to step forward, but Brielle holds my arm. I wait for her to say something to Emma, but she doesn't, she just waits. As soon as Emma has walked past us, not making eye contact, Brielle lets go of me and follows her into the building. It takes me a second to catch up, but then I see what we're doing – Brielle walks fast and we circle around so we're walking to Emma's locker from the other end. By the time Emma gets there, Brielle and I are standing on either side of her locker, having a conversation, super casual. I just see the red hair and the aqua coat out of the corner of my eye as Emma pauses for a second. Then Brielle looks right at her, staring. Emma holds her gaze for a minute, and I'm almost impressed by her total poker face. But then she turns and walks away.

Brielle watches her go and says, 'God, this is too easy.'

'Are you kidding?' I ask her. My stomach is a jumble of nerves and butterflies and a million other things. I'm so excited and angry and confused I would sprint down the hallway if it weren't so crowded. 'That was *perfect*. How did you do that?'

She rolls her eyes at me and pushes away from the lockers. 'Seriously.' Her voice carries over her shoulder as she leaves me behind again, striding to her homeroom while I scramble to catch up. 'Give me a *challenge*.'

At lunch we sit with Kyle and Jacob and talk loudly about what a loser Emma is, even though she's sitting one table over with Megan Corley.

'I heard she's with Dylan *and* Tyler,' Brielle announces. 'Like, they *share*.'

'Dude, that's disgusting,' Jacob declares, also at top volume.

Emma and Megan exchange a look, then get up from their table, grabbing their barely touched lunch trays. Brielle high-fives me as they leave the cafeteria.

Dating Dylan doesn't help Emma even when we aren't around – the whole school finds out about the Valentine's party and now *everyone* thinks she's gross. Dylan was called a man-whore on Facebook before the weekend was over. I

181

mean, *all* of his best friends have already hooked up with Emma. So far Tyler's the only one who's still talking to both of them, but the thing Brielle says about them 'sharing' becomes everyone's favourite theory by the end of Monday.

I spent all weekend talking to Brielle about what a slut Emma is, and Brielle comments on anything Emma does on Facebook with 'A slut says what?'. We're not friends with her, obviously, but she gets tagged in stuff and it's easy enough to find her on other people's pages.

Still, I don't feel any better about losing Dylan. At night, alone, I have to admit that he must actually like her. I'm not Miss Universe, but I'm not a social outcast, either – or a desperate transfer student, or a slut who's been with all his friends. I slept with him, *only* him. And then I followed him around like a . . . A groupie. A puppy.

But he wants *her*.

And we want her to suffer.

'Did you see what Emma Putnam is *wearing* today? What *is* that?' Brielle says loudly in the locker room before Gym on Tuesday. As usual, we are fully aware that Emma is standing two feet away from us. That's the whole point.

'Oh my God, I *know*,' I practically shout back. 'Do you think she knows? Maybe someone should tell her.'

Emma, who's wearing a sweater and jeans, no big deal at all, practically sprints out of the locker room.

'Jesus, she can't be sick *again*, can she?' Brielle sneers.

'I heard she's been to the nurse's office every day this

182

week,' Beth offers, eager to get in on the action.

To my surprise, Brielle doesn't ignore her this time. 'She has such a *gentle soul*,' she says to Beth.

'Oh, totally,' Beth says. Her sarcasm is about twenty notches too enthusiastic, but the three of us laugh anyway.

'Or maybe she's pregnant,' I say. I don't know what makes me think of this, but now that I've said it, we all realize it could totally be true.

A few other girls turn toward us, and one of them, Parker, goes, 'Wow. How's she going to figure out who the father is?'

I feel sick and satisfied, all at the same time. Like the other night, when I ate all the leftover Valentine's candy in one sitting – it was gross, but I'd be unwrapping another piece before I'd even swallowed the one in my mouth. Like I *wanted* that gross feeling – like having too much was the whole point.

We're playing volleyball in gym, and I hit the ball so hard every time, the girls on the other side of the net jump out of the way. Everyone knows I'm in a terrible mood; they all know I got cheated on and broken up with. I mean, there was no official breaking up – screaming at Dylan and Emma on Friday and then leaving with Brielle pretty much took care of it. And now I guess it looks like I want to murder the volleyball and everyone else on the court. But the yelling, the crying, the *thwack* of the ball on the gym floor – it's not enough.

'What do we do next?' I ask Brielle after last period. She

183

drove me this morning and needs to give me a lift home, too. Dylan's at practice, so I know Emma's on her own.

Brielle looks at me. For a second I think she's annoyed, or maybe she's not into this any more – maybe it's really not a challenge. I get scared that she's about to back out.

So before she can answer my question, I go, 'Maybe we should follow her home?'

Something that looks like pride flashes in Brielle's eyes. 'Yeah, okay,' she says, nodding. 'Let's go.'

I follow her to the Mercedes and climb into the passenger seat, bouncing a little with nervous excitement. Brielle screeches out of her parking spot, barely missing about half the freshman class walking to the bus stop, but instead of heading toward the exit she peels around to the next row of student cars.

'What the—' I start to say, but then I see what she's doing.

Emma is just walking up to her Audi when she sees it, too. Brielle has pulled her SUV up so we're right behind Emma's car, blocking her in. It's colder today than it was this weekend, but Brielle rolls down her window and casually dangles her arm outside.

'Oh, hey, slutty!' she calls to Emma, waving. If you hadn't heard the words you'd think she was talking to a friend. 'Nice car. I guess Stepdaddy thinks you're *really pretty.*'

Emma has frozen in place, still standing at the front corner of her car, not even on the driver's side yet. She's looking at me and Brielle like she doesn't know what's going to happen next.

A few other people are looking at us too, and I see a couple of guys from our class laughing. I turn a little and see Megan Corley walking the other way. I guess she doesn't feel like being on Emma's Only Friend Duty this time.

'What's wrong?' I say loudly, leaning over the centre console so I can see her better. 'Didn't anyone else's boyfriend want to give you a *ride* today?'

Brielle's laugh is short and sharp.

And it seems to break Emma out of her trance. Smoothly, as if we haven't said anything at all, she continues walking around to her car door and beeps it open. Then she looks right at us, her chin lifted a little, and goes, 'Actually, I think that's your problem. But at least you have each other, right? *Lez* be friends.'

'Oh, you little c—' Brielle is cursing and unbuckling her seat belt and opening her door all at once, but just in time I see Mr Jansen, the guidance counsellor, walking toward us. That explains why Emma thought she could talk to us that way.

I grab Brielle's arm and say, 'We gotta go.'

She looks at me like I'm crazy, but I point at the teacher, who definitely sees us now, and she slams her door back shut and puts the SUV in gear.

'You better watch your ass!' she yells at Emma, and we drive away.

'Why can't you just leave her alone?'

'Who?'

'Don't be like that. You know who.'

'I don't know what you're talking about.'

'Come on. You and Brielle are being total—' Dylan cuts himself off, his head jerking to the side, his lips pressed tightly together. Keeping the rest of his sentence unsaid.

'We're being what?' I demand. 'Total *what*?' I'm trying to keep my voice down, since we're in a corner of the library during study hall, and Ms Hillman can hear the slightest whisper anywhere in here. But Dylan started this; he came over to me and started talking. And I know he's about to call me and Brielle bitches. Which is so completely unfair I can barely see straight.

'Whatever. Just leave Emma out of this.'

'*You* brought her *into it*,' I snap. 'I didn't want to be anywhere near her, but you—' I throw up my hands. Now I'm the one who can't finish a sentence.

A look crosses Dylan's face. I think it might be regret. He reaches out and touches my shoulder and says, 'Sara, I didn't mean to hurt you.'

It's such a cliché, such a lifetime movie moment, I don't even know what to do at first. Tears leap into my eyes and they sting. Everything about this stings. He doesn't deserve to see me cry. He doesn't deserve for his apology to be accepted.

He definitely doesn't deserve for me to want him to kiss me right now. But that is totally what I want. I want him to wrap his arms around me and lean us into the Earth Science shelves and forget any of this ever happened.

Instead I say, pathetically, 'Don't you like me any more?'

He drops his hand back to his side and looks away again. Guys hate this kind of thing, I know that. Brielle has told me a hundred times, and I know I should just shut up. But I can't help it; if he can answer this question, maybe I can stop lying awake every night wondering about it. Maybe the knot in my stomach will unwind a little bit.

'You just . . . I dunno, Sara, did *you* even like *me*? It's not like you were ever around that much.'

I don't know what to say to this. I want to scream or cry or something, say anything, if only to keep him talking. But I can't figure out how to respond. I hold my breath, literally, hoping he'll say more.

Dylan shifts from foot to foot, like he'd really like to run away now, but finally he adds, 'I mean, you were always with Brielle. You didn't really need me.'

'I needed you to not *cheat* on me.' The words pop out, angry and hot, before I think better of it.

The look of regret – or something – comes back to his face. 'I know,' he says. 'I'm sorry about that.'

We're both silent again. I don't know what we're supposed to be saying. I was hoping he'd say he misses me and wants me back, but obviously that's not happening. Obviously he expects me to accept this apology, to believe him. And to *understand*.

I don't understand any of it. I don't want to.

187

Dylan takes a step back and goes, 'That's what I wanted to say, okay? That I'm sorry. And you should really leave Emma alone now. She's just . . . she's really sensitive. You guys are pretty harsh.' He lifts up his hands and looks like he's about to say something else, but then shakes his head a tiny bit. Finally he just says, 'She didn't do anything wrong.'

And then he walks away. And I just stand there.

'I was *always* around!'

'You were. You were totally there for him. He's a moron.' Brielle's voice is sympathetic, but her eyes are fixed on her reflection in the girls' bathroom mirror.

We've been in here for at least half an hour, even though she's supposed to be in Language Arts and I have French. I've told her everything about the Dylan conversation except the part about him thinking I spend too much time with her. Obviously he and Emma agree on that, so they've probably been talking about me. Or definitely. Which makes me feel like I'm naked, like everyone's looking at me and laughing and I can't do anything to stop it.

So I don't mention that part. But I tell her everything else, and of course now – now that it's a hundred years too late – I'm thinking of all the things I should have said to Dylan in the library.

'I went to every single one of his games,' I say, though of course Brielle already knows this. 'I gave him my *virgini*—'

Brielle holds up her hand before the word is even out

and goes, 'Stop. Stop, okay? We're gonna fix this.' She finally turns her back to the mirror and pulls herself up to sit on the counter. Brielle is always sitting on counters, and somehow she never gets her pants covered in water like I always do. She smooths her hair back and up in one swift motion, knotting it in a perfect updo while I just stand there, waiting for the plan.

More than ever, I need Brielle's plan.

'Dylan is just confused,' she declares. 'More importantly, *Emma Putnam* is confused. She seems to think she actually belongs at this school, with us and our friends and our *boy*friends. But she is *wrong* about that.'

'I know, but what are we supposed to do?' I can't stop myself from whining.

'God, Sara, don't be an idiot. The girl has been kicked out of, what, four schools already?'

'Actually I think she just transferred, like two ti—'

'*Details.* Fine, transferred. Well, Bitchy Bitch can just *transfer* her ass again.'

I nod, finally getting what she's saying.

'We've been thinking too small,' Brielle says, jumping back off the counter as the bell starts ringing to change periods outside the bathroom door. 'Obvs the girl is not getting the message with *flowers*.'

Brielle sneers as she says this, and for a minute I want to argue with her – the flowers were her idea, but she sounds like she's blaming me for them being lame or not working or something. But maybe it *was* my idea? Or maybe I

189

should've come up with a better one, argued with her at the time? Not that I've ever talked her out of anything before.

We grab our bags from the windowsill, leaving the bathroom just as a group of seniors is coming in. One of them is Noelle, and she and Brielle hip-check each other, like it's an old routine they've done a million times. I blink, surprised by the move and the sharp pang of jealousy that sticks in my throat.

'Hey, girl,' Brielle says casually. We're about to go through the door when she turns back on her heel and points at Noelle. 'How old is that boyfriend of yours?'

'What?' Noelle asks. Her friends are at the mirror and she's digging through her purse for something, not really looking at us.

'I mean, is he eighteen?' Brielle asks. 'His birthday was just in December, right? Was it his eighteenth?'

Noelle looks up from her bag and wrinkles her nose. 'What is it, weird question day?'

'It's just this thing,' Brielle says, waving her hand dismissively. 'I thought I remembered something from his party, but I wasn't sure.'

Noelle looks like she wants to ask Brielle another question, but then her face clears and she shrugs. 'Yeah, he turned eighteen. He got me into a club over break, actually.'

'Badass,' Brielle says. And with an ironic finger-gun at Noelle – which Noelle returns – she finally turns back to me and pushes me out the bathroom door.

'What the hell was that about?' I ask as we join the between-classes crowd in the hall. 'You guys are friends?'

'Duh,' Brielle says. 'And it's just research. You'll see.'

That afternoon, we follow Dylan's car to McDonald's. It's like a sting operation – Brielle stays a safe distance away, and we wait in her car until they've gone inside and ordered and everything. Then we walk in, like it's all a coincidence. But we walk right past the counter and over to their table.

'Isn't he a little *young* for you?' Brielle asks Emma.

She looks up from the small packet of fries and puddle of ketchup in front of her. Her eyes have that soft, sad look they always get when a boy is around. Why can't any of these guys see that she's just using them?

'Jesus, Brielle, give it a break already.' Dylan looks at me pointedly, like *We talked about this*, but I just stare back. This isn't the school library. We're allowed to be here, it's a free country, and Emma should know we're gonna say whatever we want.

'I don't know what you're talking about,' Emma says with a heavy sigh. Her hair is pulled back into a messy bun and she's wearing a chunky fisherman sweater and just a little mascara. She looks amazing. I look my best – since the breakup I've come to school every day in my nicest skinny jeans, my newest sweaters, my most careful makeup – but I definitely do not look effortless. Is that what I did wrong with Dylan? Tried too hard?

Brielle ignores her and focuses on Dylan. 'You better watch out,' she says. 'Isn't your birthday coming up? Wouldn't want to get arrested.'

Dylan's face wrinkles in confusion. 'Seriously, what are you talking about? Can't you just go eat like everyone else? Sara, can't you put a leash on her?'

'*What* did you just say?' I blurt, and at the same time Brielle goes, 'Oh, you *best* be joking!'

Dylan holds up his hands as if he's calling for a truce, or maybe just protecting his face from whatever he thinks we're about to do. But at the same time I see Emma grab her soda, trying to hide a smile behind her straw.

'You better put a leash on *that*,' I snap, jutting my chin at Emma.

'If you can even stoop that low,' Brielle adds. 'Come on, Sara. If we stand here any longer we're gonna get an STD.'

'You guys are really pathetic, you know that—' Dylan is still talking as Brielle grabs my arm and we stomp away from their table.

We still don't have any food, of course, and as we make our dramatic exit Brielle says loudly, 'Drive-thru, babe. It's the only way we know our food won't be *contaminated*.'

I feel a surge of energy from yelling at Dylan, and amazingly, I'm really hungry. I'm even smiling as we climb back into Brielle's car – this is, like, the first time ever that I've been around Dylan and my stomach hasn't been in knots. I mean, they used to be good knots. Excited knots. But since Valentine's Day it's just been an awful tangle in

192

there. Every time I see him or Emma or, the worst, both of them, I want to puke.

But now I'm hungry. I'm *starving*. I'm smiling and ordering supersized *everything*.

September

'Is Mr Wharton not joining us?'

'Do you see him here? No, he's not coming.'

'I'm sorry, Julia. I didn't mean – I just thought Sara said he was going to be in town.' Natalie shifts some papers on the table, clearly uncomfortable. She's been saying all along – and, for the past week, nonstop – that having both my parents here would be helpful, and that they definitely need to come to the trial. Obviously my dad is totally excited about *that*.

'I said he might be,' I clarify quickly, trying to see my mom out of the corner of my eye. 'But he couldn't make it.'

Natalie gives us both a level look and takes a deep breath. 'Well, I have news,' she says, and my stomach goes cold. 'The charges against Dylan Howe are being dropped.'

'What!' my mom shouts. 'How did—'

Natalie holds up her hand, interrupting her. 'The evidence wasn't sufficient. But he's still agreed to testify against the rest of you.'

'Jesus Christ,' my mom says. 'What does this mean?'

'It's not good,' Natalie says. 'And I think we need to seriously reconsider making a plea deal with the prosecution.'

I can't believe this is happening. I have to clear my throat to say, 'But I'm not guilty. I thought we said I wouldn't—'

'I know what we said last time,' Natalie interrupts, but her voice is soft. 'Honestly, though, this is a really tough case. There's so much at stake – your whole future, Sara. I know it's hard to see now . . . but this has always been my recommendation, as you both know, and now more than ever I think you need to take this option. We can plead to the lesser charges and you can go back to your life. After your eighteenth birthday your record could even be cleared, if they'll agree to that.'

My mom runs her hands through her hair and sits back, so I can't see her face without turning. She used to think this whole thing was bullshit, I know – she used to think the Putnams were crazy for blaming me for Emma's death. But I think going over all the testimony has been changing her mind. I'm pretty sure she doesn't think I'm innocent any more, even if she hasn't said so to my face.

'I think if we agree to allocute on the stalking and intimidation charges, and maybe one count of assault, we could see just twelve months' probation,' Natalie says.

'Probation?' my mom asks. I can't tell if she wants to know what that means, or if she's saying that's too much punishment. Or not enough.

'Sara would have monthly check-ins with a court official, and if she commits any crimes – whether or not they match the ones she's being charged with here – she'll be sentenced to time in a juvenile facility.'

'But I'll be eighteen in a couple months,' I blurt out. We were all charged as minors, of course – except for Tyler – but everyone's getting older. Dylan's birthday was in June, so he's technically an adult now. I know his parents got a fancy lawyer, but on his birthday, when I was busy not calling him, I kept wondering what would happen if he had to go to prison for real. Like how Tyler might have to. It's crazy. It's not fair. I don't like Tyler, but come on, *prison*? And if I'm going to be on probation until after I'm an adult—

I shake my head, but I can't stop my mind from spinning.

'Doesn't matter,' Natalie says. 'You were charged as a minor.'

'I know, but—'

'It only matters when the charges were filed, when the prosecution claims the crimes were committed,' she clarifies. Right, I think she told us all this before. I don't know. I can't keep any of this straight.

Mom's still leaned back in her chair. 'Would this go on Sara's permanent record?'

I finally turn toward her, furious. 'What are you saying? You want me to tell them I'm guilty? I didn't kill her! I didn't do anything wrong – everyone hated her, everyone was mean to her *all the time*! And even if they weren't, *she* was the one hooking up with everyone! She's the one with the problem!'

Mom shakes her head. 'Sara, you *did* do something wrong. You did a *lot* of wrong things, don't you see that? And no one's charging you with murder.'

I jump out of my chair, shoving back from the table so hard it almost topples over. 'I knew it! You send me here by myself all summer, you make me feel like you can't even be bothered with any of this, and all along you think I'm guilty!'

'I didn't say that, honey, sit down—' She reaches her hand out but I jerk away.

'No! Fuck this!' I shout. I'm so hot I can't breathe. I want to pick up the whole table and throw it across the room, or run through the wall, or just – I just – I want more *air*, there's no air in here, I'm gasping and sweating and I could *kill her* right now. My throat seizes up and my eyes are stinging.

But I am *not crying*.

I am *leaving*, I'm out the door and down the hall. And I'm shaking, but I'm in the elevator, I'm outside, I'm sweating more because it's one of those awful September days that feel like July and the humidity makes it impossible to breathe out here, either, but at least I can walk, at least there's a sidewalk around the hideous office park, at least there's a gas station right over there, and I have my cell phone, and I'm getting his number, I'm calling him, I'm

197

getting a ride because I came here with Mom and there is no way I'm getting in that car with that woman *ever again*.

Carmichael doesn't ask any questions. He seems kinda freaked when he finds me under the awning in front of the Texaco, but he's quiet as he reaches over and opens the passenger door of his dad's truck.

I climb in and I know I should just start apologizing, especially for him having to borrow the truck. But I'm too drained to say anything at all. I see him glancing over at me every few seconds. I keep my eyes forward, hoping he can't see how red they are.

I don't know what Carmichael is doing, hanging out with me. He still talks to me at school, even though no one else does. Sometimes we have coffee on the weekends, though he makes me go to the independent place downtown, saying that Starbucks is too corporate. We don't have the same lunch period, but I prefer to eat in my car anyway. The days that I feel like eating, that is. He's a friend. He's a better friend than I deserve, and he's the only person left I can call.

But after this, I swear, I won't ask him for anything else, ever again. He's a nice guy. He doesn't deserve this. No one does. Maybe not even me.

Finally he turns on the radio, flipping around until he finds a country station. I think he's trying to make me laugh, like, *Ha ha, you don't listen to country, isn't this stupid*. But it's a sad song, it's not funny. The lyrics are about not being able to forgive someone, but not being able to leave, and I just wish I couldn't relate.

The song swells and I feel a wave of nausea come over me. I have to say something, I'm gonna say something. For once, I can hear the words that are about to come out of my mouth, and it makes me sick.

'Why do you – I mean, like, why do you hang out with me?' I ask Carmichael. By the end of the sentence my voice is a rasp, and I have to swallow hard.

'Why?' he says, turning down the radio. 'Why wouldn't I?'

I just look over at him with one eyebrow raised. Well, with both raised. I don't have Brielle's one-eyebrow talent.

But anyway, he knows damn well *why*.

'All that stuff . . .' He waves a hand in the air like he's clearing it, and for a second I think of Brielle again, how she always does that. Did that. I don't know any more. But either way, Carmichael does it differently – with him it's not like he's trying to erase something, and more like he's gathering it all up.

He takes a deep breath, and a painful minute passes as he stares out the windshield, watching the road, but then he goes on. 'I know what everyone's saying,' he says. 'But sometimes what everyone says isn't the whole story.'

'No,' I say quietly. 'It's not.'

'And freshman year, when everyone decided I was a terrorist over one made-up story, you never called me Bomb Boy,' he says.

I look up at him, surprised. 'I didn't?' I say. I thought I did – it definitely seems like something Brielle and I would have done. But maybe back in ninth grade we were . . . different.

'You don't remember? Well, I do,' Carmichael says. 'And then I saw you at summer school, and with your brothers, and now that we've hung out, I don't know. You're not mean to *me*. Plus, you're weird.' He smiles, but I can't return it.

'They want me to make a plea bargain,' I tell him, finally. 'And write a statement to Emma's parents. And read it in court.'

He nods. 'That sounds like a good plan,' he says. 'You must be relieved.'

This idea stuns me so much I jerk back in my seat. 'Why would I be relieved?' I almost shout.

Carmichael hesitates. 'Because . . . well, because now you can just say how sorry you are. Right? And not . . . not go to trial, not have to deal with . . . um, whatever's gonna happen after that . . .' We stop at a red light and he turns to look at me, concern and confusion all over his face.

'*I didn't do anything*,' I say, my voice low but vicious, and he flinches. Typical. Just like everyone else, he shrinks back, afraid of me. Afraid of how angry I am. But I *am* angry – I'm furious. He doesn't get it at all. No one gets it *at all*.

But a second later he's reaching over to my side of the bench seat, trying to take my hand. It's my turn to pull away, but he stays where he is, looking me in the eye for another long second before the light turns green and he pulls the truck forward again.

'I know you didn't want her to kill herself, Sara, but you guys were pretty mean, right? You and Brielle, you guys are gorgeous, you were at the top of the, you know, the top of the high school food chain. Emma couldn't fight back against all that. Don't you feel bad about what happened to her?'

I'm breathing too fast. I feel a little faint. I'm hot and nauseated and I just have to get out of here. It feels like what happened at Teresa's all over again, like my head is trying to float away from my body. I don't even understand what he's saying – me? On top of high school? I was clinging to one stupid guy and a couple of parties and Brielle's coat-tails. I was nobody! He's talking about Brielle. And, okay, maybe Brielle was too mean to Emma. Fine, maybe we both were. But I was just defending myself! I was just trying to – to keep things the way they *were*.

Finally, *finally* the truck is pulling into our neighbourhood, and even though we're still two blocks away from my house, I take off my seat belt and grab my purse.

Carmichael reaches out one more time. I shake my head, turning toward the window. When he eases into our driveway I yank the door open and jump out.

My feet hit the pavement and Alex is already outside, running down the walkway steps to greet us. Tommy was allowed to be the one in charge today – apparently he's old enough not to burn the house down for two hours – and for a second I panic that something is wrong. And then I remember that something – everything – is totally wrong, just not with the boys.

'Mom's been trying to call!' Alex is yelling before I've even closed the truck door behind me. 'Are you okay? She didn't know where you were!'

My throat is still tight, but I shake my head. 'No,' I say. 'I'm okay, buddy, it's fine.'

At the front door I see Tommy, a dark, unhappy shape in the middle of the sunny afternoon. *We match*, I think. *But we don't go together.* He turns and slams back through the door without a word.

Carmichael's out of the truck and coming around it, saying hi to Alex and still trying to catch my eye. I wish I could just follow Tommy into the house, but I finally manage to gather my dignity and my manners and say, 'Thanks for the ride. I'm really sorry I had to call you.'

'No, I'm glad you did,' he says, and there's too much feeling in his voice. What does he think, he's going to fix this? My life? It's so broken I can't even remember what it looked like before.

Alex is looking at us like we're a puzzle he's trying to figure out. I put my arm around his shoulders and say, 'Come on, let's get back inside.' He walks with me, but he turns back to wave goodbye to Carmichael. I don't. I turn away as soon as I can, trying to keep Alex from seeing how awful everything is.

But I don't turn quite fast enough, because I still see Carmichael's face – that look of betrayal, of disappointment. Of disgust. That look that says *She doesn't understand at all.* And he's right. I really, really don't.

In my room I unfold my laptop and do what I haven't done in months – Google *Emma Putnam.*

Dylan's name comes up right away. Apparently the dropped charges are something the papers can talk about. There are a lot of recent articles about the trial coming up, and Tyler's name is in there. Brielle and Jacob and I aren't named yet, we're still just the 'minors', but Natalie says we'll lose our anonymity when we go to court. She said sometimes you can make a deal where your name doesn't get published, but Emma's parents wouldn't agree to that for any of us. And anyway, what difference does it make? Everyone knows who we are already.

All the articles talk about Emma like she was a saint, of course. Or like she wasn't even a real person. *Months of bullying* and *relationships with a few popular senior boys* and *physical assault* and *statutory rape* jump out as I skim through.

'Emma was a new student who was trying to make friends, and instead made enemies of a few vicious girls in the junior class,' the prosecutor said in a statement.

Emma Putnam was just one month from her seventeenth
birthday when she took her own life by hanging herself in the
garage of her parents' home.

I didn't know that. The birthday thing, I mean. I knew
about the garage. Everyone knew about that stuff almost
the second it happened, or pretended they did. People at
school had different stories about what she hanged herself
with. I try not to let myself picture it, though obviously
sometimes I can't help it, like that day at Teresa's.

For a long time the paper didn't print any of those
details; my mom said they probably didn't want to give
the rest of us any tips on how to commit suicide. But
obviously now that there's a big criminal prosecution thing,
the whole story is out.

All of a sudden I see something out of the corner of my
eye and nearly jump off the bed. It's Tommy, standing still
and silent in my doorway. I feel like I've been caught doing
something much worse than what I'm doing. Like by
having my laptop open, with Emma's name all over it, my
little brother can see me buying Emma those roses, putting
the sign in her yard, throwing my shoe at her and Dylan.
Or like he knows what happened that weekend right before
everything *else* happened – that weekend that was so great,
until the world just crumbled around me.

'Hey, bud, what's going on? Don't you knock anymore?'
My voice is light, or at least trying to be. Tommy doesn't
come in my room at all these days, so I'm not really mad

about knocking. I'm happy to see him.

The feeling doesn't seem to be mutual. His frown doesn't shift when he says, 'Door was open.'

'Oh. Okay. You want to come in?'

'Mom said you're in charge since you're home now. She went to the store.'

God, I'd forgotten all about Mom, and my ride home with Carmichael. The fight at Natalie's office is still pulsing in my head like a thrumming baseline, but it's just background noise to everything else. Everything is layers of noise these days – the pain of losing my friends and Dylan, buried under my family going through this, buried under school, buried under the lawyers, buried under . . . I don't even know. I feel like I'm looking up at my brother from the bottom of a deep, dark well. And even though he's standing right there, just a few feet away, it's almost like I can't really see him. I wonder if he's at the bottom of his own well, looking up at me.

'Come in,' I say, patting the bed. I close the laptop and slide it back under my pillows.

Tommy shrugs and comes into the room, but he wanders over to the desk. My textbooks are stacked up, still shiny and new, and still mostly untouched. The wall over my desk still has its giant corkboard, but it's not covered in photos of me and Dylan or me and Brielle any more. I took those down a while ago, and lately I've been hanging mix CDs up there. Some are ones I was going to give to Carmichael, but I kept chickening out, figuring he'd think I was being a dumb girl. Anyway, I guess I'll have to get rid of those now. People are just flying out of my life these days.

My brother sits down in my desk chair and spins around. That used to be his favourite thing, and I haven't seen it in a while. When he catches me smiling at him, though, he stops.

'Mom says everything's gonna be over soon,' he says darkly.

'She does?' I ask. This is definitely true, but I'm not sure how he means it.

'She said you're going to settle.'

It's such a grown-up term, but then, I guess Tommy's getting to be more of a grown-up by the second. His voice is deeper now, and God knows he's more of a moody teenager than I ever thought he'd be.

I can't help but frown, though. 'I guess that's what she thinks,' I say. 'I mean, that's what Mom and the lawyer want.'

'But not you,' he says, and it's not exactly a question.

'I don't think . . .' I pause, pulling my knees up under my chin. I've been spending so much time trying to not talk about all this with the boys that I'm not even sure where to start. Of course, now I know that Tommy was still hearing about everything, even at camp. But I still try to avoid the subject, try to protect him and Alex.

Just like with everything else, I'm obviously doing a terrible job.

I clear my throat a little. 'I don't think I did anything wrong,' I say. My voice sounds small and unsure. I've said these words a million times, but for some reason, saying them to Tommy, I'm ashamed of them. I'm ashamed, period. I can't look at him when I add, 'They want me to apologize, in court. To say I . . . that I had something to do with . . . what happened. But I didn't. Or, I mean, everyone was doing it . . .' I look down, unable to finish the sentence.

'I know,' Tommy said. He sounds like he means it. The old Tommy, who always took my side in fights with Mom or on game nights at home, would have said the same thing. 'But what are you going to do?' he asks. 'I mean – I don't want you to go to jail.'

His voice breaks on the last word and I look up finally. He's trying not to cry – he's staring at my stupid mostly empty corkboard, biting his lip.

'They won't send me to jail,' I say. 'They won't. It might be – I mean, you know about those youth home places? At the very worst it might be something like that.'

His eyes squeeze shut and his shoulders shake, just once, and I hurry to add, 'But that's not gonna happen.'

I get off my bed and come over to him. I hover behind the chair for a second, knowing he might throw me off if I try to hug him. So instead I kneel down on the floor so I'm looking up at his face. His eyes are still shut, but he's breathing evenly, and I don't see any more tears.

'It's not going to happen, Tommy,' I say again. 'Mom's right, the lawyer's right. I'm going to sign the plea agreement thing, and we're going to settle. It doesn't matter what really happened – I mean, it does, but not any more. I don't want you to worry, okay?'

He takes a long breath, then opens his eyes and looks down at me.

'I'm gonna apologize,' I tell him. 'It's all going to be okay. It's all going to be over soon.'

For the briefest of moments, I think I might be right. Tommy nods and even smiles a little. He says, 'Okay.' We both stand up and I offer to take him and Alex to get ice cream.

But when he leaves my room to get his brother, I remember.

It's never going to be over. And now – now that I know I'm just going to give up, I don't have any choice, I have to just plead out and hope it's not completely awful – now no one will ever hear my side of the story.

March

'You girls should go now.' Mrs Putnam's eyes are cold. Her whole face changed as soon as the words were out of Brielle's mouth. She obviously recognized us right away, but maybe she thought we were here to apologize or something.

'We just thought you should know,' I say, but the words get half stuck in my throat. The sky is a cold, dead grey behind us, and my feet are turning to ice in my ballet flats.

It's really terrifying to be talking to this woman face-to-face. I hate her daughter so much I can taste it, and that makes me hate Mrs Putnam, too. But she's an adult; I'm automatically supposed to be scared of her. And I am. Brielle thinks adults are stupid, but I think they can get you in trouble.

But I guess Mrs Putnam isn't doing anything to get her daughter *out* of trouble. Which is why we're standing here. We got out of school early for teacher conferences today, and we happen to know that Emma is out with Dylan right now.

'What I really think is that you should leave my daughter alone,' Mrs Putnam says. Her left hand is gripping their front door tightly, keeping it as closed as possible so Brielle and I have to stay shivering on the front porch. 'I don't know how many times I have to call the school about you two before you get the message.'

'Mrs Putnam,' Brielle says, and I can hear her best parent-speak tone coming through. That voice that seems to hypnotize everyone, that just flows so easily. 'We've made some mistakes, but now we're really worried about Emma. She's still new to our school, and she's already had so many boyfriends, and they're all so much older than she is, like Jacob, and now Dylan, who's almost eighteen . . .'

The magic voice doesn't seem to be working so well on Emma's mom. Mrs Putnam yanks herself back, as if someone pulled her, and slams the door in our faces.

'Delusional bitch,' Brielle mutters under her breath, her voice back to normal. She spins around and stomps down the porch stairs, leaving me standing there like a frozen idiot. Especially frozen – it's literally like four degrees out here – and particularly idiotic, with my one whole sentence in this conversation echoing in my cold head.

We thought you should know. Is that what we thought? I guess that could be true. I mean, I guess Emma really could be in trouble. Troubled.

And now Mrs Putnam knows.

Brielle drives us to the mall, and for a while we don't talk about anything important. We try on perfumes at

Sephora and split a pretzel at Auntie Anne's. In the food court, I've almost forgotten about Emma for two seconds when we see Kyle, Jacob, and Noelle coming toward us.

'Hey, bitches,' Noelle says, smiling prettily. She sits down next to Brielle. Jacob settles into the seat across from her, and Kyle grabs a chair from the table next to us, turns it around, and straddles it like a cowboy. 'What's up?'

'You know, plotting to take over the world, the usual,' Brielle says.

Noelle laughs and I can tell she's heard this joke before. I squirm in my chair, suddenly hyperaware of Jacob next to me. Over-eighteen Jacob. We're friends with him, at least sort of. What's going to happen when he finds out about our visit to Emma's house? Is he going to find out?

For a second it occurs to me that maybe Jacob didn't sleep with Emma. I mean, it's possible, right? Like when I was little and I'd watch movies where the couple would be kissing and the screen would go dark and I'd think they were just going to keep kissing. I know that's not usually how it works – usually they're having sex – but maybe sometimes they're not, right? What if we're wrong about Jacob? Or what if Emma—

'Dude, when're your parents going out of town again?' Kyle asks Brielle, and I snap back to the conversation.

'*Dude,*' she replies, 'it's your turn. Why do I always have to be party central?'

'Whatever, my house is the worst,' he says, slouching over the chair back. He doesn't seem bothered by having

211

the 'worst' house, though. Then he turns toward me and says, 'What about you? It's just your mom, right?'

'Um, yeah,' I say. All those weeks dating Dylan and hanging out with these seniors, but I still get awkward around them. So embarrassing. 'But my little brothers, too. They're always, you know, there.'

Jacob laughs. 'Gotta send the baby bros to Vegas or something.'

Brielle laughs too, and I smile, but I don't get it. Or maybe I do, and it's just not funny. At least it gives me a chance to look at Jacob's face for a second. He's already looking away, though, at someone else in the food court. I follow his eyes and see Irish O'Irish – Seamus – walking by with some girl I don't recognize.

'Whoa, that loser has a girlfriend?' Jacob sneers.

Brielle looks too, and says, 'Ew. Look what the band camp dragged in.'

The girl isn't that bad – she's got that kind of mousy hair that never quite looks right, and her black coat looks old and beat-up, but she's kind of pretty – and Seamus looks happier than I've ever seen him.

But Jacob is already out of his chair, striding up behind them. He puts one arm over each of their shoulders, startling them both. They're all still walking, but we can hear Jacob bellow, 'Little man! Who's the hottie?'

Brielle and Noelle laugh, then turn back to each other and start comparing manicures. But I can't stop staring at Jacob, Seamus, and the girl. Jacob is still talking to them all

212

chummily, turning his head back and forth between theirs. Seamus and his girlfriend look scared. They stop and try to get out of his grip, but only the girl succeeds. Jacob hangs on to Seamus's shoulders and shakes him a little bit, his mean laugh echoing all the way back to our table. The girl looks like she wants to run away, but what is she supposed to do?

It's like I'm watching a movie or something. And it's, like, freakishly good timing – I was just feeling kind of guilty for going to Mrs Putnam, so even though I've seen Jacob act like an a-hole a million times, today feels like it means something. I mean, I want to get Emma in trouble, or at least I want her to leave Elmwood and never come back. But I always kind of thought Jacob was basically a decent guy, if a little more macho than necessary. I guess there was the cheating on Noelle and hooking up with Emma and . . . well, okay, maybe I don't think he's a decent guy.

And now he's pulling Seamus's head down, rubbing his hair in a hard and embarrassing noogie. The girl takes a step backward and for a second I think she's for sure going to bolt. I would. But she stays.

Finally, Jacob pushes Seamus away and comes walking back to us, all cool, like nothing happened. Seamus stands there, rubbing his head, not making eye contact with his girlfriend.

Jacob comes back to our table and I wonder if anyone's going to say anything. I glance at Brielle but she's playing

213

with her straw. Jacob's already talking to Kyle about something. Finally Noelle rolls her eyes at Brielle and goes, '*Boys*.'

'Totally,' Brielle says.

I look at Jacob again, and for some reason, just for a second, he looks like Tommy to me. I blink and it goes away – but I still feel sick. I'm officially done being here.

'Brie, I need to get going,' I say. She rolls her eyes at me, like I knew she would, but starts putting on her coat at the same time.

'Okay, if you guys are all gonna be lame, we can hang at my place Friday,' Jacob says, finally turning back toward us and Noelle. 'Good plan,' Noelle says to him. I can't tell if she's being sarcastic or not.

'Awesome,' Brielle says. 'Text me later,' she says to Noelle, who flashes her a nonchalant peace sign.

We walk out the other way, so we don't pass by Seamus, and I'm happy we've turned so I can't even see him on the other side of the food court.

The cramp in my stomach feels tighter, though. 'Do you think Jacob will get arrested?' I ask Brielle. 'Like, if Emma's mom calls the cops or something?'

'God, no,' she says. 'Or even if he does, his parents will get him out of it.' I think there's an edge of worry in her voice, but she's walking so fast I can't be sure. 'Whatever, guy's a creep anyway,' she adds.

I can't argue with that.

Brielle and I swing by my brothers' school to pick them up, and then she drops us all at my car back in the Elmwood lot. It's mostly empty, except for a few athletes' cars, like Dylan's. I wonder where he and Emma went during their free half day. I kind of thought we'd have seen them at the mall, but I guess after that scene at McDonald's they're probably lying low. Good.

Tommy and Alex are beating each other up in the backseat because I wouldn't let either of them sit up front today. I can't even hear them over the roar of worry in my head, and when we pull up to the house it just gets louder – it's not even five yet, but our mom is already home, which just feels like a bad sign.

I can't even explain why I keep sitting in the car while the boys and all their crap form a kind of Tasmanian-devil hurricane through the garage and into the house. I'm still out in the driveway – the garage only fits Mom's car – and staring at the lights inside. It should look warm and inviting and all that stuff. Instead it looks like the mouth of hell. What am I going to do in there? Sit around while Dylan doesn't call? Text Brielle and hear about whatever hilarious thing Noelle said since we saw her at the mall two seconds ago? Like it's not bad enough that their names freaking rhyme, they're practically turning into the same person. It seems like lately I only really talk to Brielle when we're talking about Emma.

The scene on Emma's front porch keeps rolling over and over in my head. Mrs Putnam's hard eyes, her sharp fingernails against the door. Brielle standing up for me – for Dylan, for Kyle, for all of us, trying to tell this woman anything that will make her take her daughter away, so she'll leave us alone – but in the process, also basically telling her to get Jacob arrested, maybe even Dylan, after his birthday. And then I think of Jacob and Seamus, or Jacob and Emma, or Emma and Dylan, and I'm back to where I started.

I freaking *hate* Emma Putnam. I wish she'd never been born. The surge of anger gives me the energy to yank my keys out of the ignition and stomp into the house, but as soon as the inside garage door slams behind me, I know my first instinct – to pull the car back out of the driveway and speed away – was dead on.

'Why did I get a call from a Valerie Putnam today?' my mom asks. Her voice is as scary as Mrs Putnam's was. Scarier.

'I don't know,' I say. I throw my bag on the kitchen table. The boys have disappeared into the house, obviously not worried that Mom is home so early, even changed out of her work clothes already and starting dinner. Not that I'm looking at her that closely. I don't actually look her in the eye at all as I reach into the fridge for a water, like nothing's wrong, like this is a totally normal day.

'You *don't know*, huh?' she repeats after me.

Well, great. Apparently *she* knows, and this is one of those *Tell me the truth and you won't get in trouble* deals. Which are really not deals at all, as everyone with parents has already learned the hard way. Even Alex doesn't fall for that one anymore.

I grab a bottle of water and turn back to her slowly, letting the fridge door slam shut behind me. 'What,' I say, not even bothering to pretend it's a real question.

'Have you been threatening her daughter? Is there something going on I should know about?'

By now, she probably *should* know about it, but if she doesn't, I'm not gonna be the one to fill her in. 'I don't know,' I say. 'But her daughter's a bitch, did she tell you *that*?'

'Sara, that is ridic—'

I've ripped the cap off the water bottle and now I throw it across the room, momentarily shocking both of us into silence. But after a second I spit out, 'Little Miss Perfect *Emma Putnam* is going out with *Dylan* now. So if she wants to complain about *me*, that's just *fine*. That's perfect.'

My mom looks at me like I'm not making any sense, but also like she's sorry for me, or sorry I'm upset at least. She liked Dylan, I know, and I never actually told her why we broke up. Another thing she should've known by now, but whatever.

'Her mother says you've been hassling Emma,' she says quietly, almost whispering. 'For a while?'

I just stare at her, my lips clamped shut. If she can't see that Emma's the one bothering *me*, not to mention half the school, I really can't explain.

Mom pauses for an extra minute before seeming to

realize I'm not going to say anything else. She lets out a sigh. 'Listen, maybe just leave her alone. I know you're not a mean person, but they're obviously taking it the wrong way. And I'm sorry about Dylan. I know it feels like the end of the world, but I promise, it's not.' She reaches out to touch my arm, but I flinch, stepping out of reach. She lets her hand drop. 'He's graduating anyway, right?' she adds. 'So maybe this is even for the best. Long-distance relationships are so hard, especially when you're so young—'

She's still talking, but I just leave the kitchen. I cannot talk to her. Obviously I already have a long-distance relationship with my own mother. If only it was *literally* long-distance, everything would be way better.

'So I guess you're gonna need another plan to get Little Miss Loser off your boyfriend.'

'What? What do you mean?'

'Didn't I tell you? Nothing really happened with Jacob. Or anyway, that's the story he's sticking with.' Brielle jerks her head to the side, throwing her hair over one shoulder. A couple of strands don't make it, but she can't use her fingers because the manicurist is spraying them with the antibacterial stuff. 'Noelle believes him, which, you know, whatever.'

'But I thought – so, wait, they didn't have sex?' I lower my voice, embarrassed, and bracing myself for Brielle's reaction to this almost definitely stupid question.

She just shrugs. 'Probably everything but,' she says. 'Noelle says Emma called Jacob in a big panic, so I guess it could've worked. Who knows, maybe they'll still pull Emma out of school. You could get lucky.' The manicurist is massaging fancy lotion onto Brielle's hands now, and Brielle stares at them absentmindedly. 'But of course, Jacob's parents are crazy litigious, so maybe they just made it go away. Remember that pool their neighbours were going to put in?'

I shake my head a little, trying to keep up. It hadn't been my plan to get Emma in trouble for hooking up with Jacob. That had all been Brielle – though, I mean, I'd wanted it to work. But she'd really come up with the whole thing. And now she's acting like it's not a big deal at all.

'Pool?' is all I can manage to say. My own manicurist is faster than Brielle's, and she's already applying bright yellow polish to my nails. I stare at the paint; it looks like each nail is being lit up, one at a time. Like candles.

'You know, Ronny Davidson's parents? Wanted to build a pool in their yard? Next door to Jacob's house? *Anyway*, it was back when Jacob's sisters were really little, and apparently the fence was too low and they said it was, like, a drowning hazard. So they couldn't build it.'

I still have no idea what she's talking about, but I'm afraid to set her off again, so I nod like I get it.

She can always tell when I'm lying, though, and she rolls her eyes at me. 'So my *point is*, even if he'd, like, gotten her pregnant or something, Jacob's parents would've slapped the whole thing down in a second. It's, like, a hobby for them.'

I nod again. I actually feel a little better, knowing that no one's getting arrested. 'Her parents should still put Emma in another school,' I say. 'An all-girls' school.'

'I know, right? She'd probably just sleep with one of the teachers, though.'

'Totally.'

'Anyway, what are you wearing tonight?' Brielle asks, flipping her hair again.

My nails are done, but I stay in the chair next to hers, describing the tank top and jeans I have picked out for the thing at Jacob's. It's not really a party, so I'm trying to not look like I'm trying too hard. But Dylan will probably be there, so I want to look better than Emma.

I don't say that, but Brielle gets it anyway. When our nails are dry she pays, and then we go to Forever 21 to look for better shirt options. By the time we leave the mall I have a new top with aqua sequins and pretty yellow nails and a smile on my face. Brielle and I haven't spent this much time together, just the two of us, in forever. It's nice not to have Noelle or the senior guys around.

I wish we could stay out until it's time to go to the party-hang-thing, but I'm already in enough trouble at home. Mom wanted me back in time to take Alex to practice, and when I called to tell her I wouldn't make it, she hung up on me. Clearly she's gonna be mad about Mrs Putnam's call for a while. When Brielle drops me off I just stand outside the door for a minute, wondering if there's a way to sneak off in my car. But I hear yelling inside, and I figure I should go in to make sure the boys aren't being punished just because Mom's mad at me. Besides, I need my gas allowance from her. It's really for driving the boys around, but I'll need it before tonight.

I step through the door and the volume of the yelling goes way up. 'A couple hundred dollars to fly out here is not too much for your daughter!' Mom's shouting. There's a pause. 'I work too, Doug, don't give me that crap. She's our *daughter*. There's obviously a prob—' another pause.

Great. She's on the phone with Dad again.

For another minute I just stand there, still holding my bags and wearing my coat. Mom's in the kitchen but she can't see me from here. I look down at my new nails and wonder how they can be so damn cheerful.

'It's on Wednesday afternoon,' Mom says into the phone. 'I'm leaving work early and—' Pause. I guess he keeps interrupting her. 'Yes, she's going to be there, she—'

I look up. Wednesday afternoon? She? What the . . .

'I'm worried, okay?' I hear my mom's voice drop from a yell to a tired, pleading tone, and my throat seizes up. 'I'm just worried. I just think you should come out. You can stay here for the night. The principal really wants us both there, and the other girl's parents are definitely going to be—'

There's another pause and my mind goes wild trying to figure out what's happening. My parents, together, having

221

some kind of meeting at my school? That I have to go to, it sounds like. With . . . who? Not Emma's parents? If my dad is actually coming out for it, during a work week, I must be in a massive amount of trouble. Right? What else could they be talking about?

I wiggle out of my coat, dropping it and my bags on the main stairs, and practically run down to the basement. Tommy and Alex are sprawled on the old sectional couch, in the dark, watching a movie on TV. One look and I can see it's not something they're supposed to be watching – even if I hadn't glanced at the screen and seen guns, I'd know from the way they both sit up guiltily, Tommy grabbing the remote like he was just about to change the channel.

'Whatever,' I say, waving my hand at him. 'I won't tell Mom. I think I'm in trouble, anyway, so it's probably easier if you are too.'

Alex's eyes are wide. 'What were *you* watching?' he asks.

I surprise myself by laughing. Then I go over and ruffle his hair, which he hates, and scoot in between the boys. 'Don't worry about it, little A,' I tell him. Turning to Tommy I say, 'What is this? Isn't there, like, a Kardashian episode on?'

'Ewww,' both boys groan at once. We're not allowed to watch those shows, either, even if they're not violent. I secretly do, though. Mom has a lot of TV rules for someone who's put a television in the basement and computers in her kids' rooms. Though I guess we follow a lot of those rules anyway.

'It's kind of dumb,' Tommy says, pointing the remote at the TV. Two guys in masks are holding up a bank. 'They're surfers, but they rob banks? And they wear costumes, like the Joker in that Batman movie?'

'Hey, you weren't supposed to see that movie, either!' I say, grabbing the remote from him and hitting the Info button.

'I know,' Tommy says sheepishly. 'Duncan had it. We watched it at his house.'

'Hmm,' I mutter. 'I never did like that kid . . . Oh, hey, I've heard of this movie. *Point Break*. It's supposed to be funny.'

'It is?' Alex asks incredulously. 'I don't think it's funny at all . . .'

'No, I mean, it's supposed to be so bad it's funny. Like, you laugh at it, not with it.'

'That's mean,' Alex says.

'Everybody does it,' Tommy informs him, in his older-wiser-brother voice.

'No, not everybody,' I'm quick to say. But as we turn back to the TV I'm thinking, *Not everybody. But pretty much.*

September

'Guess our lawyers have us on different schedules, huh?'

I look over, startled. Brielle is walking up to the elevator bank with her parents. I'm waiting here alone. I see my lack of adult supervision register on Mrs Greggs's face. Her mouth goes all pinched and disapproving, but then, it usually did that even back when Brielle and I were allowed to hang out.

'Brie,' her mom says warningly.

Brielle rolls her eyes, not even turning back to her mom to respond. 'After that day in the parking lot I thought I'd run into you again,' she says.

My eyes dart to Brielle's parents, but they're staring straight ahead now. I wonder what she means. Was I supposed to try to, I dunno, meet up with her secretly? I guess that would have made sense.

'Um, yeah,' I say. 'It's weird. That we, you know – um . . .' I can't form a sentence but Brielle is nodding like I am. She seems even softer around the edges than she

224

did this summer.

Ding. The elevator doors whoosh open in front of us and we file inside.

'Where's your mom?' Brielle asks. Her parents still aren't talking to us, but her dad reaches past me to hit the tenth-floor button. I wait a second, then press eight.

'She had to work,' I say. Mrs Greggs sniffs, maybe disapprovingly, maybe just because she had to sniff. I keep staring at the elevator buttons, feeling shy and weird next to Brielle. 'How's, um, the – what is it, like, homeschool?'

'Oh, yeah, it's so lame,' Brielle says easily.

'Brie,' her dad says, his voice a low growl. I wonder if her parents just walk around all day saying her name in threatening tones of voice. It's working on me – I'm counting the seconds until we reach Natalie's firm and I can get away from them.

'Whatever, I guess it's better than Elmwood,' Brielle adds. 'But so is, like, prison—'

'All right, that's enough,' Mrs Greggs goes, but just then we finally reach the eighth floor and I scramble to get myself on the other side of the doors.

'See ya later,' Brielle says to me. 'You know, at the plea thingy.'

I turn back, surprised, and see her giving me a little wave as the doors shut again behind me.

So we're all accepting plea deals, I guess. And everyone knows what's going on with everyone else, except me. As usual. I mean, Brielle always knew everything about

225

everyone. Some things, at least, haven't changed.

As soon as Natalie's secretary lets me into the office I practically shout, 'Brielle got a deal, too? So there's, what, no trial at all anymore? What's going on?'

Natalie doesn't even look up from her papers. 'Hi, Sara,' she says. 'Have a seat.'

I look around. There's a chair with only one document box on it, so I move that and flop down.

'What the hell?' I say, still trying to get her attention. 'Brielle's lawyer is upstairs, you know. She said I'll see her at the settlement thing? Are we all going in at the same time?'

Natalie's writing something down, but she nods. 'Yes, just like it would've been if we were going to trial. You'll each be read your charges, allocute, and deliver your statements. Which is optional, but I still highly advise—' She finally looks up and then stops. 'Where's your mother?'

I sigh. 'Where is she always?'

'Jesus,' Natalie mutters. 'Well, I guess it's fine, this is going to be quick.' She takes off her reading glasses and squints at me a little. 'You don't have to give a statement. But I think it would be a good idea. This will be the judge who's going to sentence you, and while I'm not expecting more than a year's probation, you never know. It's an inflammatory case. The judge is a mother. You don't want to risk it.'

I nod. She told me all this last time. I'm pretty sure Mom

knows about it too, since they do at least talk on the phone now and then.

'It could also help with down the road, when we go back to expunge your record. So. Have you written anything yet?'

'No.'

She pauses. 'But you're going to?'

It's my turn to pause. I still don't want to do this. It feels phony, and kind of pointless. Hasn't the worst already happened? What can I say that will make anything better for any of us?

But I think of my little brothers, and what I said to Tommy the other day. I think of the reporters that have started calling again. The reporters who will almost definitely be at the hearing, and the articles that will end up online alongside the 'Poor Emma Putnam was so abused by her classmates she just couldn't go on' articles. At least I'll get to say *something*. At least something I say will be heard, maybe, and maybe even written down.

'Yeah, I guess so.'

'Good. I should read it first, you know.'

'Really?' I ask her. 'Why?'

She lets out a little chuckle. 'Because, Sara, I'm your lawyer. Remember?'

I sigh. 'Fine.'

'Great. How's the end of the week? You can just email it over. Now, I'm sorry to have dragged you in here, I keep thinking your mom will be coming too and we can get some things done . . . but it's fine, I'll be in touch with her.'

She turns back to her papers, glasses forgotten as usual, sitting on the table beside her. I hesitate for a second before I realize this means we're done. Basically I came all this way to accidentally run into Brielle and her parents. And get a lecture about my statement.

Whatever. I guess I wasn't doing anything today, anyway.

'Here, why don't you try writing something down now? We can talk about what comes up.'

'It's fine, I'll just do it at home.'

'No, no trouble, I have a whole stack of notebooks . . . Ah ha! Here you go. Use this.'

Teresa hands me a legal pad and a pen. She smiles but I just stare at her for a second, wishing this wasn't happening. I know I have to do this, but now? Here?

The notepad sits sideways on my knees and the pen is still capped, in my left hand. I feel frozen like this, like I'm a doll someone wants to pretend is doing her homework.

'Now. What is it you think you'd like to say?' Teresa asks.

I look at her.

'You don't have anything to say?'

'Besides that I wish Emma hadn't killed herself?'

'Good! That's an excellent place to start.' Teresa smiles and sweeps her hands toward me and the notepad, as if she can bring me to life, set this whole story in motion.

'But, I mean – *no one* wants someone to kill themselves. It's not, like, some big revelation.'

Teresa tilts her head to the side. She's wearing a sort of normal peasant-y blouse today, but it's in this intense shade of orange. I feel like I'm squinting back at her.

'Do you think Emma's parents feel that you wanted her to commit suicide?'

I pause. My mouth opens, then shuts again, without any words getting out.

Usually Teresa would just wait me out, but today she leans forward and adds, 'I can see that it might look that way to you. Just as it might seem obvious that you did *not* intend for Emma to do such a thing. This letter is your chance to clarify all these feelings, Sara.'

I look down at the pen in my hand and blink. The orange of Teresa's shirt stays behind my eyelids, making me tear up.

'You can write a dozen drafts of this, a hundred – you can tell them how angry you are, how hurt by what Emma has done.'

I let the pen drop to my lap, resting on the notepad. 'No, I can't,' I say. My voice is soft but bitter.

'Of course you can. Why can't you?'

'That's not – that's not the point, is it? That'll make the judge hate me. And everyone else. I mean, they already hate me, I guess, but I'm supposed to . . . like, Natalie says this will maybe make sentencing easier and everything . . .' I trail off, suddenly unsure what I'd been

229

meaning to say when I started.

'Well, I think everyone agrees that a suicide is a tragic thing,' Teresa says.

'Yeah, but for *them*,' I say, a wave of anger bringing my voice back up. 'No one cares about me – or Brielle or the guys.'

'Don't they?'

Carmichael's face pops into my mind, then – his messy hair and his black T-shirt, leaning over towards me in his dad's truck. And his words – what was it he said? That I could finally say how sorry I am?

'I just don't see why I'm the one apologizing!' I blurt. 'I'm not the one who ruined everything! *Emma* did that, and she did it *all by herself*. She killed *herself*!'

Teresa's gaze doesn't shift. She looks at me steadily, like I'm a fixed point on the horizon. I can't look back at her for more than a second before I need to look away again, back at the blank paper on my lap. There's a long moment of silence.

'We all make mistakes, though, right?'

I don't know what to say to that, so I just shrug.

'Believe me, we've *all* done things we wish we could undo. If there's anything you wish could be undone' – she waves a hand at the paper and pen again – 'this is a very good opportunity to say so. Don't add silence to your list of regrets.'

I look down and see my hands uncapping the pen, turning the notepad right-side up on my knees. My mouth is dry, my stomach is in knots, my life is over, my heart is broken.

I start to write.

There's about thirty seconds, sometimes a little more, every morning, when I forget. Or I don't remember yet. I'm just a little bit awake and my brain is just listening, I guess – wondering if it's time to get up, wondering if it's Saturday yet.

And then I feel the buzz, the low hum of panic that's always there now. On really bad days I don't even remember after it starts, not right away, because the buzz feels a lot like excitement. Sometimes it's the same feeling I used to get on any day I was going to see Dylan. If I wake up when it's still dark out, I can actually start to feel happy, because my whole body thinks it's winter and time to pick out a cute outfit because I have a boyfriend and things to do and maybe we'll—

No.

And it comes rushing back.

The buzz has almost always turned into a full-blown alarm by the time I'm getting out of the shower. I give myself about twenty minutes between waking up and leaving the house, just enough to pull my wet hair up in a bun and throw on some mascara, grab a Pop-Tart, and throw my bag in the backseat of my car while the boys run out of the house. The panic pushes me forward, or maybe I'm trying to outrun it. Either way, I don't pause. If I

231

stopped for a second, I'd throw up. And then I wouldn't ever be able to move again.

Today I have a strawberry toaster cake, still in the aluminum wrapper, clamped between my teeth, and my wet hair is still resting on my shoulders, getting my shirt wet. Of course I wore the grey T-shirt, it'll be all splotchy now. I picked it because it was nondescript, like everything I wear these days – something to be forgotten in. Dumping my bag on the driveway next to my car, I hurriedly pull my hair back and rub at my shoulders, hoping the shirt dries before I get to school.

'Front seat!' Alex yells, as always, careening out of the house with his own crappy breakfast.

And as always – these days, this school year – Tommy is strolling out behind him, going, 'Whatever.' He's too cool for the front now.

Alex bounces on the seat as we drive the fifteen minutes to his school. He still talks about what's going on that day, which today is some project about American government that I remember doing with the same sixth grade teacher.

We drop off Alex first, now that Tommy's in junior high. He jumps out, slamming the door behind him, and I glance at the rearview mirror. 'Don't you want to move up?' I ask Tommy. We're still idling in the crowded Pleasant Hill driveway, my hand hovering over the gearshift just in case. 'I feel like a chauffeur with you in the back all the time,' I tell him.

232

'Nope,' he says, and I sigh. 'You sound like Mom,' he adds under his breath.

'What? I can't hear you back there,' I say loudly, trying to turn it all into a joke. 'Don't worry, sir, we'll be at your destination in just a moment.' My attempt at a British accent is extra lame, and it doesn't cheer either of us up.

It's only another five minutes to the junior high, and then Tommy's out of the car, meeting his new friend Liam at the low wall in front of their school. I pause to wave, but they don't look back at me. Liam's wearing yet another hugely oversize T-shirt with baggy jeans and giant sneakers. The rest of Tommy's school is pretty preppy, and they're not allowed to wear baseball caps or anything, but Liam has one on, a crisp White Sox hat that I'm pretty sure he just thinks looks tough. I watch them shuffle into the building like a couple of baby thugs and try not to worry about my brother.

But the other anxiety, the Big Fear, comes back like a wave then, washing over me as I put the car back into drive and crawl toward Elmwood. When it was Dylan making me nervous, there'd be a moment when I finally saw him, and the awful buzz would turn into a happy pulse. Like tuning an old radio from static to music. But now I'm stuck. It's just static.

From the student parking lot at Elmwood all the way to my locker, no one even looks at me. The static fills my head, my stomach cold and hot and tense. Down the hall I see Carmichael, but I can't tell if he sees me.

233

The one person who didn't hate me, and I pushed him away. I think of how Hamlet treated Ophelia so badly and then she was dead, gone, like Emma, like everyone I used to have in my life. I see Beth talking to Megan Corley and I have to bite my lip. I'm going to throw up. We've been back at school almost three weeks, but it's not getting easier. Next week – in six days, actually – I go before the judge. I see Jacob and Brielle. I say I harassed Emma Putnam. I accept the charges.

I apologize.

Carmichael is walking toward me now, but only because he needs to get to the classroom on this end of the hall. But still, there he is, a few feet closer, and I move forward like there's a magnetic pull coming from his flannel shirt.

'Hey, Carmichael,' I say. From the corner of my eye I see Megan's head whip around, but I can't worry about that now.

Carmichael meets my eyes but he doesn't smile. He looks like he did at the beginning of the summer, like I'm a stranger.

'I just—' Someone bumps into me, shoving their way into homeroom. I don't know if it's on purpose or not, but it shuts me up. The impact literally snaps my mouth closed, and that's good, because it gives me one more second to think before I say something stupid. I don't even know what I was going to say, but when I catch my breath I manage a quick 'I'm really sorry.'

'What for?' Carmichael says. Not exactly cold, but not warm either. Tepid.

'For – you know, for everything on Saturday. For making you give me a ride. I – I really appreciate it.'

'Okay.'

'Okay. And . . .' I pause. What else do I say? 'And I want to make it up to you. I want to . . . um, we could have coffee? Again? Or I could—' Someone else bumps into my shoulder and this time I'm pretty sure it was on purpose. I step a little closer to the wall, trying to shield myself, but stay close enough to Carmichael that he knows I'm trying, close enough that he doesn't turn and walk away.

'Look, Sara, it's no big deal. You needed a ride. I don't need any coffee.' And then he does start to leave and I reach out, grabbing his wrist, the one with the tattoo.

'Please,' I say. I sound pathetic but I can't stop. 'I don't have anyone else. I didn't mean to be mean, I just – I'm just scared—'

He gently twists his arm so my hand falls away. 'I know,' he says. 'But I'm not here to make you feel better about everything. I have my own problems.'

I look up into his eyes and I just want to die. Of course he has his own problems, I know that. Don't I? I mean, no one's problems are as bad as mine . . . or maybe they are.

He waits for another minute, but I can't think of anything to say. I don't even know what I'm asking him for, really, except to not leave me alone, not to abandon me when I'm already so lonely.

'I gotta go,' he says, and then he's walking away. And I was wrong – he wasn't on his way to class. He's walking out the door.

The last bell rings and I'm still standing in the hallway, watching Carmichael's back getting smaller through the glass doors of the school, turning the corner outside towards the bike racks. I don't know where he's going. I don't know him very well at all. And I need him so much. But he doesn't need me.

I have to run to Mr Bastow's room, sliding into my seat just before the bell, but once I'm in it I can't get a deep breath. I don't know how much longer I can live like this, never being able to relax or breathe or feel okay at all.

'Took them long enough,' I hear Estrella Santos saying.

She's talking to Chris Black, but for some reason I think it's about me.

'Everyone knew he didn't do anything,' Chris says. 'They just messed up his whole life for no reason.'

'He's going to the U in the spring, I heard,' Estrella says, and that's when I know – Dylan. They heard about Dylan.

'Yeah, but baseball . . .' Chris shakes his head. 'The whole thing was stupid. I mean, she was his *girlfriend*.'

'I know. He must be *so sad*.' Estrella shakes her head too, her ponytail swishing and bouncing.

I sink a little farther into my seat.

'He was always so sweet. He wasn't like *them*,' Estrella adds. She glances over her shoulder and I look down. My hands are wrapped around my stomach, trying to hold it

236

in. I think of the breakfast I forgot in the car, still in its foil wrapper, probably melting on the dashboard right now. I don't even have anything to throw up.

Finally Mr Bastow comes through the door in a rush of polyester and papers and 'Calm down, everyone.' But I don't look up again. Maybe if I just don't move, I can finally just disappear completely.

March

'You look hot, okay? Jesus, Sara, I tell you this every time we go out! Would you stop? Just – oh my God, stop doing that!'

'What?' I drop my hair, which I've been trying to pull into a messy knot on my head, and look at Brielle. She's driving, eyes on the dark road ahead, and waving her right hand frantically in my face. I bat it away, yelling, 'What? *What?*'

'That!' she yells back. 'That updo business! you always try that and it's always a disaster!'

In the back seat, Noelle laughs, and I can't keep the whiny, defensive tone out of my voice when I say, 'I don't *always* try it. I was just – I just wanted to pull it back for a minute, I—'

'Ugh, *hopeless*,' Brielle insists. She's teasing me, I know, but she's also showing off in front of Noelle, pointing out how lame I am. But I can't help it – I'm crazy nervous. Every time I know I'm going to see Dylan, especially if

Emma's going to be there, I get nervous. Going to school is like getting up on stage – I want him to see me, but my hands are sweaty and my mouth is dry and it's just scary. I don't know. Sometimes yelling at him or Emma, like at McDonald's, makes me feel better. But then by the time I see him again I'm like this – a walking ball of panic.

Brielle used to understand, I think, but now she's over it. She and Noelle are talking about the weed that Jacob, or Jacob's cousin or something, is supposed to have tonight. Brielle's always wanted me to smoke with her, but I never have. So now I'm feeling nervous *and* totally third wheel. Perfect.

Jacob lives in an older part of town, where the houses aren't fancy but the trees are tall. We have to park on the street but it seems to be like Jacob said – just a few people – and immediately I notice Dylan's SUV. And then as soon as we walk inside, he's the first thing I see. I haven't been here before, and you'd think I'd be distracted by the oversized photos of Jacob and his sister over the fireplace – really embarrassing posed shots from a cheesy portrait studio, taken a few years ago when Jacob had total Bieber hair – but all I see is Dylan, sitting on the couch, talking to Kyle, drinking a beer.

And then he looks up and sees me, and he smiles. Like a *Hey, what's up* smile, an easy smile.

'Yo, Crazytown,' Brielle says behind me, poking me in the back. 'You gonna let us in the door?'

I've stopped in the doorway, I realize, and I jump

out of the way like a spaz.

Jacob walks up to Noelle and kisses her. Then he looks at us and goes, 'Coats in my room, right?' It's weird to see him being all party host. It's a nicely non-douchey look on him.

'Come on, I'll show you guys,' Noelle says, and we follow her down a narrow hallway, covered in more family photos.

'This is seriously embarrassing,' Brielle says, laughing and pointing at another soft-focus picture of Jacob.

'Don't even get me started,' Noelle says. 'His mom wants to hire someone to take our prom photos.'

'Ew! No!' Brielle shrieks.

'I'm like, "Get an iPhone, lady,"' Noelle goes on, opening a door at the end of the hall.

Not surprisingly, Jacob's room is plastered with those porny girl posters they sell at the mall. There's a really old Pamela Anderson *Baywatch* one, and some Rihanna posters, and then I have to basically stare at the floor because the walls are just a boob festival. I wait for Brielle to say something about the posters, but I guess she's not surprised, either. Or maybe she thinks it would hurt Noelle's feelings to make fun of Jacob's personal decorating.

I suddenly remember how Dylan's room just has a few college football posters, the rest of the room decorated really tastefully by his mom. This room feels like no one's mom has ever been inside it, or ever should be.

We drop our coats on the bed – which is at least made,

with a Green Bay Packers bedspread – and Noelle goes, 'You want to stay in here to smoke? We can open the window, it's cool.'

Brielle looks over at me like we haven't had this same conversation a hundred times. 'You wanna?' she asks.

I hate that I have to say no again, but I'm also glad she asked – I still feel left out, but a tiny bit less than I would have if she'd just ignored me. I'm starting to shake my head when Noelle adds, 'It's good stuff, totally mellow.'

'I'm cool, thanks,' I say.

Jacob and another guy I don't know come into the room behind me and I can tell that this is where I'm supposed to leave, so I do. I'm barely out the door before the other guy has shut it behind me, and I hear them all laughing. Not at me, I know. Or I'm pretty sure.

Brielle doesn't understand why I don't smoke weed, and sometimes I don't either. There's something about the thought of staying in that room with them that just scares the hell out of me. Like, in this house I don't know, with people I don't really know – even with Brielle there, it just feels scary and lonely. Like being driven out into the woods and left there. At night. Brielle says it's better than doing prescription drugs or something, which is what the real dropouts at school do. But whatever, it's all too much for me.

I stare at one of the photos in the hallway, an airbrushed shot of Jacob when he was maybe five or six, posing with a toy fire truck. My only option now is to go back to the front of the house, where Dylan and Kyle and Noelle's friend Amy are hanging out. I still don't really know Kyle that well, and I've only talked to Amy maybe once ever. And I don't know Dylan any more.

At least Emma isn't here. I take a deep breath and force my feet down the strip of plush carpeting.

The first thing I see when I walk back into the living room is Dylan's face, smiling at me. My whole chest swells, like it's being inflated, just because of that smile – pointed at me again, after all this time. I almost can't stand it.

He's obviously a little drunk, but I don't care. When he pats the couch beside him, the universal *Hey, sit here* gesture, I glide across the floor and take a seat. It's dangerous and sexy; *I'm* dangerous and sexy. Never mind the me that wouldn't smoke weed a second ago – this Sara is accepting a can of beer from Kyle and smiling at Amy.

'You guys are so cute,' Amy slurs, smiling back at me and Dylan. I think maybe she's being sarcastic, but I can't tell. I decide I don't care about this, either.

'Dylan looks good with everything,' I say boldly and, I think, cleverly. Like Brielle's voice is coming out of my mouth. 'He's just got one of those faces.'

'Hey, what's that supposed to mean?' he asks, teasing. 'What's wrong with my face?'

'That's my point, dummy,' I say, poking him playfully in the arm. 'Nothing's wrong with your face. It's a *great* face.'

I'm looking right in his eyes and grinning like an idiot. I was never this obvious with him when we were actually

242

dating – I never talked like this, flirted so openly. For some reason I feel like I can now, now that he's not my boyfriend. Now that he's dating a stupid slut, a girl everyone laughs at. I'm doing him a favour. I'm *rescuing* him. He could be with me instead. It's not too late.

'Where'd Tex go?' Kyle asks Amy. I figure he means the other guy I saw in Jacob's room, which is confirmed by Amy's response. She just holds her fingers to her mouth in an imitation of smoking pot and Kyle goes, 'Oh, right.'

'Where's Emma?' I ask Dylan, but quietly, so the other two can't hear me. I keep my expression blank, or I try to – but just in case, I lift the beer can and take a long drink. It's cold and sharp and I instantly feel a rush of warmth all the way to my knees. Beer and Dylan's smile, his body next to mine on the couch . . . dangerous combo.

He frowns and shakes his head a little. 'She's . . . I don't know. She said she's grounded or something.'

I hesitate, wondering if she's grounded because of what Brielle and I did, what we said to her mom. With a jolt I realize that Dylan might know everything already – didn't Emma's parents call Jacob's? But why would he still invite us over? God, Brielle didn't explain anything to me. I have to just play it cool.

'Don't you believe her?' I ask, taking a big gulp of beer.

'Sure, I guess. But she wouldn't tell me why.'

I nod sympathetically, relief flooding me even faster than the buzz from the beer does.

Dylan's frown deepens. 'Come on, you don't care about

243

me and Emma,' he says. 'You hate her.'

For some reason, his words slice right through me. If I were trying to act like a wounded puppy, I couldn't come close — but there are tears in my eyes suddenly, and I have to clear my throat before I can say, 'She stole my boyfriend.'

Dylan just looks at me for a second. He looks at me like he never really saw me before, but then he turns back to his beer, taking a long gulp. He stands up, and I think he's going to walk away, but when he's on his feet he turns back to me and holds out a hand.

'You want to get out of here?'

Holy crap. I've never wanted anything more *in my life.*

We're in the back of Dylan's car and it's old times again, it's like it should be. It's better than old times too, because I'm not scared. I know him, I trust him. He needs me.

I'm the one moving things along — I take off my own shirt, and I don't go limp when he starts tugging at the waist of my jeans. I don't care that we didn't even move the car off the street near Jacob's house. The other houses are far apart and there are so many trees, it feels all wooded and private. And I want to be here so badly — I want to be close to him more than I've ever wanted anything. Before, I don't know — I think I just wanted to have a boyfriend or feel like he liked me. But now that I know what it's like to have him and lose him, I can't let go. I won't let go.

But Dylan pushes away. I'm lying across the backseat

and he lifts himself up, looking down at me.

'This isn't – I don't think we—'

'It's okay,' I say in a rush. 'I'm okay.'

A look crosses his face that I can't really read. I don't want to read it – if it's second thoughts, I don't want to hear them.

I pull him back to me and we keep kissing. And then I'm having sex again, for the second time in my life, with this perfect, perfect guy. He's perfect and he likes me. He didn't really leave. He's back. We're back.

When it's over, he doesn't move right away, and I wrap my arms around him. He's still wearing his sweater but I don't mind. It's cute. It's warm. Then when we both sit up and rearrange ourselves. I feel like laughing. I feel better than I have in a hundred years.

But when I look over at Dylan, his eyes are down. And he goes, 'I'm sorry. I guess I just . . . I don't know.'

I open my mouth to say something, but I'm stuck again. What's happening? What does he want to hear?

'It's . . . okay,' I finally manage, though I don't even know what I mean. Why is he apologizing?

He shakes his head. 'Emma really is a nice person,' he tells me. The sound of her name feels like a punch to the gut, but I sit silently and wait for him to say more. 'It's just so hard . . . She's had such a hard time. Not just at Elmwood or with you guys or whatever.'

I want to point out that Dylan wasn't a big Emma defender himself, back before Valentine's Day, but I guess he wasn't as mean as Jacob or Tyler. He didn't really do anything at all.

I clear my throat. If we have to talk about this, fine. He's going to break up with her, obviously. So maybe I can feel a little sorry for Emma Putnam, just this once.

'I heard she sees a therapist,' I say.

'Yeah, she does. But not like that,' he adds, and now he's looking at me, his eyes pleading for me to understand, even though I obviously don't. 'At her old school it was just really hard, and her parents thought it would be good to move to Elmwood. Or her mom did, I mean – I don't know, it seems like her stepdad is really a jerk.'

I can't help but snort at that. 'Yeah, okay. I'll take a jerky stepdad who buys me a freaking Audi any day,' I say. And I would. I don't understand how half the kids at Elmwood walk around like they're suffering so much. I haven't even seen my real dad since the world's crappiest day-after-Christmas visit last year. He brought the boys some sports equipment and then he handed me an unwrapped Taylor Swift CD. I just stared at it, unable to even begin explaining what a ridiculous excuse for a 'gift' it was.

Dylan runs his hands through his hair and I wonder if I'm messing things up right now. Emma's the emotional mess – I'm the easy one, the one who doesn't have problems. I'm the drama-free girlfriend, the girl he wants to be with.

I scoot over on the seat and lean my head on his shoulder. 'I'm sorry you had to deal with all that,' I say, reaching for his hand. 'But I'm glad things are better now.'

246

His whole body tenses up under me, his shoulder flinching out from under my cheek. 'Uh, Sara, this—'

I lean back and smile at him, letting him see how happy I am. Somewhere in the pit of my stomach I can feel something bad coming, like when you first realize you're going to have to puke, that glimmer of nausea before the retching starts. But I'm ignoring it. I'm fine. This is fine.

'This was a mistake,' he says. Whispers. 'I'm really sorry.'

His voice is so soft and low, but it echoes in my head like he's screaming. The nausea starts to rise.

'Are you—' I start to say, and then I have to stop. My voice is scratchy and there's so much in my throat – vomit and tears and, like, a whole pile of giant, painful lumps – that I can't get any other words out. I swallow and swallow again and he's not looking me in the eye. By the time I open my mouth again my voice is barely a squeak, because I can't get any air, but I sort of croak, 'What are you saying?'

'I'm really sorry.' He's still whispering. He's sad. But he's saying it anyway. 'This can't happen again. I'm sorry.'

I can't move. I can't feel my arms or legs or anything inside, either – I'm not frozen, because that would feel like something, that would feel solid. I'm heavy and limp. I'm speechless. I'm never going to be okay again.

'Hey, listen, do you need a ride home? Let me take you home.' Dylan fumbles in his pocket for a minute before smacking his palm to his forehead and going, 'Duh, obviously my keys are in the car!' He makes a sound kind of like a laugh and looks over at me, but I'm still not

247

moving. I am too humiliated to blink, much less look at him and laugh about his car keys.

'So . . . okay,' he says uncertainly. 'You just . . . you can just stay back here if you want. I'll . . . um . . . I'll just . . .' He doesn't try to explain anymore, he just gets out of the backseat and into the front. When the doors are open big gusts of cold air sweep into the car, and suddenly it smells damp and earthy, that early spring smell that tells you all the snow and ice is melting and some day the sun will come out again.

And maybe it will, for some other girl. Maybe for some girl who isn't being driven home chauffeur-style by the boy who doesn't love her, who doesn't need her. The drama-free girl who isn't exciting enough for anybody. The girl who tries to be a good friend and a good girlfriend and just isn't quite good enough.

I guess the sun will shine on Emma Putnam's pretty hair, and her life that's so freaking difficult will be happy again. Dylan will make it happy.

But I'm the girl in the backseat, in the dark, with the tears coming down her face, crying about nothing, to no one.

September

'I want you to start cooking dinner one night a week.'

'What? Why? I have a million things to do! And I don't know how to—'

'*One night*, Sara. Come on. And you do know how, you help me with the mushroom chicken all the time. Or you could make chilli, or mac and cheese out of a box.'

'How nutritious.'

My mom stops chopping the onion on the cutting board and points the knife tip at me. 'I'm serious. You come home, you disappear into your room. We don't see you. I get that you've been upset by all of . . . what's going on.' She waves the knife in a circle, then seems to realize she's pointing a weapon at her only daughter and sets it down carefully on the counter.

'I have a lot to *do*,' I insist.

'Next week this will finally all be over,' she says. 'We can go back to normal. But you need to help us go back to normal.'

'I didn't *normally* cook before.'

'Tommy!' Mom yells over her shoulder, ignoring me. 'Enough! Get your brother for dinner!'

'Why don't *they* have to make dinner?' I ask. Now I'm just whining and I know it, but I can't stop. I was just about to disappear into my room, exactly like she said, and I swear I'm going to go insane if I don't get out of this kitchen in two seconds.

'They do. They will. That's part of the plan,' Mom says, and she throws the onion bits into a hot, buttered pan, where they start to steam and sizzle. '*Tom!* I don't hear you!'

Thump. Thump. Thump. 'Okay, okay,' we hear Tommy saying. We don't see him, but we hear his footsteps continue from the basement stairs around through the front of the house and up to the second floor.

'God, what did the stairs ever do to him?' my mom says. Her face breaks into a smile and for a second I don't know why it looks so weird. And then I realize – she doesn't smile any more. Ever.

'I'm just gonna—' I say, starting to move away, but she stops me.

'You're just gonna set the table. In the dining room.'

Sigh. 'Right, exactly,' I say. *Back to normal.* Whatever that means.

I'm sitting on my bed, staring at the notepad from Teresa's office, when there's a quick knock and then my door is being pushed open.

'What the—' I start to say, expecting one of my brothers. But instead I see my mom.

'Can I come in?' she asks, hovering in the open door. She's changed into her night clothes, yoga pants and the old Huskers sweatshirt. Her hair is up and she's wearing her glasses, which always make her look younger. She used to come into my room every night around this time, just to talk, just to spend a little 'girl time' at the end of the day. Obviously that never happens anymore. And obviously this must be about something else – I mean, who has time for 'girl time'? Not us. Not the girl who killed Emma Putnam and that girl's mom.

'Yeah, okay,' I say. I shove the notepad behind me, under a pillow, and pull one of my textbooks closer, as if I'd been working on . . . right, European history. I don't think I've even opened this book more than once. And in fact, it snaps when I flip it to a random page now, that obvious new-book sound making me flinch. The pages slap open in the middle of a chapter about the Holocaust. A gruesome black-and-white photo of three emaciated men with giant eyes stares at me. I shut the book again.

Mom is at my desk, looking at my corkboard, just like Tommy did the other day. 'Did Carmichael make that for you?' she asks, pointing at one of the CDs. Of course it's the one with *Carmichael Is Awesome* Sharpied onto it. It was supposed to be a joke, back when I thought we were the kind of friends who made jokes. Or any kind of friends at all.

'No,' I say, hoping she'll drop it. Luckily she just nods.

'Listen,' she says, finally turning around and walking closer to my bed. For a second she hesitates, since the whole mattress is covered in my books and backpack. I reach out an arm, knocking my English and science books on to the floor. I see her roll her eyes, but she sits on the part of the duvet I've cleared and goes on. 'Natalie and I spoke about the statement you're writing.'

I don't respond or nod or anything. I know all this, or anyway I figured.

'She said you're going to let her read it?'

'Yeah, I think I have to. She's the lawyer and everything.'

'Sure,' Mom says. 'Do you think – I mean, would you mind if I read it too?'

I blink. She – what? 'Why?' I ask, too startled to make more words.

She shrugs a little, that one-shoulder shrug that she and Alex do exactly the same way. One of those weird, random family traits. Like, after the zombie apocalypse, I'll know who I'm related to because of how they shrug.

'I've spent the last six months wondering . . . I just want to know how you are,' she says quietly. 'You don't talk to me.'

I can see there are tears in her eyes now, and I take a breath to say . . . I don't know, but I need to say something, don't I? But she reaches over and grabs my hand quickly, holding it in her soft, lotioned hand, the hand that wears a curled sterling silver ring instead of a wedding band.

'You don't *have* to talk to me, Sara. You're growing up so fast, I know. I know you have a life outside this house. I know things are . . . complicated.' She stares at our hands and so do I, the shapes of our fingers so similar and so completely different at the same time. My nails with their chipped grey paint and hers with their almost unnoticeable pink at-home manicure. My wrist wrapped in a rubber band from the school binder that's already falling apart, hers still wearing her slim gold-and-silver watch. The watch her mom gave her for her high school graduation. I think I'm supposed to get it for mine. I'd totally forgotten about that. When I was little I thought I'd be so happy the day I finally got that watch. I thought I'd be so grown-up. Pretty and confident. With hands like my mother's.

'I thought it might be easier to tell me, you know, how you feel, if it was in writing, that's all.' She looks up again and smiles, the tears gone. 'I remember how much I hated talking to my mom when I was seventeen, eighteen. She didn't know *anything*.' Mom laughs, and I find myself smiling too. Grandma is pretty cool, though we don't see her much since she moved to New Mexico a few years ago. Mom obviously doesn't have a problem talking to her any more – they spend like three hours a week on the phone now – but I always like hearing stories like this.

But I guess it's not a story night. Mom lets go of my hand and sits back, glancing at my books on the floor. As she picks them up she says, 'So anyway, if you want to show it to me, I'd like to read it. But of course I'll be there on Tuesday, too, when you read it.'

She stacks the books back on the foot of my bed and gets up to leave. I still haven't said anything. My hand is still warm from where she was holding it. I didn't even realize how little I've said to her all summer, all year – I thought she was the one not talking to me. But maybe it was the other way around? Maybe I've had everything wrong, mixed up, the whole time?

She's at my door now, but she stops and looks back, like she can hear what I'm thinking. 'You know, baby – you know I love you, right?'

I nod, still mute.

'And I'm proud of you for doing this. I'm not – I don't like what happened, you know. I don't like everything I've heard about in Natalie's office. I remember high school, I know how brutal it is. And I know Brielle. She's got a strong personality. She's exciting to be around. I know how you can get pulled into all that . . .'

I swallow. Mom's said all this stuff before, though not often since, like, ninth grade. For a while she wanted me to not hang out with Brielle so much, but after a year or so I think she finally gave up. At the time I was just happy she wasn't bitching about Brielle's 'influence' on me any more.

But I don't remember her ever saying what she says next.

'I'm on your side. I'm your mom, I'll always be on your side. The idea of you ever wanting to kil— of ever doing something like what Emma did . . . I just don't

254

know how I'd be able to go on. I'm just – I'm just so glad it wasn't you.'

I feel numb, but she's looking at me so intently, I nod.

'And I'm glad you agreed to do this, to talk in court. Because no matter how hard this has been on us, I can't imagine how much worse it is for them. I think if I were Emma's mom, it would mean a lot to me.'

She presses her lips together, pursing them to the side a little, like she's wondering whether to say something else. But she doesn't. She just smiles, kind of sadly, and quietly closes my door behind her.

And I sit there, the corner of the notepad digging into my back from under the pillow. Waiting.

Overnight, everyone at school figured out what's happening next week. They even all know the word *allocute* suddenly, like it was on a test or something. Many of them have loudly declared their opinions on the subject. *Unfavourable* would be the word. 'You should go to jail for the rest of your life' is the longer-winded version that most people seem to prefer.

By lunchtime I still haven't seen Carmichael, though I've been looking everywhere. I'm afraid he's skipped the whole day, but when I walk out the back doors to eat my sandwich in my car – I haven't set foot in the cafeteria all year – I finally spot him with his bike. I take a deep breath and go over to him.

'Hi, it's me again,' I say, ignoring the fact that I sound

like a moron. 'Can we talk?'

He looks like he was just about to take his bike lock off the rack, but he stands up and turns to me and puts his hands in his jeans pockets. 'Sure,' he says.

'I acted like an asshole,' I say. I push my shoulders back slightly, trying to be taller, braver. More confident. 'I'm really sorry.'

'Okay,' he says. He's looking at me like he doesn't really know what to think, or hasn't decided yet at least.

'Maybe you could let me take you out to dinner this weekend,' I go on. 'I mean, if that's good for you. I just – I'm not sure where I'll be next weekend. So this weekend would be good, if you can.'

He nods slowly, his face softening a little.

'I didn't say that to make you feel sorry for me.'

'Okay,' he says again.

'But if you feel sorry enough to say yes and go out with me, that's cool.'

Finally, like a miracle, he smiles. I'm so happy and relieved that I smile back instantly. I almost laugh out loud, but I resist.

Carmichael takes a step, closing the space between us, and touches me, feather-light, on the nose. Just the tip of his finger, just for a moment, but it makes my head buzz and my heart pound. 'Thank you for that,' he says, his hand back in his pocket.

'You're welcome,' I whisper. We're still standing too close, and I'm dizzy from having his hand on my face like that, like when your eyes are closed but you can tell someone is nearby. I remember learning why that was in biology at some point, something to do with survival instincts. I don't remember exactly – that was another science class I shared with Brielle, so mostly I recall that every time I'd close my eyes after that day, she'd hold a pencil up to my forehead or wave her hand in front of me, laughing hysterically when I would jump.

That's just how Brielle was. That's what no one gets, I think – she would tease you even if she did like you. *Especially* if she liked you. And then if someone was mean to her, or to one of her friends, she'd turn that teasing on to them. It would be a lot less nice, of course. It was pretty tough sometimes. But – and suddenly I know this, standing here with Carmichael, in the middle of passing period, in the middle of nowhere – that was her survival instinct. That's just how she deals.

And without her, I can't deal. Because my instinct is to just disappear. Thanks to Emma Putnam, I'll never be invisible again, no matter how hard I try. With Brielle, I could've turned into a yearbook girl, a popular girl, a confident girl. Emma turned me into a mean girl.

Right? Didn't she? Or did Brielle do that, too?

I wouldn't have been so mean all on my own, would I?

I blink, refocusing on Carmichael's face in front of mine. He steps back again and says, 'Yeah, I'm around this weekend. Maybe I should take you out, though. More traditional.'

'You don't seem that hung up on tradition,' I point out.

He shrugs again and says, 'You still don't know me that well.'

My cheeks burn, and suddenly I wish I had just gone to my car and left this alone. I can't see my life past next week – past that courtroom I'll be standing in, speaking in. I can't see how life is going to keep going after this. I know we're settling the case, but part of me still feels like the judge is going to hear what I say and go, 'Never mind, put her in jail.'

And maybe that would be easier. Because what do I do here? Make new friends? Figure out how to be someone that people can actually forgive?

Be someone that Carmichael can forgive? That would be a start, I guess. I think that's what I'm trying to do.

'There's time, though, right?' I say finally. 'I could still know you. If you want.'

It's the craziest, bravest thing I've ever said to a boy. I think I'm going to fall over right there on the pavement and die of embarrassment.

'Yeah, that's what I was thinking,' Carmichael says. 'So I'll pick you up on Saturday, okay? Take you out for a last meal.'

I smile at his joke, at his offer. 'Okay,' I say.

'Okay. I'm gonna go now,' he adds, gesturing back at his bike. 'You all right here?'

I nod, watching as he unlocks the bike and pulls it off the rack. 'See you later,' he says, and pedals away.

My heart is still thumping away in my chest, practically kicking me, but I feel calmer, too. I feel like I've just accomplished something.

I look toward the parking lot, wondering if it's too late to hide in my car for a while. And right then a group of girls, including Alison Stipe, walks past me. I start to lift my hand to wave at Alison, but then I see her turn to one of the other girls. Lindsay something. Alison whispers to Lindsay and Lindsay looks over at me. They both laugh. The sound sends a shiver up my spine.

I drop my head, staring at my shoes, wishing my hair were longer and covered my face more. I don't know what to do here.

'Slut,' one of the girls hisses.

I feel like I've been slapped, but I keep my head down and wait for them to pass.

If survival instincts were worth anything, I would run away now. But there's a different set of rules in high school. And then a whole other set for me. If you're me, you just stand still while the wolves circle, licking their chops.

Even if there's life after my court date, I don't think I'm gonna make it.

But I have to. I can't just give up. Like Emma did. That's not the answer.

Keeping my head down, I turn and walk back in to school, back to my locker. I can feel the stares, but I think about Carmichael instead, about how I'm going to get to know him better. Because he's giving me the chance.

Behind my curtain of hair, I find myself smiling, just a tiny bit.

Something about this small glimmer of happiness feels wrong, but I can't think about that. I just hold onto the glimmer, the shred. I let myself feel a tiny bit happy. Even though it kind of hurts.

March

omg, you missed everything.

u didnt rlly leave with man-ho dylan?

text me back, stupid.

???

god, whats yr problem?

emma is fuh. reaking. out.

kyle says she went apeshit on d-bag.

where the forks are you?????

I roll over in bed, ignoring the five-millionth buzzing of my phone. It's almost noon and I've already been up for a whole day, practically – Alex needed a ride to his game, Tommy needed help with a diorama thing for his science project, Mom needed me to go to the store for the bananas she forgot to buy – but now they're all having lunch and I've escaped back to my room. Of course my bed hasn't been made, which just means it was that much easier to crawl back into it. I didn't even bother to take off my jeans first.

I figure the buzzes are texts from Brielle. I should've told her why I disappeared last night, but whatever, she shouldn't've left me alone with Dylan. I'm sick of being her charity case. Or, like, the diorama thing in *her* science project. Social science. I tried to do what she told me to do, and look how well it turned out.

I just want to sleep, but every time another text comes through I wonder what's going to happen at school on Monday. If I can even manage to drag myself there, I mean. Obviously I'm not going to tell anyone what happened, and obviously Dylan doesn't want anyone to know. He wishes it hadn't happened at all – or at least, not with me. Is he not sleeping with Emma already? I mean, that's why he wanted to sleep with me, right? I guess I don't actually know that. But I thought that's what was going on. What the hell were we doing, anyway?

Whatever it was, it's a secret. It'll stay a secret. If Dylan doesn't want to break up with Emma and be with me now, he's not going to tell anyone. Especially Emma.

Right?

If he tells Emma I'm so, so screwed. She's the one who's the slut – she's the one whose fault this is in the first place.

But if Dylan doesn't want to leave her, then people are just going to think I'm the slut now.

I'm the most recent slut, so I automatically lose.

God, this is so humiliating. I am never leaving this bed again.

When I first started dating Dylan I used to like how people suddenly knew who I was, how I could talk to senior guys and they were nice – or nice enough – and I felt less like Brielle's plus-one and more like an actual popular girl, a girl who'd be in those pages in the yearbook with the photos of people just having fun. Those photos are always of the same few groups, the kids who have shiny hair and nice cars and letter jackets. Brielle ends up on those pages sometimes, but the closest I've come was sophomore year, when half of my head was in one photo. Next to Brielle's smiling face, but cut off, because there was a big group of us, with Alison and some of the guys we used to hang out with before Rob and Dylan and all them. Being Brielle's BFF has always made me more popular, but I've never really been *in*.

And I mean, I know, with Facebook and everything, it's not like the yearbook is that big a deal. But my mom's yearbooks are still in the basement and she's like the *star* of those things. When I was little I used to flip through them and think that all that would just happen to me – that I'd just grow up to be a girl like that, a cheerleader and a girlfriend to some great guy and a smiling face in a black-and-white montage that said *Seniors Rule* or whatever.

263

Except now it's the end of junior year and I'm not a cheerleader, I'm not anyone's girlfriend, I'm not the star of the yearbook. I'm the same nobody I was when Brielle plucked me out of nowhere in eighth grade.

Buzz.

Fine. I will read the damn messages. I'm not going to school ever again, obviously, but I'm kind of curious what's so freaking important.

Um. *What?*

The phone starts buzzing again while I'm still holding it, reading the texts I missed, and I jump about a mile. It's Brielle, but this time she's calling – the photo of her at the pool last summer, the one that was her profile picture for*ever* – jumps up at me. I just stare at her face for a second, my heart pounding and my thumb hesitating over the answer button.

Right next to it, the Ignore button stares back at me. Can't I just hit Ignore instead? Can't this just go away?

'Hey, Brie.'

'*Sara.* Jesus, where have you *been*? You just disappear into the freaking night, apparently with *Prince Charming*, and then you don't answer your phone?'

I fall back onto my bed, face-first into my pillows. 'Mmph,' I say.

'Well, that is simply not good enough, missy,' Brielle says. 'Why is Kyle telling me that Emma's lost her shizznit? Where did you and D-Bag go?'

'Nowhere. Well, I mean, he brought me home,' I tell

her. 'I have no idea why Emma's freaking. Isn't that what she always does?'

Brielle makes a little *pshh* sound, her version of a laugh. 'True,' she agrees. 'And it's her lucky drama-queen day, because she's already grounded for, like, ever. Mama finally responded to our tip on Jacob, I guess.'

I sit up. 'Is Jacob in trouble, too?'

'God, no. Weren't you just at his house last night? I *told* you, nobody actually *cares*. Or not once they start talking to those crazy parents of his, anyway. They make mine look like normal people, for Chrissakes.'

'Oh. That's good. I guess.'

'Yeah, it's awesome, Jacob can live to hump minors another day,' Brielle says dismissively. I can practically see her waving a hand in the air, brushing this aside. 'Anyway, you still haven't told me what *happened*! Did you guys totally bone? You totally boned. You're totally boning and back together and Emma is going to run away in shame to some girls' boarding school, *finally*.'

If only I could just agree with her. But instead I'm mad that she's making it all sound so easy. Everything *is* so easy, for her – she's got plenty of other friends, she's got all the money in the world, she's pretty and effortless. Why did I think I could be that way too?

'Nope,' I say finally. 'Nothing happened. He just took me home.'

'Boo!' Brielle yells. 'Booooo. You know what would be a way better story? The boning thing. In fact, I think

265

I'm going to make sure that Slutty Putnam hears that version of events. Let me just . . .' Her voice trails off and I hear tapping.

'Wait. What are you doing?' I ask, panic clawing its way up my throat.

'Ooh, this is good. Why didn't we think of this before? Whatever, it's genius now. And there's the fact that you and D-Bag were actually hanging out last night, so she's totally going to believe this.'

I sink my face back into my pillow. I know what Brielle is doing – maybe not exactly – but it doesn't take a genius to figure out she's starting another rumour. Or maybe just emailing Emma directly, who knows. Yesterday I would've been helping her, too; yesterday I would've even made up a story that pretty much matches what I did last night, just to get back at Emma. Now I'm just . . . tired.

'Okay. I'll pick you up at two, yeah? Wear something cute.'

'Why?' I don't remember having plans with Brielle today. After last night I kind of figured she'd still be hungover, or still hanging out with Noelle. I feel a rush of energy all of a sudden. How does Brielle do that? Just the words *I'll pick you up*, and I'm up off my bed, walking to my closet.

'Duh, the game! Jesus, what is with you today? Did D-Bag say something last night?'

'No,' I lie. I know I can't, but suddenly I want to tell her the truth so bad. She'd think it's awesome – but at the same

266

time, she wouldn't understand. And it's too embarrassing. God, I'm such a loser. I open my closet and there it is – nothing to wear.

'Well, you can say hi to him when we get there. And Emma will find out you guys were hanging out again, and she'll put on another freak show, and then boarding school, here we come! La la la la.'

I'm actually kind of smiling as Brielle sings out a loud 'Goodbye!' and clicks off. But my sour mood rolls back as soon as her voice is gone. What is Dylan going to think when he sees us at the game? It's totally going to look like I'm stalking him.

A series of options runs through my head, even as I'm pulling my best jeans out of the laundry pile on the floor of my closet. I could take my brothers with us; call Brie back and say I'm sick; just drive myself to Mexico right now – but I can't. I can't even convince myself that I *want* to do any of those things, because I know the truth. I want to see Dylan. I want him to see me. I still think he might pick me. And just maybe, *maybe* Brielle is right. Maybe Emma will transfer. Maybe the rest of the school year can go back to the way it was supposed to be, with me at Dylan's prom, at his graduation. At the parties. In the yearbook. Maybe at college parties next year . . .

It's okay that Dylan made a mistake, that he made out with Emma on Valentine's Day. Maybe a couple of other times too, I guess. It's okay that he's confused now. But the warmth and power and excitement I felt last night had to be the real thing, he had to be feeling that too. We're good together, he likes me. Emma is just a horrible distraction. And she's in trouble now. She won't be around at all for the rest of the weekend – she won't be at the game. She'll be hearing that I'm at the game, just like she heard I drove away from a party in Dylan's car last night. She'll break up with him. Or he'll break up with her.

It doesn't matter. All that matters is I need to find a stupid sweater right now and then everything is going to be *fine*.

Finally.

'I didn't think you'd be here.'

'Yeah, I mean – Brielle was coming, and I really miss this. Coming to your games, I mean. I just – I don't know. I'm sorry.'

Dylan rubs his hair, still wet from the shower. Brielle is down the hall, talking to Marcus, and I'm leaning against the wall next to the locker room Dylan just came out of. The game was at the indoor field at the Catholic college downtown, and the concrete brick walls are all painted a blinding combo of blue and yellow. I feel like I'm squinting at Dylan – when I can force myself to look right at him, anyway, which isn't very much.

All my clever flirting from last night has evaporated. Now I'm just a stalker with nothing to say for herself.

But Dylan shrugs and smiles a little. 'It's nice to see you,' he says quietly.

I look up at him hopefully.

'We're gonna get something to eat. Maybe at that diner down here?'

My heart does a little leap. I know the place he's talking about – it's one of those old-fashioned silver-sided places like in movies. Downtown has a couple of cool places that make this feel like a real city, and that's one of them. I don't know why I'm so excited about a restaurant, but I nod more enthusiastically than I should and keep holding my breath until—

'Do you guys wanna come?'

'Yes! Yeah – I mean, yeah, let me just tell Brielle, okay?'

I pause as Dylan picks up his bag and walks away, over to another group of guys. I can't believe this is actually happening.

'Dude, check this.' Brielle is suddenly at my side, holding out her phone. I look down and see a picture of me from just now – talking to Dylan, smiling. Brielle has just posted it on Facebook. 'Operation Boarding School is *on*, bitches.' She pulls her phone back, putting it in her coat pocket. 'Did he invite you to the diner, or what?'

'Yeah,' I say, trying not to laugh out loud. 'Can we go?'

'Can we *go*? We are already *there*!' Brielle turns and strides toward the gym doors, swinging her arms up in a grand gesture. 'What a photo op! I am a *genius*!'

At two in the morning I'm still online, scrolling through the mobile uploads Brielle put on her wall, my wall, the

269

baseball team's wall. Me and Dylan in the hall, me and Dylan wedged into the diner booth (seating arrangements by Brielle), me and Dylan at the cool music store a couple of blocks from the diner, me and Dylan at 7-eleven buying gum. I expand the diner shot again, peering at our faces. Can you tell we're in love? Everyone can see it, right? Not just me?

We all hung out downtown for hours, walking around in the cold and going into random stores. Brielle unceremoniously disappeared with Marcus around ten, and Dylan offered to drive me home again. I was so happy that I totally forgot I hadn't called my mom all day and I'd probably be in trouble when we got there. Well, happy, and nervous. It's not like my last trip in Dylan's car had been so stress-free.

But tonight was like a brand-new everything. We didn't even talk, really, while he drove. And when he pulled up in front of my house we both just sat there.

Then he said, 'Listen, I'm sorry about – everything.'

'Me too,' I said. I took off my seat belt and glanced over at him. His short hair was tucked into a wool cap and his long eyelashes glittered a little in the streetlamp light coming through the windshield. I took a deep breath, closing my eyes halfway, smelling his aftershave.

'I don't know what to do now. I really like you.'

My eyes snapped open again. 'I really like you, too,' I said, the words rushing out. 'I've always really liked you.'

I was sure I'd said too much, but then Dylan leaned over

and kissed me. Really soft, gently. Like a kiss goodbye. Except it felt more like a hello kiss, a new beginning.

He pulled back a little bit, just enough so we could see each other, and breathed in, like he had more to say.

But before he could, I said, 'Can we start over?'

He started to answer me but I couldn't stop talking. 'I'm really sorry about everything, before. I just think Emma is – I just think she's using you. But if you want me to be nicer to her, I can do that. I just miss you so much.'

I stopped, biting my lip, trying to swallow down the giant knot in my stomach.

'I'm sorry, too . . .' he said, but then he stopped.

'It's okay,' I said quickly. 'You don't have to – I mean, never mind, it's fine. I had a really nice time today. Thanks for driving me home.' I managed to smile at him again before I bolted out of the car and into the house.

I close my eyes now, blocking out the laptop screen in front of me and the rest of the memory of tonight, with my mom bitching about me not calling and all the crap around the house I'll have to do tomorrow. I keep my eyes closed until I've picked up my phone yet again. It's still open to the text I got an hour after Dylan drove away.

i had a nice time too. talk to you tmrw.

And yet again, my stomach tightens and then flips over happily, nervously. I turn back to my computer one last time and see I have a new email.

Emma Putnam is following you on Twitter!

What . . . the . . .

271

God, she's pathetic. Is she stalking me now? I guess after Brielle's posts today, Emma is – what? I don't even know. I link through and I'm about to just deny her – I'm not really on Twitter that much, but this is creepy – but first I decide to check her feed, just to see.

And that's when I see that maybe Emma isn't actually on Twitter that much, either. Maybe not at all. I mean, not the real Emma.

Her photo is of a pig. And the posts are all the photos Brielle took today, with captions like 'The guy I stole prefers nice girls'. They're all tagged #EmmaPutnamisaSLUT.

Yikes. I know Brielle is trying to have my back. But this . . . this is bad timing. Dylan's going to think it was me, or at least that I knew about it. And Brielle might think it's funny, but maybe it's not any more. Maybe it's just making everything worse.

My chat window pops open. Of course it's Brie.

#emmaputnamisaslut, bitches!!!

I shake my head and type back, *You can't. Dylan will think it was me.*

thbbbbbt. yr no fun.

And then she's offline again – she just hangs up on me. I glance back over at Twitter and see a new Emma post pop up.

I don't have any friends boo hoo cuz #EmmaPutnamisaSLUT

This is not good.

I close the computer and put it down on the floor next to my bed, hoping that Brie will stop soon and this will all just go away. For now, I'm going to sleep. I'm going to dream about Dylan, and about my life, which is finally back on track.

October

'Order up! Extra chips!'

'That's me, that's me!'

'Okay, now, here you are . . . Let me just get your salsa . . .'

'Nooo! Not on *pancakes*!'

'No? You don't take salsa with your extra chips?'

'They're extra *chocolate* chips!'

'Oh, I see. Well, if that's really what you want . . .'

'*Daa-aad!*'

Alex shrieks and giggles like he's gone back in time five years. I roll my eyes, but it's okay, because no one can see me – I'm still in the hall, out of sight, not in the kitchen with everyone. It's nice to hear Alex laughing, but without even being able to see them, it's painful to witness Dad doing that thing where he pretends to be all fatherly. It's hard even to listen to.

I can also hear that he's turned back to the stove. The pan sizzles with more butter and the spatula scrapes, and then I hear him say, 'Tomcat, you're a salsa man, right? Puts hair on the chest!'

Alex laughs even harder at this, but Tommy just says, 'No, I'll take just plain chocolate chips, too.'

He sounds a little weary. Like me. I want Tommy to like his dad – our dad – but a part of me is glad that I'm not the only one who sees what a fake he can be, how *not enough* this all is. Besides, it's way too early to deal with all of it. And it's Saturday – it's supposed to be our day off. Or, I mean, it's supposed to be the boys' day off. I'm already practically vibrating with nerves about my own plans for the morning, which include an extra fun trip to Natalie's office.

Another scoop of batter hits the pan, making the butter hiss, and my stomach drops a little lower. I feel like I've had ten cups of coffee or something. I don't think I can go in there without throwing up on everybody.

'Doug, you know where the fields are, right?'

At the sound of my mom's voice, I jump. I thought she was still upstairs, or out – anywhere but having a cozy pancake breakfast with Dad. Her tone is suspiciously friendly.

'Of course. Been there a million times. Right, guys?'

'Yep!' Alex says, his words muffled by a mouthful of food, I'm guessing. I don't hear Tommy answer. It's not like he has to – just like with our rides to school, he's perfected the art of letting his little brother talk for him. Kind of like I figured out a long time ago, when these little visits from Dad first started to make me upset instead of happy.

'Julia, you want more?' I hear Dad ask my mom. His voice has that edge to it – they can't say anything to each other without it sounding vaguely like a threat.

'God, no. But thank you for cooking,' she says, and there's a clatter of dishes in the sink.

I take a deep breath and peek around the doorframe. I don't know why I can't just go in there, but I can't. There are so many reasons why not, but mostly, right now, it would just be impossible to have the chocolate-chip pancake discussion one more time. I don't like them, and no one, particularly my little brothers, can understand why. And Dad will think I'm just being a brat to spite him, like I live my whole life to thwart his crappy efforts at playing Good Father. I can't explain that there's nothing to even thwart, so why would I bother trying?

And Mom will want to say something about my outfit or whatever. She's been really nice since the other night in my room, but it's basically an addiction with her, to look at me and immediately find something that needs improvement. And of course *everything* about me needs improvement. I just don't need to talk about my T-shirt and cutoff shorts right now.

I can't see very far into the kitchen, but I watch Mom at the sink, her hair pulled back into a loose, pretty-but-weekend-y ponytail. I'm surprised to see she's wearing jeans too – usually when we go to Natalie's she wears something she'd wear to work. They're nice jeans, of course, with a nice shirt.

Then my dad comes striding into view, carrying the skillet to the sink. He's in chinos and a polo, the Saturday uniform of absentee fathers everywhere. I didn't even know he was coming today, and actually it seems like he must've gotten in last night – his hair still looks a little wet from a shower. Wait, is he staying *here*?

'Thank you,' Mom says to him, taking the pan and adding it to the pile she's rinsing and then putting in the dishwasher. 'And thanks for cooking, this was nice.'

'Of course. I'll get the boys to their games and then meet you at the lawyer's office.'

'Okay, but no rush, stay with them as long as they need. Tommy's just a couple fields away from Alex today, so you can go back and forth, maybe, and then bring them home.'

They're talking like they're still married, like it's just another weekend. Most people probably wouldn't hear the tension in their voices, or see the way my mom isn't really looking at my dad. But still. I realize how much easier this last six months would've been if we were a two-parent household. Even two parents who still pretty much hate each other.

My stomach does another sloppy flip, like a broken, half-cooked pancake. I take one last look at my parents and finally back away, unseen, going around the long way to the front door. I have my keys and my bag already. I guess we could drive together, Mom and me, but my car is in the driveway, and Dad's isn't blocking it – he parked on the street, his bulky black car looking like the FBI came to stay with us or something. I take that as a sign, and without really thinking I get into my car.

I don't want to go straight to Natalie's – if for no other reason than I'll be way too early – but I need to go somewhere. When I pull up to the intersection with the Albertsons on the corner, I make a split-second decision to turn. I'm not even expecting Dylan to be there, but then I see his car, and I park hastily, not giving myself time to think.

The store is freezing, as always. Outside the temperature has dropped fifteen degrees, an early preview of what fall will feel like, if we get more than a couple of days of it before winter sets in. But it always takes a few days for places like school and the grocery store to catch on and turn their thermostats up. I haven't caught on, either – even my emergency Teresa sweater is still in the car. Goosebumps pop out on my arms as soon as I walk through the automatic sliding doors.

The sight of Dylan doesn't make them go away, that's for sure. He's right at the front, unloading boxes of apples, standing with his back to me at one of the first tables inside the produce section. It's been a long time since I've seen him – outside of stalking his Facebook page, I mean – and the sick-excited feeling I've had since I woke up gets even more intense. Just watching his back as he leans over and opens another cardboard box, pulling a tray of Granny

Smiths up and setting them on the table, makes me dizzy.

Plus I realize I have no plan here, no agenda, no point. Did I just want to see him? Just one last look before he goes to college, which I'm assuming is what he'll be doing next – starting late, or moving to some off-campus housing until spring semester, or—

I don't have a chance to decide what I'm doing, though. Suddenly he turns, looking at me so directly and immediately I wonder for a second if I didn't say his name out loud. We're staring each other in the eye, me shivering in short sleeves, him in his dumb blue apron.

He doesn't look surprised to see me, really. We're standing too far away from each other to talk without yelling, so I kind of angle my head back, toward the door I just walked in, trying to silently ask him to come outside. This makes him raise his eyebrows, maybe because we're usually in the back, hiding from everyone. But maybe that's not what he's thinking. I don't think I've ever really understood how Dylan thinks.

'Hey, dude,' he calls out to another blue-apron guy, who's stacking cartons of caramel apples a couple of tables over. 'I'll be right back.'

The other guy looks like he wants to argue, but Dylan's already walking toward me, untying his apron, running a hand through his hair. For another minute I just stand there, letting Dylan walk right past me and through the sliding doors. Then I turn and follow.

Yep, still cold outside. *Brisk*, my mom would say. Dylan

has found a bench to sit on, one of the ones that line the outside walls of Albertsons and the half-dozen other stores in the strip mall. There's an overflowing ashtray/garbage can at the end of the bench, and between that and the cold I want to suggest we go sit in my car, but instead I sit down, still shivering.

'What's up,' he says dully. His apron is crumpled in his hands, one escaped string dangling down as he rolls the fabric into a tighter and tighter ball.

Now that I'm here I can't remember what I wanted to say. If there was anything at all. So I go with the truth, or part of it.

'I just wanted to see you,' I tell him. We don't look at each other – we're both staring out at the parking lot, or down at the cigarette butts crushed on the ground.

'Good timing, then,' he says. 'I'm moving to Lincoln next week.'

'Really?' I'm surprised it's so soon. And – suddenly – really disappointed.

'Yeah, you know, with Rob and them, they have an apartment.'

'Oh, right. That sounds good.'

'Yep.'

We're silent for a minute, staring off some more.

'So,' Dylan says finally. 'You guys got a plea.'

'Not as good as you,' I say without thinking. 'You're off the hook completely.'

His head snaps around fast and suddenly we're looking

280

eye to eye, but it's awful. He looks so mad. Betrayed.

'I didn't *do* anything,' he says.

I think of those times this summer, those days I'd visit him on the other side of this same building, those pointless hookups. It had felt so good to hang on to each other in the middle of everything falling apart – or maybe it hadn't felt good, but it had been a little raft of not-awful in the freaking ocean of very-awful. And we'd been *together*. We were the wrongfully accused, the innocent.

And now I can tell from his eyes that it wasn't that way at all. He'd been innocent, and I'd been . . . not.

'Did you ever even like me?' I ask him.

'C'mon, Sara, what kind of question is that?' He shakes his head a little, then sits back on the bench and faces forward again with a big sigh. The apron drops out of his hands, onto his lap, one big blue wrinkle. 'Not everything is about *you*.'

'I know . . .' I say, but my stomach is twisting itself into another knot, and the pain makes me just angry enough to defend myself. 'But it's *partly* about me. I mean, I'm on trial too – or making a deal, or whatever – and I was the one you . . .' I trail off, unsure again of what to say. Dylan *is* innocent. Or at least, he hasn't done anything you can put on paper, and that's basically the same thing.

There's a long pause while we go back to staring forward, like we're in a car, like the view in front of us is important, like it's going to change. A few people pass by on their way into the store, ignoring us. I don't see them, either.

Finally Dylan says, 'I'm glad you guys aren't going to trial. That would've been really hard.'

'I wasn't exactly looking forward to it,' I say honestly.

'Yeah, well, I kind of meant, you know, Emma's parents. It was gonna be really hard on *them*.'

I frown. 'They're the ones who wanted a trial, though. They *started* this whole thing.'

He turns to me, his eyes locked onto mine. His hair got longer over the summer but now it's freshly cut, leaving his ears a little too exposed. He has a little nick on his chin from shaving. He smells like the aftershave he always uses, a sharp, boyish scent mixed with that other smell that's just . . . him. He shifts on the bench and his shoulders are like a swinging door, blocking everything else out, closing me in. I want to lean on them. I can't.

But I see his face clearly, like it's the first time. Except I'm pretty sure it's the last time.

'Nobody wanted this,' he says slowly, evenly. 'Nobody.'

Then he stands up and walks away.

March

When I wake up Sunday morning – not late, like I wanted to, but insanely early, before it's even eight, because my nerves are still wired – the first thing I do is go online and find that the Emma Twitter is still active. There are lots of 'I'm pathetic'–type posts, and lots of followers and replies. Who's online that much on a Saturday night? Everyone, apparently.

And on Facebook, a bunch of people are talking about how cute Dylan and I are together, how we make a better couple than he and Emma do. There are even a few 'Good for you, bro' posts on his wall, though I have no idea what that means exactly. That they're happy he's back with me (or that it looks like he is, anyway)? Or that they think he's a stud for having two girlfriends at the same time?

It's still the weekend. The boys have more sports stuff. Mom is still mad at me for being out late Friday and then all day yesterday and probably won't let me go anywhere. But there's got to be a way to see Dylan again. If I see him

I can explain that I'm not doing this, that everything I said yesterday is still true. If I can see him we can . . . I don't know. I just want to see him.

So when my phone buzzes, I grab it, my heart leaping into my throat, so sure he's texting me.

It's Brielle, though.

911 my house now!!!!!

Brielle is a lot of things, but she's not an abuser of the 911 text. I throw on some jeans and a sweater and hurry downstairs, bracing myself for a flurry of lies to get out of the house. If I can get out to see her, maybe I can get over to Dylan's house too.

'*You're* a pinhead,' I hear Alex shouting as I come into the kitchen.

'Language,' Mom says, but her voice is tired and doesn't sound very threatening.

'Yeah, pinhead, *language*,' Tommy snarks.

'You started it!' Alex shrieks.

'Yes, he did,' Mom agrees. 'And I don't know why, but you're both going to your room now.'

'But *Mom*—' Tommy starts to say.

At the same time, Alex goes, 'I'm still eating my cer—'

But then Mom drops her coffee cup into the sink so loudly that they both stop talking at once. The clatter of the metal cup in the metal sink is momentarily deafening, and way scarier than anything she could say right now. In the perfect silence that follows, my brothers get up from the table and leave the kitchen. Alex gives me big googly eyes as he leaves, but Tommy smiles, like, *She's all yours.*

I'm stuck in the doorway, not sure if I should still try to get my keys from the hook by the back door or just retreat to my room. But when Mom sees me, she just goes, 'You're up.' Then she turns back to the sink and starts washing the dishes.

Slowly, I walk over to the other side of the counter, between Mom and the back door. 'Yeah,' I say. 'And I kind of have to . . . go . . .' I gesture lamely at the door, waiting for her to start yelling at me.

'Fine. Be back by noon.'

She doesn't look at me and I hesitate, wondering what's wrong. Isn't she still mad about yesterday?

Slowly I reach for my keys on the hook, carefully lifting them so they don't jingle. I don't know why – the water in the sink is loud, and Mom's tossing the dishes into the dishwasher like they're all unbreakable (I guess most of them are, thanks to having two little boys in the house). I'm actually surprised I can hear her when she speaks again, because her voice is low, like she doesn't have the energy even to talk anymore.

'Enjoy it. I don't know what they're going to tell us about you at this meeting on Wednesday, but I'm betting you won't be driving that car anywhere without the boys in it for a long time.'

I'm looking at the keys in my hand, the doorknob in front of me, the whole life I have on the other side of it. Shit. I'd forgotten about that meeting, that phone call she was having with Dad. That was three lifetimes ago.

'Just go,' she adds. 'Just get out.'

So I do.

'Wait, first you need to sit down.'

'And have some coffee.'

'Yes! This is totally sit-down-and-have-some-coffee news.'

'Can we smoke in here? It's *really* have-a-cigarette news.'

'Sara doesn't smoke. But we could go out on the deck.'

'Yuck, no, it's freaking freezing outside.'

'Oh, I'm sorry, Your *Highness*.'

'Damn straight! Keep calm and *don't freeze your ass off.*'

Brielle leans against the kitchen island, laughing, and Noelle doubles over on her chair. 'Keep calm and *wear some damn mittens!*' Brielle shouts.

'Keep calm and *what the hell does that even mean!*' Noelle answers.

I'm standing at the other edge of the island, trying to laugh – or even just smile – but they aren't paying any attention to me. They're in their pyjamas still, so obviously Noelle has been here all night. Brielle isn't wearing makeup yet. She wipes her eyes and turns back to the coffeemaker, going, 'Where were we?'

'You were keeping calm and telling Sara the good news!' Noelle crows.

'Oh my God!' Brielle whirls back around to face me. 'Are you sitting? For the love of Christmas, sit down!'

I walk around to where Noelle is perched on one of the tall bar chairs. Brielle's kitchen is huge, with a big table and this wide island area. One wall is just windows, overlooking their giant deck with its own table, chairs, and bar area, next to a large sunken hot tub. Beyond that the trees seem to go on for miles – maybe they do, I don't know; Brielle and I haven't been back there in years. It's a grey morning, the branches wet from rain and starkly black against the flat metallic sky. Driving over I thought there was something ominous about the weather, but I guess I'd just overreacted to Brielle's text. Whatever's going on, it's obviously hilarious. To her and Noelle, anyway. Stupid me, thinking I'd be the first person to hear about it.

'Here, stop pouting,' Brielle says, reading my mind. She sets a heavy Le Creuset mug in front of me and I lean over to look at the suspiciously thin brown water.

'This is coffee?' I ask. I don't really mean to sound insulting, but it looks wrong.

'Shut up!' Brielle says, and Noelle cracks up again.

'I told you that wasn't enough scoops!' Noelle shrieks.

God, this is all giving me a headache.

Brielle is stomping back to the coffeemaker, pulling out the kettle part and dumping the rest of the watery liquid down the sink.

'You are so going to get fired from Starbucks,' Noelle says.

'I don't have a *job*, silly.' Brielle smiles.

'Guys, hey,' I say, finally, 'You sent a 911? What's going on?'

They both look at me like I haven't been sitting here, the subject of their little coffee one-act play, for ten minutes. Brielle's smile widens and she says, 'Oh. Oh, *yes*.'

Noelle squeals, hops in her seat, and claps her hands. I've never seen her so perky. Though obviously I'm not her BFF, like Brielle.

'I have one word for you,' Brielle goes on. '*Tyler*.'

I just stare at her for a minute, then look back over at Noelle. Why are they trying to make me feel stupid? I feel stupid most of the day, anyway.

And I must look stupid, because Noelle goes, 'Tyler *Chang*.'

'That's two words,' Brielle says, but she's still smiling.

'What about Tyler?' I ask.

'Tyler and *Emma*,' Noelle says.

'Last *night*,' Brielle adds.

Jesus, at this rate, I won't know what's happening until summer.

'You guys, just tell me!' I beg.

They look at each other, and for a second I think they're going to start laughing about some other stupid inside joke, but finally Brielle comes up to the island and leans over again, looking at me excitedly.

'Tyler and Emma hooked up last night.'

'For real,' Noelle adds.

'It's all over for Emma Slut-nam.'

'Sayonara, slutty!' Noelle says.

'Wait – what are you saying?' I ask, blinking.

'Well, Emma was grounded—' Brielle starts.

'I know, I know,' I interrupt her.

But she holds up a hand and says, 'Let me finish! Emma was grounded. But Tyler, ever the gentleman, saw all the stuff about you and Dylan online—'

'Um, thanks a lot for that, by the way,' I say, but she gives me such a dirty look that I stop, pressing my lips together tightly.

'Do you want to hear this or not?' Brielle asks. She's not angry, but she looks like she will be in about two seconds.

I clench my teeth and nod quickly.

'Okay. So Tyler goes over to Emma's house – I don't know, he like sneaks in, or something – and tells her everything, and they totally have sex.'

'Totally,' Noelle chimes in. I really want to say *Thank you for the echo*, but I'm keeping my mouth shut.

'And then – this is *totally* the best part – Emma *called Dylan*.'

'Wait, what?' I blurt out, so surprised I can't be quiet anymore.

'I know!' Brielle says triumphantly. 'This morning! Or last night, maybe, do we know?' She turns to Noelle, but Noelle just shrugs. 'Anyway, she felt so guilty that she *told him*. I. Mean. *What*.'

Brielle pushes back from the counter and just looks at me as she fans her hands out in the air, like she's just served

Emma's head up on a silver platter and is waiting for me to say thank you. Which I guess is kind of what just happened.

'That . . . I don't . . .' I can't really form words. This is good, right? Brielle and Noelle think it's good, obviously. So . . . good. Right?

'She is so transferred,' Noelle says.

'Oh my God, they're going to transfer her twice,' Brielle says.

'Wait, her parents know?' I ask.

'Um, kind of,' Brielle says sarcastically. 'Marcus said Tyler told him they found Tyler sneaking out, so, um, the parents know for sure.'

Noelle nods, still in Brielle-echo mode. I wonder what happened to the cool senior who barely knew us – but she's obviously the one who stayed over last night, not me. I look back at Brielle's messy morning hair, her favourite house-hoodie from Abercrombie. She never makes coffee when I spend the night. No wonder it's so bad.

'Ohhhh . . . my . . . shizz . . .' Noelle says, her eyes suddenly big and round.

'What?' Brielle and I ask her at the same time.

'Tyler is eighteen,' she says solemnly.

'You're kidding me,' Brielle says, her eyes widening too.

'I am totally not. His birthday was like a month ago. Remember?'

Suddenly I do – it was like a week before Valentine's Day, so obviously I'd forgotten all about it until now. But a bunch of us decorated his locker. I remember him talking about going to adult emporium, this store that sells porn and stuff outside of town. A lot of the guys talk about going there when they turn eighteen. I always assume they're joking. But I guess with Tyler – or Jacob, for that matter – it might not be a joke.

Brielle claps her hands together, just once, loudly. 'That stupid bitch!' she cries. 'I could kiss her!'

'Uch, don't,' Noelle says, wrinkling her nose. 'You'd definitely catch herpes, at least.'

Brielle and Noelle high-five. 'Did I tell you, or what? It all works out in the end. That slut just did our job for us!'

'Sounds like she did a lot of *jobs*,' I say, and Brielle and Noelle nearly do spit takes from laughing so hard. But my heart isn't really in it. I kind of just want to get out of here – suddenly I just want to see Dylan, make sure everything's okay. I mean, I've wanted to see Dylan since I woke up, but now I'm starting to feel a little panicky. Did this change things? Will he be . . . what? He'll be happy, right? Because nothing else matters now. It doesn't matter what happened in his car on Friday, or all the stupid stuff Brielle put online yesterday. We can just be together, and no one has to know anything else.

Brielle is talking, Noelle is laughing, but I can't hear them anymore. The nervous feeling in my stomach climbs into my head, making everything sound like fuzz, like it's at the other end of a long tunnel.

'I should . . . go,' I say, but they're ignoring me. Brielle is back at the fridge, getting something out, and when she turns back around I see it's a bottle of champagne.

'Mimosas!' she's saying, and Noelle is pulling out glasses. I notice she's only holding two.

But I'm getting off of my chair anyway, picking up my keys. 'I'm gonna go find Dylan.' I finally manage to speak loud enough for them to hear me, for the words to reach my own ears, and Brielle just raises the bottle up high.

'To getting your man back!' she cries.

'Hear, hear!' Noelle says, holding up the two empty glasses.

I think I smile at them, but I'm not sure. All I know is, I'm back in my car and pulling out of the driveway and driving, hoping that when I finally find Dylan, when I see him, when he touches me – maybe then I'll be able to breathe again.

October

'It's too cold to be wearing that, Sara.'

'You let her dress this way to go to the lawyer's office? To *any* office?'

'She's seventeen, Doug, relax.'

'You both need to relax. I'm fine. Natalie's seen my knees before, okay?' The truth is I'm still freezing – I found an old hoodie in the trunk of my car, but I didn't have time to go home, so I'm still wearing the shorts I stupidly put on this morning. But I'm also still numb from talking to Dylan, so what difference does it really make?

'Here you are!' Natalie greets us at the door, looking organized, for once. She waves us all in with a big smile and I'm relieved to find that her personal office is a lot warmer than the rest of the building.

But then I notice that the cold had been distracting me from the waves of panic, the beating thrum of *last time, last time*. Last time I'll be in Natalie's office before . . . Last time I'll see Dylan before . . . last time I—

'Everyone have a seat, great, right over here is good.' Natalie's talking a little too loudly, but she seems excited. Not only is the heat on, someone cleaned up in here – we can actually all sit down at the table without rearranging any boxes, and it turns out there's a coffeemaker on the side table. Natalie goes over to it and pours two cups for my parents and I try to remember what's usually sitting on that spot. Piles of paper, I guess, like everywhere else. Normally.

'Sara, you don't take coffee, do you?' she asks brightly. 'I guess with Starbucks, kids are starting younger and younger . . .' She carefully sets the other cups on the table, then turns back to pick up some sugars and a little container of milk.

'I sometimes—' I start to say, but I'm cut off by my dad.

'Kids think they're drinking coffee, but those things are more like milkshakes with a little caffeine in them,' he gripes. I've heard this one before. 'For six bucks a pop,' he adds.

'They do make a mean Frappuccino,' Natalie says with another big smile.

I pull the sleeves of my sweatshirt over my hands and tuck them under my knees. Natalie turns her smile to me and I know what's coming next.

'Sara, I don't think I've gotten your letter yet – did you have a chance to email that over?' she asks, just like I knew she would.

I can feel Mom and Dad turn, on either side of me, to

294

see what my answer is. 'Not yet,' I say, and my voice is barely a whisper. I try to take a deeper breath before adding, 'I can get it to you la—'

'This is important, young lady,' my dad says firmly. He just can't let me finish a sentence. 'Natalie needs to see that in plenty of time before we're in the courtroom. She's our attorney, she needs to advise us on these things.'

'What *us*?' I ask, but I'm whispering; no one hears me.

'It's all right, Mr Wharton, I'm sure Sara just needs a little more time to figure out exactly what she wants to say,' Natalie says smoothly. 'It's not the official allocution statement, of course. We should go over that while we're all here – shall we get started?'

She gets up again from the table and grabs a bunch of file folders from her desk. Dad's still looking at me, his lips pursed angrily, I can tell. I don't have to look back to know he's annoyed, waiting for something else to yell at me about.

But I haven't finished the statement. I wish I had; it's like the worst possible homework assignment that I just can't get done. I think about the notepad Teresa gave me, stuffed under my bed. I'd finally given up on trying to write the thing longhand. Now there's just a bunch of words in a document on my laptop at home. Words that don't fix anything, don't change anything, don't say anything. Don't fix what happened, what went so completely wrong.

Natalie comes back to the table and smiles at me. 'Why don't you go in the conference room and work on the letter while I talk to your parents?'

'I need my laptop,' I say.

Mom rolls her eyes. 'No, you don't,' she says wearily.

Natalie's already handing me a legal pad, and my dad slaps a pen on the table in front of me, hard.

'*Okay*,' I say, but I barely whisper it. I pick up the pen, wondering what it would be like if he'd just handed it to me.

I pick up the notepad, too. Everyone's giving me blank pads of paper these days.

'There's a room across the hall, you know the one,' Natalie says. 'It should be empty.'

I sit there for a second, not moving yet. 'Can't I . . .' I stop.

'What is it?' Natalie doesn't seem impatient, not like my mom and dad, who are sitting like their chairs are on fire, all jumpy and weird. Like they would leap right out of them and into a courtroom this instant, if it meant this would all just be over.

'Can't someone else write something, and I could just read it?' I ask, finally. 'Like, you? Couldn't you just tell me what to say?'

'It's still optional—' Natalie starts, but Dad interrupts her.

'Absolutely not!' he practically shouts. 'You owe everyone an Apology, young lady, and you're going to make it yourself!'

I stare at him. Mom and Natalie are looking at him too,

watching his chest rise and fall with fast, angry breaths.

'I'm sick of this whining!' he goes on, his face getting flushed. 'You and your friends and your – your pranks – and now a girl is dead, and you've avoided a trial and jail time by *this much*—'

'She wasn't going to jail—' my mom says quietly, but Dad doesn't seem to hear her.

'Take responsibility, young lady!' he shouts at me. 'It's time to grow up! Can't you see that you've been acting like a *child*?'

Natalie is holding up a hand, trying to get him to calm down – he's leaning out of his chair now, over the table, like he wants to hit me or, I don't know, throw the table across the room or something. And before I know it I've shoved back, out of my chair, stumbling a little bit but hanging on to the pen and paper.

'*You're* acting like a child!' I yell at him. 'You don't know *anything*! You're never here! Neither of you! You act like you know what happened, you act like you know who I am or what I did. But you don't!'

I hate that tears are coming down my face now, and I furiously try to wipe them away, but the stupid pen and notepad are in my hands, so I have to wipe with the backs of my wrists and it doesn't work at all. Mom and Dad are staring at me, and Natalie is too, though I can't really see their expressions. Everything is blurry from the tears. The stupid, childish, irresponsible tears.

But then I see Dad sit back in his chair and throw his

hands up. 'I can't work with this,' he says, still angry. 'This is ridiculous. Can't you make her behave?' he asks my mom. Or maybe he's asking Natalie. But they don't answer him.

I manage to take a big, shuddering breath. For some reason, I feel a little calmer. I'm not shrieking when I speak again. And I look right at my dad's face. He doesn't scare me any more.

'Maybe I *am* a child, Dad,' I say. 'Did you ever think of that? Maybe I'd know how to grow up if anyone had ever *taught* me.'

For once, he doesn't have anything to say to that. And even if he does, I'm out the door before he can.

I'm thinking *This is the last time I'll visit Therapist Teresa* when I flop down on her couch. But it doesn't take long to find out I'm wrong about this *last time*.

'I've already recommended you keep coming to see me as part of your probation period,' she says, twirling her pen in her hand. 'Or another therapist, if you'd rather, but I'd like to keep seeing you if you're happy with the work we've been doing.' She's wearing a silver ring on almost every finger, and her scarf today is a blinding swirl of oranges, reds, and yellows. I wonder if I'll wear scarves like that when I'm, what, forty or fifty years old? Is it a requirement?

'Okay,' I say to her. 'I don't know what we're going to talk about, but sure.'

'Oh, I think we both know that there's more to talk about in high school than any other time in your life,' she says with a little laugh.

'I don't do anything, though. Especially not now. I don't even have any friends.' I feel a blush creep up to my cheeks at the thought of Carmichael, but I don't want to tell Teresa about that right now.

She gives me one of her looks, one of those long, studying stares. 'Sara, you do realize how much adult responsibility you've taken on?'

I think of what Dad said to me at Natalie's office and laugh, short and bitterly.

'No, really,' Teresa says.

I nod, not laughing any more, not wanting to explain why what she's said seems ironic right now. 'You mean, like, my brothers and everything?' I say. 'That's not really so much. I just drive them places.' I'm still wearing my sweatshirt, and now that my parents aren't around I can tuck my knees up under it. Mom would yell at me for stretching out the material, and Dad for putting my shoes on Teresa's couch. But I know she doesn't care about the couch. And the hoodie sort of pulls my knees up so I'm kind of balancing on my butt, anyway, and not really touching anything.

'Your brothers, yes, that's a lot,' Teresa says. 'But your relationships with your peers, too. Your friendship with Brielle. Your sexual relationship with Dylan. These are very intense situations.'

'I don't – I mean . . . Everyone has sex,' I stutter, embarrassed.

'Not everyone does in high school.'

I snort. 'Well, they're *supposed* to.'

She tilts her head. 'I know it's hard to see it now,' she says softly, 'but this is a lot to take on, to process. You have very adult feelings, but everything you're experiencing is for the first time. There's a tremendous weight on all of it.' She holds up the hand holding her pen and turns it palm up, pulsing it up and down, as if she's holding something heavy, weighing it. 'These are complicated feelings, complex relationships, for women even in their twenties and thirties. Even older.'

I'm tipping a little to the side, and I have to pull my legs down, out of my sweatshirt, sitting like a normal person. Like an adult. Who has complicated feelings and relationships.

'If that's true,' I tell Teresa, 'then everyone at school needs a therapist.'

I'm joking, but she doesn't laugh, or even smile. She just shrugs one shoulder and says, 'Maybe so. But you're here now. Let's talk about you.'

My stomach lurches. 'I haven't finished the letter, if that's what you mean.'

She tilts her head to the other side. 'Why did you think I was talking about that?'

My eyes practically roll themselves at this – of *course* we're back to Twenty Questions.

'Because it's Saturday?' I say. 'And I just went to see the lawyer with my parents, and I'm supposed to be ready to go to court on Tuesday?'

'And you're not ready?' Teresa asks.

'No,' I say with a sigh. 'I don't think I'll ever be ready.'

I drive home the long way. The very long way. Somehow I end up in Emma and Tyler's neighbourhood, which is only on the way to my house if you're trying not to get to my house any time soon. But it's as if my car just goes where it wants now, like how it still seems to be able to find Dylan's SUV. Well, used to.

I turn onto Emma and Tyler's block and immediately have to slam on the brakes. TV reporters, with their network-logo-antenna-topped vans, are lined up along the curb. I couldn't drive past if I wanted to. It's not like we're such a big town that we have so many TV stations or something – but it looks like maybe there are some national ones here too. Great.

Only a couple of them seem to be actually set up; it's not like there's anything going on right now. Emma's house sits, as always, at the top of its sloping lawn, the line of columns across the front looking austere and dignified. This neighbourhood is old enough that the trees are big and stately, too, and the leaves are all starting to turn and fall. *It's a pretty scene*, I think, and then I figure: *That's what the news is going to say. 'What a pretty place. You'd never think something like this could happen here.'*

Creeps.

There's a driveway to my left that isn't blocked, so I pull into it and turn the car around. I head for home, for real this time.

'Hey. You look nice.'

I stare at Carmichael. 'So do you. Your shirt has a . . . A *collar*.'

Carmichael looks down at his dress shirt. 'I clean up pretty good,' he says modestly.

I can't help but smile. Because it's true – it's just a navy button-down, nothing earth-shattering. But it's not a black T-shirt. And it looks terrific on him, with his clean, combed hair and a nice pair of dark jeans. The evening sun is all glowy behind him, and I realize this is probably the first time a boy has come to my front door to pick me up on a Saturday night. This just wasn't Dylan's style at all. I never would have thought it was Carmichael's style either, but he is full of surprises.

I look down at my own outfit, a merino sweater and jeans. Normally this ensemble would make me *twice* as dressed up as Carmichael, but now I'm not sure. 'Should I change? I should go change,' I say, backing into the house.

'Nah,' he says, but I'm already on the stairs.

'Be right back!' I call, hurrying to my room. I have a skirt here somewhere, and a cuter pair of shoes, and . . .

And for the first time ever, I get to do that thing of walking down the stairs while a boy waits at the bottom, looking up at me. It's not the prom or anything, but I'll take it. He's even talking to my mom, and they both smile when they see me. Like it's just a normal night, like I'm allowed to be this regular girl.

It's fully dark outside by the time Carmichael turns us onto Harney Street, scanning the rows of cars for somewhere to park. We're downtown, and there's a big weekend crowd I've never really seen before. Actually, the last time I was here was—

'Hey, um, we're not going to the diner, are we?' I ask him quickly.

'No, why, you want to?' he asks. I shake my head, but his eyes are still on the sides of the street. 'It's not really worth getting dressed up for,' he adds.

'I want to go – wherever we're going.'

He turns at the corner and, magically, someone is just pulling out. 'Excellent,' he says, either about the parking space or what I've said, I'm not sure. Both, maybe.

This part of the city has been kept the way it's been since the 1800s, with cobblestone streets and old brick warehouse buildings still standing. Inside them are little boutiques, shops, and fancy restaurants. When Carmichael leads me to one of the nicer Italian ones, Vermicelli, I get another small wave of nausea. This is too nice. It's too much. I don't deserve this. My parents used to go here sometimes, for special occasions – I've never even been inside. This is the kind of place I would've gone before prom with Dylan. If that had, like, been able to happen.

303

And now, Carmichael is holding the door open, and here I am. The ceilings are tall and dark; the brick walls have candles set in sconces here and there, and the back wall is open to the kitchen with a big wood-burning stove. It's like the cellar in an old castle or something. Romantic.

'This okay?' Carmichael asks.

'Yeah, of course,' I say.

The hostess puts us at a tiny table near the back, close enough that we can watch the kitchen, and hands us menus the size of poster boards. I look at Carmichael, tempted to make a joke about how huge they are, but he's just studying his seriously. So I do too, and by the time our waitress comes, I've found the cheapest pasta so I can order that.

We don't talk about Emma, or the trial, or anything, really. I ask Carmichael questions about stuff, trying to keep my promise to get to know him better. He tells me about the BMX competition he has the next weekend. And his older sister, who goes to college in Denver. And he asks me about my brothers, about where I might apply to college. We're in a different world, a parallel universe.

By the time the waitress asks if we want dessert and Carmichael says no, I feel comfortable enough to say, 'Why, you think I'm getting fat?'

'Obviously not, no, I wasn't—' Carmichael shakes his head, and I realize my little joke has thrown him, made him flustered. But then he finally lets out a small laugh and says, 'We're going somewhere else for dessert.'

It's gotten colder outside, and when Carmichael takes

my hand leaving the restaurant, for a second it almost feels like he's just trying to keep me warm. It works – a shot of heat races through my whole body, up my neck and into my cheeks. He walks us toward a popular ice cream place, one where they hand-mix whatever candy you want into your soft-serve, and keeps talking about nothing, like nothing unusual is happening. I love every minute of it. I love being someone, something *usual*. I love that tonight feels so special but so normal at the same time.

But when we reach the door to the ice cream parlour, I pull Carmichael past it, on toward the park that lines the edge of the marketplace. There are lots of people out, and most of the benches are taken, but we find one and sit down.

'I've had a really nice time,' I tell him.

'Yeah,' he says. 'Sorry it's too cold for ice cream.'

'That's not it. I just . . . I mean, thank you for all of this. But you don't . . . you don't know . . .' I stop. We're still holding hands, and I can't look down, can't acknowledge my fingers wrapped in his. But I can't look him in the face, either.

'I *do* know,' he says softly, but I'm shaking my head. I can feel tears coming but I take a deep breath, swallow them back down. I want to just say this.

'I just want you to know – I just, if this is the beginning of something, and I don't know if it is, but I should just tell you – I did so many horrible things,' I say in a rush. 'I hurt so many people. I still think what Emma did . . . I think it was really selfish. I don't understand why I have to take the blame for something I never wanted to happen.'

Silence hangs between us. Our bench sits at the top of a little hill, overlooking the sidewalk that follows along a creek. A few people, on dates like ours, walk by, stroll over the footbridges, stare at the city lights reflected in the water. Above us the sky has turned a clear, deep black, the stars just visible beyond the glow of downtown. A few blocks north of us there's a skate park, and I can just barely hear the sounds of wheels on the pavement, rolling, then *up*, that break in the noise, that moment of held breath before they come crashing back down, rolling forward again or stuttering to a stop.

Finally a tear escapes, falling fast and landing on my sweater sleeve. Then another. Carmichael is still silent but I keep going.

'I've been talking about her, about everything we said to her, for so long,' I go on. My chest is tight and I try to breathe in again, but I can only take little gasps of air. 'And I'm trying to figure out how to . . . how to apologize. I have to say something in court, or at least I have to try. At least they're letting me talk. But how do you apologize for this? I know what I did, I know it was bad, some of it was *really* bad. But how am I supposed to fix anything *now*? What do I—' But I have to stop talking again because the tears are coming faster, so hot on my face it feels like they're burning me.

Carmichael picks up my hand and holds it against his

lips. The rush of feeling distracts me and I feel myself calming down, breathing more evenly. The crying slows. He covers my fingers with his other hand and holds it there, in the air, like an offering.

'I don't know what to tell you,' he says, finally. 'I don't know if anything you say now is supposed to fix anything. But I don't think it can hurt, either. You have a chance. I think Emma—' He pauses. 'She didn't give herself another chance, you know? Maybe she didn't think she deserved one. Maybe she thought it wasn't possible.'

He stares at the water, then up at the sky, my hand still in his hands.

'Does that make sense?' he asks, almost a whisper.

I don't say anything for a second, a minute, a year.

'Yeah,' I say. 'It does.'

March

'Yo, it's D, do that thing.'

'Hey, Dylan, it's me – it's Sara. Sorry, I sent you a couple texts, I was just wondering . . . Um, you must be busy, but if you get a sec, can you call me back? Thanks. Uh, okay. Bye.'

I hit the end button and sit back on the kitchen stool, staring at my phone. Dylan wasn't at his house. He hasn't answered my texts. He's not answering his cell.

The pit of dread in my stomach just gets bigger and bigger. It's the Grand Canyon right now. Things are not good.

I wander around the house, wishing I could drive Tommy and Alex somewhere. Or fight with my mom. Anything to get my mind off of this – this whole stupid weekend. Where is Dylan? Is he breaking up with Emma? Does he know about Tyler?

I start to send a text to Brielle, then stop. I walk toward the door, reaching for my car keys, then stop again.

I go upstairs. I open my laptop. Without even a pause, I open up Emma Putnam's Facebook page and post a new comment.

Why are you such a slut?

Then I go to Tyler's wall.

Enjoy the herpes you got last night.

The knot in my stomach tightens, but it feels better, too. It feels like I'm *doing* something.

Back to Emma's page.

So, let me get this straight: You steal my boyfriend and then CHEAT on him? Nice.

I click on the Post button and wait a second, then add: *What's it like being a skank?*

Suddenly another post pops up, not from me. From Brielle!

I hear the weather's nice in slutsville this time of year.

I laugh out loud, sitting alone in my room. I click in the comment box below Brielle's post and write: *Warm with a chance of STDs.*

Then there's a post from Noelle: *Who farted? Oh, that's just Emma.* Someone has tagged Emma's name.

Then Kyle is there, too. *Thanks for banging all my friends,* he writes, and then, *Gotta go take another shower.*

The four of them keep writing, trying to top one another. Brielle posts on Tyler's wall too. She opens up a chat window with me separately, but we mostly use it for saying *HAHAHAHA.*

I look at the corner of my screen and see that an hour

has gone by, but it feels like no time at all. With a jolt I realize that Dylan still hasn't called me back. I guess he's probably not going to . . . I mean, I promised to be nice to Emma. Didn't I? I don't even remember. I don't even care. Fine, let him be with that loser. Screw them both. I'm the one with friends – he and Tyler can just fight over who gets to be with the girl that everyone hates. The girl that's definitely going to transfer schools now – I mean, how's she gonna come back to Elmwood after this?

That gives me an idea, and I post one last comment to her page.

You're gonna have to move to Canada now. You've slept with everyone in the U.S.

I can't quite bring myself to type the F word, but I think this makes my point anyway.

Downstairs I hear the garage door opening, so I sign off with Brielle and close my computer. I go downstairs, feeling light and relaxed. I'm okay now. If I can just not think about Dylan, I might be okay for a little while.

He doesn't text. He doesn't call. On Monday I forget my shyness around the guys and walk right up to Jacob, blurting out, 'Where's Dylan? Have you seen him?'

Jacob does this big flinch, like I'm acting crazy, but he goes, 'No, man, I heard he called in sick.'

Kyle has just walked up to Jacob's locker too, and he laughs loudly. 'Yeah, he's sick, all right.'

'Sick of dealing with Emma's bullshit,' I say, and both

310

guys look at me, surprised.

'Uh, yeah,' Jacob says.

'Is Tyler here?' I ask, and now they look less surprised, and more like they don't understand why I'm still bothering them.

'Yeah, I guess,' Kyle says.

Jacob slams his locker and shrugs at me. 'See you,' he says, and he and Kyle walk away.

I scan the hallway and find Brielle. With Noelle, of course, but at least Noelle gives me a little wave as I make my way over to them.

'What up,' she says, but it's not really a question.

I turn to Brielle and say, 'Did you hear Dylan stayed home sick today?'

She snorts, like I knew she would, and goes, 'God, are we still talking about that douche? Seriously, Sara, you need to move on.'

Noelle nods knowingly. I start to say something, even though I have no idea what to say, but then Alison Stipe walks up and goes, 'You guys, that stuff this weekend was hi*lars*. Stupid Emma.'

'Yeah, whatever, we were just killing time,' Brielle says, sounding like she couldn't care less either way.

'I heard she's gonna transfer to Central,' Alison says.

'You did?' I ask, surprised Brielle didn't already hear this.

'Well, I mean, she *should*,' Noelle says. 'Right? Who the hell wants her here?'

311

'Tyler, I guess,' Alison says, but Brielle and Noelle both laugh at this so loudly that she looks embarrassed, like she wishes she hadn't said anything.

'Oh my God, Tyler did Dylan a favour. He did everyone a favour,' Brielle says. 'I don't know how they all missed the skank memo, but now they know. But Tyler wanting to hang out with Emma *now*? I *really* don't think so.'

The bell rings and Alison races away, throwing us a little wave but looking relieved at the same time. Noelle and Brielle roll their eyes at each other, and Brielle says, 'Back stairwell?'

'Yep. Be there in ten,' Noelle replies.

I wait for them to explain what they're talking about, but Brielle just raises her eyebrows at me. 'Don't worry about the D Train,' she says. 'I don't think he and Emma were really doing it, so if you really want him back, he's probably syphilis-free.'

'Unless *you* have it,' Noelle says, and they both laugh again.

I smile as if I think it's funny too, but like Alison, I'm kind of happy to be getting away from them and going to my own homeroom. For one wild second I wonder what it would be like not to be friends with Brielle anymore – not to get teased like that all the time, not to always be her best punchline. But that's crazy. Brielle's been my best friend forever. We have so much fun, we're so close. I watch her walk away with Noelle and remember it's not my choice, anyway. If Brielle wants to hang out with you, she does.

312

And if she doesn't, you walk to homeroom alone.

Nothing really happens for the rest of the day. Right before gym I pass Principal Schoen in the hallway and I remember the meeting my parents are coming in for on Wednesday. Jesus, I keep forgetting about that. My stomach lurches. Why didn't I think to call in sick today too? I feel sick all the time.

Emma isn't in Gym class, and I have Brielle to myself, so we spend the whole time trying to avoid playing any basketball. Turns out if you go to the far end of the gym and pretend to play H-O-R-S-E, you can pretty much just stand there and no one cares.

Emma's not in History, either. It finally occurs to me that she might be with Dylan. I can't remember the last time I saw her, or saw them together. The weekend is starting to feel like I dreamed it. That night in Dylan's car might as well have happened a hundred years ago.

But it still hurts. That part feels pretty damn fresh in my mind.

I pick up the boys after school and we go to Taco Bell again, this time with an actual ten-dollar bill I got from my mom that morning. The sun still hasn't set by the time we get home, but the sky is turning pink, and Tommy actually stops for a minute to look at it when we get out of the car.

'It's pretty, right?' I say, leaning against the Honda next to him. Alex has already run inside, excited to have first dibs on the Wii.

He wrinkles his nose – the boys hate even the word

313

pretty, much less the idea that they might think anything is – but he goes, 'Yeah, it's cool.'

'I used to think that kind of sunset was good luck,' I tell him. I'd forgotten all about it until the words pop out, but it's true – when I was little I decided a pink sunset meant, I dunno, that the pony I wanted for Christmas would actually show up, or whatever.

'Is it? Good luck?' he asks me.

'Oh, I don't know . . . I think I just made that up. But maybe.'

'Yeah, maybe,' he says.

We stand there for a few more minutes, just long enough that the sky starts turning greyer, darker. Without either of us having to say anything, we turn and walk into the house together, where it's warm and light and smells like the popcorn Alex put in the microwave.

I find out the next morning.

Everyone's standing outside school, not going in. It's cold and windy and the sun isn't shining, but it looks like the entire school is huddled together on the sidewalk.

I drove myself because Brielle didn't want to shuttle my brothers today, so as soon as I park I pull out my phone and look for a text from her. There's nothing, which actually worries me more. But who knows, maybe there was just another fake bomb threat. Like the time that weird guy Carmichael supposedly called one in. We got the day off, and nothing actually happened, so I kind of hope that's it.

I see Brielle's SUV pulling in at the other end of the lot, so I wait by my car, assuming she'll park near me. But she doesn't – she pulls into the first empty space, kind of crooked. I start walking toward her. She and Noelle both jump out, and they both look kind of panicked – but I don't know, maybe it's just because I'm already panicked, so that's how everyone looks to me.

When I'm closer I wave, and they definitely see me, but they don't wave back. We meet about halfway, next to this, like, red Nissan. I think, *That's such an ugly car*, and then Brielle says:

'Emma Putnam killed herself last night.'

And then there's just nothing.

Not nothing. There's an assembly. They don't let us into school – the doors are locked, that's why everyone's outside – until after eight thirty. They make us sit in the gym because the auditorium isn't big enough for the entire school to sit down. They use a lot of words like *tragedy* and *counsellors* and *process*, like, 'We want to help you *process* this.'

'What a stupid, stupid bitch,' Brielle says under her breath. No one hears her but me, so no one knows why I'm nodding. But I can't say anything back. Across the gym, about five rows up on the bleachers, I can see Dylan. He's got his face in his hands. I can't tell if he's crying, but he keeps his head down the whole time.

The guidance counsellor gets up to talk. I've only seen

him once, at an assembly they made us go to about picking a college, but now he starts talking about supporting each other and getting through this difficult time. I don't know, I'm not really listening. I'm watching Dylan, so I see when he moves – he finally drops his hands from his eyes and stands up, all in one motion. He shoves his way past everyone in his row and takes the stairs down, two at a time. The bar on the gym door makes this loud squeak when he pushes it open, hard, and everyone in the gym is looking as the door closes behind him. It's set up so it doesn't slam, but that almost makes it worse. It takes a long, long time to close. Finally it clicks shut and I think, *Dylan must be in his car by now. Or anywhere – wherever he's going.*

And I think, *He's never going to talk to me again.*

And that's the saddest I feel all day.

We get dismissed for the rest of the day. Brielle and Noelle are going to Brielle's house, so I go too. They smoke weed but I don't. They call Kyle and Jacob, who come over, and then Marcus is there, and Brielle pulls out a bottle of vodka from her parents' cabinet. I drink a little, but I'm not used to having vodka in the middle of the day, and when I go upstairs to use Brielle's bathroom I think, *I'll just lie down for a minute*, and then I'm waking up, like, two hours later, which is totally embarrassing. I go downstairs, expecting everyone to make fun of me, but they're all watching the local news and laughing. It's all about Emma, of course, and I don't know what's so funny, but I hear Jacob say something like 'Who doesn't just take pills?' and Kyle goes, 'She was too stupid to figure out what pills to take. She would've tried to OD on, like, advil.'

It's two thirty already so I just sneak into the kitchen, grab my bag, and leave. I have to get my brothers, I have to go home. My mom must've heard about this by now. Suddenly I remember our meeting at the school tomorrow – that's cancelled, right? Is my dad still coming out? I guess I didn't really want to see him, anyway. I didn't want to go to that meeting, but – shit! That meeting was about *Emma*, wasn't it? So . . . so now what?

There's a light snow falling when I pull up to Pleasant Hill, and both boys come running out of the school with their arms spread out, trying to catch it. One of Tommy's friends is with him, yelling, 'Snow day! Snow day!'

They do their usual front-seat shove-match, which Tommy wins, and crash into the car. Alex yells, 'We're gonna have a snow day tomorrow!'

'It's March, dummy, there's no way there's gonna be enough snow for that,' Tommy says, but he's grinning and his cheeks are all red from the running and the cold.

I notice that I'm shivering, even though I've been in my warm car this whole time. Suddenly I realize I forgot to eat lunch. The inside of my stomach is cold. I'm used to it being upset, in knots, stressed. Now it's just . . . Empty. I don't even say anything to the boys. I just drive home, hoping I don't get us in an accident along the way. My hands are so numb I can't really feel the wheel.

I can't really feel anything.

It's obvious as soon as we're home that Mom already knows. She sends Tommy and Alex up to their room and tells them we're going to order pizza. They're almost as excited by that as they were by the snow, and we hear them thump up the stairs, yelling about what kinds of toppings they're going to get.

Mom and I just stare at each other for a minute. Finally, she says, 'Are you okay?'

'Yeah,' I say. It feels like I haven't used my voice at all today, it comes out all scratchy. I guess I haven't talked much, but of course I'm okay.

'Is – is everyone okay? Brielle? And – oh, God, what about Dylan?'

I just shrug.

'Of course,' she says. 'Of course this is hard for all of you. God, I can't believe this. She was *sixteen* . . .' Mom sits down heavily on one of the kitchen stools and just stares at the counter for a while. I stand nearby, not sure what to do.

'I'm just gonna . . .' I have to stop and clear my throat. 'I'm gonna go to my room, okay? I don't care what kind of pizza. I'm not really hungry anyway.'

She looks up at me, her face stricken and worried and, like, ten years older than it usually looks, but she just nods. So I go.

The next morning, there are news vans parked outside school. That afternoon they're outside my house. By the end of the week everyone knows that Emma Putnam stayed home that Monday, she waited until her parents went to work, and she tied a heavy-duty extension cord around her neck. She tied the other end to the exposed beams in her parents' garage.

And everyone knows that Emma Putnam didn't just kill herself. She killed herself for a reason.

And that reason was Brielle. Dylan. Kyle. Jacob.

And me.

A special prosecutor brings charges against us. The Facebook stuff has already been on the news. Emma's crying parents are on *Good Morning America*, sitting next to the lawyer, talking about bullying and suicide and Emma's *bright future cut short*.

Megan Corley goes on the *Today* show and tells them how 'some girls' painted the word *SLUT* on Emma's locker on Valentine's Day. I'm watching it on my computer in my room, and when she says that I almost choke. And when the interviewer asks if she means the girls 'in the lawsuit' and Megan nods, I scream. I push the laptop off my bed and for a second I think – I hope – it's broken, but it's not. The video is just paused, with Megan's stupid, tearstained face looking up at me from the floor.

Mom is at the door of my room in two seconds. 'I told you to stop watching that stuff,' she says.

'But they're all *lying* about *everything*—' I yell, but her hand is up, stopping me.

'That's it!' she yells, louder. 'No more news in this house! Turn it *off*, Sara, I mean it!'

I close the laptop, leaving it on the floor. We stare at each other for a minute, and then she turns to leave again. She doesn't even tell me to get ready for school. We both know I'm not going.

As soon as I hear her car leave, I go downstairs and turn on the TV. At first I'm just planning to watch cartoons or something, but I put it on MSNBC and there's Emma's face again. Mom says the news is national because Emma was pretty and her parents are rich, but I know it's because there's a lawsuit, too. It's a 'groundbreaking anti-bullying' lawsuit, one of the toughest ever brought against a group of minors.

I text Brielle to see if she wants to go to the mall. She's been skipping a lot too, but now she just writes: *can't talk. Lawyerzzzz. :p*

I don't know what that means. I look back at the TV and see another screenshot of all our posts on Emma's Facebook wall, the day before she died.

What's it like being a skank?

My profile picture and my name are blurred out, but I know that one was mine. Under the comment you can see there were twenty-two likes, but the people on the show are just talking about me now, about how girls are passive-aggressive or something, I don't know. There's a child

320

psychologist on. I've never met him and he has no idea what he's talking about.

'*Shut up!*' I yell at the man on the screen. '*Leave me alone!*'

But of course, he can't hear me. No one can.

October

'You look nice,' Alex says. He's got milk on his chin from the oversized spoon of Cheerios he just stuffed in his mouth. It actually sounds like he just said 'Ooo ook ice,' but it's sweet. Probably the sweetest thing I'll be hearing all day.

'Thanks, bud.' I look down at my navy skirt and dark-red sweater. I look like I'm running for student council president, but I figure it follows the rules Natalie gave me. The first time we went to court, which was really just a weird conference room with a judge in it, I wore a bright-yellow shirt. I thought Natalie was going to kill me when she saw it. It was hot outside that day, but she made me put on a grey cardigan she had in her car.

Anyway. It's cold today. And I think my outfit says *I'm taking this seriously.*

I sit down at the table with Alex and Tommy, but I can't eat. Just watching them inhale their breakfasts makes me feel like throwing up. If I only *could* just vomit, even half as often as I think I'm going to, I'd probably feel a lot better.

Or a lot worse, I guess, I don't know. Alex slurps the last of the milk straight out of his bowl and I look away.

'You sure you got it all, little man?'

Dad's voice makes me jump – it's always too loud, too much *him*. My stomach lurches again. Across from me, I see Tommy tense up too, but Alex grins at our father, his mouth still white with milk.

'Hey, Dad!' he says. 'Are you gonna pick me up from school today?'

'I dunno, kid,' Dad says. He throws open the cabinet with the mugs in it, slams one down on the counter, fills it with coffee. Leaves the cabinet open. 'This thing might take a while. I think your mom set up a ride for both you guys.'

This thing. I shrink a little in my sweater. *This thing* has already taken a while. It's taken over my entire life. It will be with me forever.

'Oh,' Alex says, disappointed.

'I don't know why we can't go too,' Tommy grouches.

I raise my eyebrows at him, but before I can say anything, Dad jumps in again.

'Nah, you don't want to go, trust me,' he says. He leans against the counter with his coffee. I'm still not really looking at him, but I can feel his presence, his overwhelming height. He's in a dark suit. He's *looming*. 'It's not going to be any fun.'

'I know,' Tommy says. His voice is quiet now, but still defiant. 'I didn't think it was going to be *fun*. I just thought we should be there.' His eyes meet mine for just a moment, and I give him a little smile.

'Thanks,' I say to him, but I really just mouth it. He shrugs one shoulder, like, *I tried*.

I figure my brothers have just given me the strength to get through *this thing*. Unfortunately, Dad's right; they don't want to actually come with us. Too bad my father's going to be there instead. And Mom – whatever. When Dad's around, she gets so distracted, I don't know. Like, she's not even down here yet. What is she doing?

'Where is that mother of yours?' Dad asks, reading my mind. Again, it's like he wants us to think he's being light and funny, but he sounds furious.

'I'll go find her,' I say, thrilled for the opportunity to get out of here, away from him for another two minutes.

But I'm barely out of my chair when she walks into the kitchen. She has on a dark-grey suit with a silky lavender shirt underneath. It's the outfit she wears when she has a meeting she's especially worried about. I don't know how I remember that, but I do, and it makes me feel even more nervous.

'Okay, guys,' she says to my brothers. 'Maggie's waiting for you outside. She'll pick you up, too.'

'I thought I was dropping them off?' I say, startled. I'd really been looking forward to the twenty minutes of alone time between Tommy's school and the courthouse.

'No, I asked M—'

Dad cuts Mom's explanation off with, 'There's no

324

way you're showing up there by yourself. How would that look? We're going together.'

I look back at Mom and she nods.

Together. Why couldn't that make me feel supported? The way Dad says it, it sounds like punishment.

And it is. The drive feels like a lifetime. I sit in the back of my dad's rental car, holding my statement. It's folded in half, pressed between my sweaty hands. None of us speak. There's traffic, but not enough to actually slow us down. So while I feel trapped in the car for eternity, we also get to the court building way too fast.

There are news vans everywhere, dozens of them. Dad has to slow to a crawl, waiting for the cop who's directing traffic to guide the cars ahead of us into the parking lot. A reporter from the channel we always watch jogs past our car. For a split second I think, *Oh!*, like I've just seen a celebrity. Then I remember.

God, I hate those split seconds. I wish I could stop forgetting, even for a moment. Being scared and sad and tired all the time sucks, but it's so much harder when I think, even for the blink of an eye, that things are normal.

Even for the brief moment on Saturday night, when Carmichael drove me home and pressed his lips so quickly, so gently, to mine. I close my eyes and remember that, hold on to it. We talked on Sunday and I saw him at school yesterday, of course, and we both acted like nothing happened. But in the dark of his dad's truck, at the end of such a nice but long night, that instant was perfect. It was relief.

The car jerks forward and I open my eyes again. There's a spot right next to the building and Dad pulls in, yanking the gearshift over to park. We all sit there for one more quiet moment, and then, like we've choreographed it, my parents and I each open our doors and let the flood of noise hit us.

I hurry around the car and they stand on either side of me, and we walk, trying not to run, past the screaming reporters and the blinding lights. I'm that girl now. I'm that girl walking into a courtroom, not looking at the cameras. Suddenly Natalie is there, but I don't even know how I see her, because I keep my eyes down, on the sidewalk. *Foot foot foot foot. Don't trip.*

The doors are held open by security guards and we rush in, the relative silence of the building swallowing us whole. I suck air into my lungs, realizing I've been holding my breath, but I don't stop. Natalie hasn't stopped, she's still leading us ahead, so we all trot down a hallway, and then another, and then finally there's a bench, and she stops, turning back to us.

'Okay!' she says brightly. 'That was the hard part.' She gives us all a warm smile, but I guess we don't look like we believe her, because she adds, 'Really. Everything is going to be fine from here on out. We'll have to see them again when it's all over, of course, but you don't have to talk to them. In fact, I really recommend that you don't. We'll meet tomorrow to talk about media interaction, but they'll lose interest pretty quickly, don't worry. This time next month, no one will remember your names.'

'Excellent,' my dad says.

My mom puts a hand on my shoulder, so lightly I almost can't feel it. 'That will be nice,' she murmurs. I nod. It *will* be nice. For them. I, on the other hand, still have to go back to school.

'And now we wait,' Natalie says. 'My new intern should be here in a minute, and she can get us some coffee, if you'd like. But just have a seat. Sara, you all set? Is that your statement there?'

I nod again, trying to loosen my fingers from the page. It's a crumpled mess at this point.

'I have another copy if you need it,' Natalie says, her voice a little lower, sympathetic. 'Do you want to go over anything again?'

Dad heaves a big sigh, like he's sick of talking about all of this, and sits down heavily on the bench. Mom wavers. I know she's dying to see my statement, which I haven't let her read. I know why she's pausing now, that she wants to be here if I tell Natalie, *Yes, let's talk about this stupid piece of paper I'm holding, even though we just went over it yesterday*, but I stay silent, so finally she sits down on the bench too.

Now that Mom's hand is gone from my shoulder, Natalie moves to my side and puts her whole arm around me. 'You've done really great,' she says, her head close to mine, speaking even more softly, just to me. 'I'm proud of you. I know this hasn't been easy or fun or – or what you thought it would be. But you really toughed it out. You wrote an excellent letter, too. Things are going to start getting better now, I promise.'

I look down at the paper in my hands. It's still folded, blank side up, but the shadows of the typed words are just visible through the white. The dark truth, just on the other side of the thin – paper-thin – wall.

I nod yet again, but only because Natalie wants me to. I think about saying *Thank you* or *I appreciate all your help* or something. I would mean it. But I just can't make myself talk at all. I stare at the faint outline of all those words I have to say – now, any minute now – and think about how I'll never be able to unsay them. And I think about all the things I've already said, and written, that can never be unsaid, unwritten.

So for now, I just want to be quiet. Natalie lets me go and I step over to the bench, lowering myself down next to my mom. My parents. The paper sits on my lap and I wait.

We all just . . . wait.

'You may be seated.'

The sound of chairs scraping against the floor fills the room. This part reminds me of the times I used to go to mass with Brielle, way back in junior high when her parents still made her go. Stand up, sit down, stand up again. Pay attention when the guy in the robe walks in. Or in this case, the woman.

She's younger than I expected, and prettier. Her hair is long and blonde and down on her shoulders, kind of casual. And she smiles at everyone, like she wants us to sit down and *relax*, not worry, enjoy this. Like that's even possible.

I wish I'd asked Natalie what this was going to be like, look like. She asked a million times if I had any questions about today, but I just couldn't focus. Now everything is catching me off guard – the pretty judge, the pretty room. Unlike the first place we went, for the allegations or whatever, this is a real movie-style courtroom. It's old, wooden. Half the room is pews (again, like church), and then there's a low wooden gate, and we're on the other side of that, at a big mahogany table. Well, I assume it's mahogany, I don't know.

There are high windows on either side of the room, and the judge sits up in a booth, just like you'd think. There's a witness stand next to her. But we don't have to use that. There's a podium set up between the tables – the one thing that looks like it doesn't belong here, with wires running across the floor – where everyone's going to talk.

I keep staring ahead at the judge. She's just going through some papers, talking to the court officer, but I can't look to either side. On my left, Jacob sits with his lawyer and someone else, maybe another lawyer. On my right is Natalie, and then Brielle with her lawyer. And then on the other side of the podium, Emma's parents and their lawyers. Behind us I hear the snap of cameras and the murmurs of all our parents, the reporters, who knows who else. I picture my mom and dad, sitting together a row behind me, holding my coat and purse. Like I've just run to the bathroom and I didn't want to carry them.

The judge looks up at the Putnams' table. 'Counsellor?' she says.

And it starts.

They go through all the charges, and then the charges we've agreed to accept so they'll drop the other ones and leave us alone. It takes a while since there's three of us, and despite my nerves I kind of zone out here and there. But then they call Brielle up to the podium for her individual allocution and everything snaps back into focus.

She gets up with her lawyer, and finally I look over. But I immediately wish I hadn't. Brielle looks like *she's* the lawyer – her hair is smooth and swept back, and she's wearing a dark navy suit with a pencil skirt and heels. She looks about twenty-five years old, and her lawyer is this older guy who's obviously won a million cases. He has a leather binder he opens on the podium, and when he says hello to the judge you can tell he's met her a bunch of times. Like they're always playing tennis and having scotch at the lawyer-and-judge club, or whatever.

He speaks, and then the judge reads Brielle's charges and Brielle says 'Yes' a bunch of times. And then the judge goes, 'If you've prepared a statement, you may read that now.'

Everyone holds their breath. Brielle turns to the back of her lawyer's binder, to a different page, and gently clears her throat. When she starts to speak, I immediately recognize her special for-adults voice. It feels like I haven't heard it in years, and it makes me more nervous than ever. I know it's not a competition, but this isn't debate class – Brielle and I aren't on the same team. If it's a contest, she'll win. She's winning.

But I guess it's too late for that, actually. We're both here to admit that we've lost. We give up.

'Thank you, your honour,' Brielle says. Like she does this every day. 'Mr and Mrs Putnam, I can't tell you how sorry I am. I didn't know Emma that well, but she was a beautiful girl, and I can't imagine what this loss must mean to you. I will always regret anything I did to make her feel less than welcome at Elmwood High, and I will always hold your family in my heart and in my prayers. Thank you.'

There's a moment of stunned silence as Brielle's lawyer reaches over and shuts the leather binder, takes it off the podium, and guides Brielle back to our table. She said all the right things, but – but what? Why does it feel wrong?

Then I hear Emma's mom take a big, gasping breath. A sob. She quiets down again almost instantly, but I figure, okay, if Brielle made her cry . . . I guess she definitely said the right thing.

But, I don't know, maybe it's me – she just didn't sound that sorry.

Is that what I'm going to sound like?

My heart is beating in my throat and I wonder how I'm going to manage not to vomit and pass out in this fancy room full of formal people when the judge calls *Jacob's* name next. I look at Natalie, panicked, but she just pats my hands, which are knotted together in my lap.

'Don't worry,' she mouths. 'You're fine.'

Jacob goes through all the same things, though as we already know, he only has to accept a couple of charges, fewer than Brielle and I do. And Tyler – God, I've forgotten all about him. His case is separate, but I know he's doing a plea too. I close my eyes while Jacob's lawyer talks to the judge and try to imagine this being over. Not, like, later today, but next year. What will next year look like? Will things be normal? What's normal anymore?

Jacob's statement is even shorter than Brielle's, and his voice wavers like he's going to cry. You can tell he wrote it himself. He just says, 'I'm really sorry about all of – all of this. Emma was such a sweet girl. I really miss her. I'm really sorry. I'm – I'm just really sorry.'

I swear, if the whole room could get up and give him a hug, they would. *I* would, and I remember what a jerk he always was. I can hear Emma's mom really crying now as I watch him walk back to our table, head down, his grey suit looking a little too big for him, like he's a kid at his cousin's wedding. Jacob's lawyer has his hand on his shoulder. I don't know if he's trying to say, 'Hey, look, this guy is just a kid,' but that's what I think of.

332

Suddenly I wonder if the lawyer told Jacob to wear that suit, because he knew it would make him look younger. If he wrote that speech for him, like Brielle's lawyer obviously wrote her speech for her.

God, I'm an idiot. This whole thing is rigged. We're not even on trial anymore, but everyone is still playing the game. Playing the system. Or maybe I'm just paranoid. I don't even know.

But the little glimmer of anger quiets my stomach, so when the judge says, 'Sara Wharton and counsel, please come to the stand,' I don't throw up all over the table. I follow Natalie to the podium, and my legs are shaking, but I'm still standing on them.

Because it hits me, right then, all of a sudden. I'm the only one who's actually sorry about all this. Not just about being in trouble, not just about Emma ruining my life. I'm sorry about that, too – I still wish to God she'd just held on another day, switched schools, tried to just get along like the rest of us have to get along. Tried to get up and make the best of it, like we all have to do, even when things are horrible and painful and pointless.

But while Natalie talks to the judge and they call on me to accept harassment charges, one minor assault charge, and one count of stalking, I keep my head up. I say I understand, I say I accept. And when the judge asks if I have a prepared statement, Natalie steps aside and I smooth my stupid, unprofessional piece of printer paper on the podium, lay it flat, hope the sweat from my palms hasn't smudged the ink. I stop for a minute. I take a breath.

'Emma and I weren't friends. For a long time, I thought we were enemies. I thought she'd done things to hurt me – and I did things to hurt her back.'

I take another breath. Natalie doesn't touch me, but she has her hand on the podium, and I look at it for a second. It's like she's holding it down, holding me in place. My hands are shaking and so is my voice, but Natalie's hand is still. I look back at my notes.

'But I see now . . . I know now that she was in a lot of pain. More pain than I'll ever really understand, though I definitely understand better now.'

I look up at the judge as I say, 'I don't think that pain is anyone's fault, exactly,' and then I look over at the Putnams' table, finally. Mrs Putnam's eyes are red, and to my surprise, so are Mr Putnam's. They look small and sad. I keep looking at them and say, 'But I made that pain worse. For no good reason. I was thoughtless and cruel and I never meant for any of this to happen, but it did, and I'll be sorry for the rest of my life. I'm so, so sorry—' I stop, afraid I'm going to start sobbing, and I don't want to sob. They deserve to hear this. I want to say this, I want them to know. I'm not even looking at my notes anymore, because I know what I want to say.

'I'm so sorry that I made that pain worse, that I made Emma's life harder. I know I did. I know I hurt her. And I hurt you. I can't forget that, I won't ever forget that. I promise you I won't ever forget. I wish I could – I wish

I could do more. But I swear, I'll always remember.'

We stare at each other for a moment, the Putnams and I. I'm shaking but I stay standing, gripping the podium, hoping they believe me, hoping they understand. I think about what my mom said, about if she'd lost me. I think about my dad, how I can't imagine him crying about me ever – but he probably would. Of course he would.

My heart is pounding and my last words come out as barely a whisper, because I want to say them just to Emma's parents.

'I'm so sorry for what you've lost,' I say softly. 'I wish I could take it all back.'

I swallow. There's nothing else on my piece of paper, I don't have to look at it to know that, but this doesn't feel like enough. There should be more.

The room is still silent, but I can hear people starting to shift in their seats, like they think I'm done. I turn back to the podium and blink at my written statement, my hands, Natalie's hand. The judge leans forward, about to say something, but right before she does I look up and say, 'Just one – just one more thing.'

She stops. Everyone stops. For that minute, I realize I'm not nervous anymore, my mouth isn't dry. I'm not scared of talking right now – because this is important. I want people to hear me. I want Emma to hear me. So I say one more thing.

'Emma, if you're out there . . . I just want you to know I'm sorry. I wish there was something more I could say. But

I really mean it. I'm really, really sorry.'

And then I fold my paper, and Natalie's hand is on my shoulder, and we sit back down. Tears roll down my face, one after the other, fast, falling, falling. And I let them.

November

'Oh my God, this one is about this guy who volunteered with sick kids in *Sudan*. I did not do that. I mean, I *could* do that . . . I think . . .'

'You have to stop.'

'But I just want to see what's – here! look at this one! She overcame an eating disorder and . . . crap, and then she saved her friend from *drowning*.'

'Maybe she could write your college essay for you too.'

I look up at Carmichael, my eyes wide. 'That's not funny. I am so dead. I mean – I didn't mean that. I just don't know how I'm going to compete with this!'

'You have to *stop*,' he says again. He reaches across the kitchen table and tries to pull the laptop away from me, but I hang on to it.

'This is crazy!' I insist. 'I just wanted some examples, but it's all, like – these people shouldn't be applying to college, they should be, I dunno, running for president! Or at least going away to be in the Peace Corps or something.'

'I'm sure that's where they'll all go next. But I just don't think everyone at UNL has gone on humanitarian trips and rescue missions, okay?'

I frown at him, but he frowns right back.

'And anyway,' he adds, 'you're freaking me out too. Now close the computer!'

Slowly, reluctantly, I lower the screen.

'*What's* freaking you guys out?'

We both look up and see Tommy coming in, making a beeline for the bowl of chips beside us on the table. He pulls out a chair and plops down casually, but as always, his eyes are fixed on Carmichael. Now we'll never get anything done, but that's okay.

'College essays,' Carmichael tells him. 'You're supposed to write something really meaningful, something that tells them what an amazing person you are and what you've been doing your whole life. Your sister here keeps looking up these crazy, extreme examples online.'

Tommy chomps loudly on another chip and glances at the closed laptop in front of me. 'Yeah? Like what?'

'Like there was this guy who BASE jumped into the Grand Canyon and got stranded and made a *movie* about it,' I say, but at the same time, Carmichael goes, 'Like we need to think about our own essays!' and glares at me.

'So it's like a test? Before you even go to school?' Tommy asks.

'Exactly,' I say.

'That doesn't seem fair,' Tommy says.

'*Exactly*,' I repeat.

'But it's not really that big a deal,' Carmichael insists. 'And see, they give you a couple of different topics and you can choose one . . .' He pushes the application form he printed out across the table and Tommy studies it.

'It's a pretty big deal when you haven't *done* anything,' I say. 'I mean, I just went to school. I wasn't even captain of the basketball team or something.'

Both of them give me this weird look. 'Basketball?' Tommy says, and they crack up, like this is the funniest thing they've ever heard.

'What? You know what I mean!' I lay my head down on the closed computer and moan.

'Here's the one you should do,' Tommy says, pointing at the paper. '"Write a letter to someone you can't talk to about how he or she has changed your life."'

I lean over to see where he's pointing. 'Why that one?' I ask.

'I don't know, it sounds cool. You could do, like, Kurt Cobain or Darth Vader.'

I narrow my eyes at him. 'Those are your examples? What have you been reading?' I turn to Carmichael and say, 'Is this your influence?'

He lifts his hands defensively and goes, 'I don't know what either of you are talking about.'

'I'm in *seventh grade*,' Tommy huffs. 'I know who Kurt Cobain is, jeez.'

Carmichael lifts himself out of his seat, leaning over the

table to read the question. 'It says the person had to be alive at some point, though, so I think Darth Vader is out.'

'That's too bad,' I say. 'He had such an impact on my love of light sabers.'

Tommy shrugs, unoffended. 'That's the one I'd do,' he says.

'And you'd write to Kurt Cobain?' Carmichael asks.

'Maybe,' he says. 'Or, like, maybe, I don't know . . .' He gives me kind of a sideways glance and shrugs again. 'Maybe, like, Emma Putnam.'

My stomach does a little flip. But just a little one. I stare at my little brother for a second, and I can see he's holding his breath, a little scared of what I might say.

'Well,' I say, 'I kind of already did write a letter to Emma.'

Tommy looks back at the table in front of him and shrugs. 'I just mean, you know—'

'Wait,' I say. 'That actually gives me an idea.'

He looks back up. 'An idea for the essay?'

'Well, no – I mean, maybe, yeah, I think I have someone I could write to. But what if—' I pull the laptop back to my side of the table and open it, starting a new Google search. 'I've just been thinking a lot about, like, what if there was something I could do that might actually help Emma? Or not Emma, exactly, but people – people in a similar situation?'

I bite my lip and look at my brother and Carmichael, suddenly self-conscious. I haven't said this out loud before, and they're both studying me pretty closely, waiting for what I'm going to say next. I'm not really sure yet, but it's true – we were in court a month ago, and afterward the papers all printed our statements and I made the mistake of reading the articles online . . . And the comments. People were not happy at all. Apparently making plea agreements wasn't punishment enough, and I guess no matter how sorry I am, people still hate me.

I know I can't be sorry enough. But I can't go back in time, either. Mom says I have my whole life ahead of me, and that I deserve a chance to make something of it. Technically I think she's right, but some days my 'whole life' feels too long. That's a long time to feel like it's too late to fix the past.

But maybe I don't have to just hide, just wait for people to change their minds or give me a second chance. Maybe I don't even have to apologize to everyone or explain myself. Maybe I can try to do something good.

'What if I started a website where people could write to people, like this essay, people they might not be able to talk to in real life? Does that sound dumb?' I ask Tommy.

'No,' he says. 'What kind of site?'

'I mean, maybe someone's gone but you want to apologize to them, or you just have something you need to say,' I go on. Tommy nods. 'Or maybe someone who's still around, but you're too embarrassed to talk to them in person.'

'Like the opposite of Facebook,' he says.

Carmichael laughs, and so do I.

'Right,' I say. 'You'd say nice things. But anonymously, maybe. If you wanted to.'

It feels kind of cheesy, but the idea makes me excited. Maybe there are other people like me, people who said all the wrong things and just want a chance to apologize, or to try to apologize. Or just to say something – but maybe it's too late for them.

Even when it's not too late, sometimes it's really hard to admit that you've been bad to someone. That you've said bad things. Been a bully.

'Then what about your essay?' Tommy asks.

'I have an idea for that, too,' I tell him. 'Don't worry.'

At the front of the house, the garage door starts rumbling open. Tommy jumps up; the sound means our mom is home with Alex, and he wants to get to the video games first. Alone at the table again, Carmichael and I look at each other.

'I was thinking maybe I'd write to Brielle,' I say quietly. Carmichael reaches across the table, past the application form and the laptop, and holds my hand. 'Is she really not coming back to school?' he asks.

I shake my head.

'And you miss her.'

I look down at our hands. Carmichael's is covered in dark ink, doodles from being bored in class that haven't worn off. But they're proof that he goes to class now. He doesn't skip. He won't be in summer school – he'll graduate, with me. He'll go to UNL with me too, maybe. Hopefully.

'I did,' I say. 'This summer and everything – I missed her a lot. It's like . . . sometimes it's like it was Brielle who died, you know?' I hold my breath. It feels like a terrible thing to even say, to even think. But now that I've said it I realize it's true, that's how I feel.

We're allowed to talk to each other now, but we don't. It took me all summer and half of the fall to notice that I feel better when I'm not around Brielle Greggs. I was *someone* with her, I guess – I was popular, or close enough to it. But I was toxic. We were toxic. We hated on everyone. I don't think she even liked Dylan. She gave everyone a mean nickname – everyone was a loser if they weren't someone she needed or wanted to be with right then. Even toward the end of last year, she only wanted to hang out with Noelle, and she barely even talked to me except when we were going after Emma.

I thought I needed Brielle. It was definitely better to be her friend than her enemy. Because those were the only two choices.

And since that day in court, she hasn't even texted me. So I figure, maybe it's for the best that it's over.

But still. She was my friend for a long time. I know she's lonely, deep down. I know she needs people. I know she lashes out because that's what she does. I know her pretty well, actually, and I do miss her. But I can't talk to her anymore.

I'm still looking down at the table, at the line where the

laptop intersects the grain of the wood, but I can feel Carmichael's eyes on me. His hand on mine. Mom and Alex are banging into the house now, and Carmichael gives my hand one last squeeze before letting go and sitting back in his chair again.

'Hello?' Mom calls. She comes into the kitchen and sees us, sees Tommy in the den with the TV on. 'Oh, good, everyone's here,' she says. 'We're having tacos! You know what that means!'

I groan, but I get up and help her unload the groceries she's carrying. *Tacos* means I'm cooking – because they require practically no cooking at all. Mom's actually making good on her promise to spend more family time, though I gotta say, spending every Saturday night learning to steam broccoli or not burn rice is already getting a little old. But tacos are easy, at least. And you can put lots of cheese on them.

Mom smiles at me, tossing some avocados on the counter. *She smiles more now*, I think. Maybe we all do.

'Can I help?' Carmichael asks. 'I can make guacamole.'

'Excellent!' says Mom. 'Yes, I will get you a knife and a bowl, and let's see . . . '

I open the package of hamburgers and get out a skillet. In a minute the kitchen is filling up with the smell of the meat. Mom is asking Carmichael about his essay, and he tells her he's writing about a BMX race where he took a really bad fall but finished anyway. She tells him it sounds perfect. Tommy comes back in and washes the lettuce, I think just so he can spend more time around Carmichael. I cut up a tomato and line up bowls on the counter: tomato, lettuce, salsa, shredded cheese, black olives.

In my head, though, I'm thinking about my letter.

Dear Brielle, What were we so mad about?

Was I a terrible friend?

Were you?

Dear Brielle, I'm sorry.

I'm sorry.

Finally Alex feels left out enough to come in and set the table. I hand him the litre of soda Mom's letting us have – only because it's Saturday – and he gleefully starts shaking it up. 'Hey!' Tommy and I yell at the same time. Alex is still grinning, but he stops. He puts the bottle on the table and comes back for the bowls of taco toppings, transferring them two at a time.

'Can I put peanut butter on mine?' he asks.

'Gross,' Tommy declares.

'You don't know,' Alex says. 'Maybe it's good! You never tried it.'

'I do know,' Tommy tells him. 'It's gross.'

'Okay, guys, let's sit down,' Mom says. She pours herself a glass of wine and lifts it, smiling at me. 'You'll drive them to the ER when they get sick on peanut butter tacos, right?'

'Yep,' I say. 'You can drink the whole bottle if you want. I got this.'

Tommy rolls his eyes, embarrassed, but by then we're all fighting over the shredded cheese and the olives,

345

overstuffing our taco shells, making loud crunching noises as we start to eat.

For a minute I just look around the table. It's not, like, the perfect American family or anything, I know that. It's not what I thought I'd be doing on a Saturday night my senior year. It's pretty boring, definitely.

But I take a deep breath and smile. I take another breath. And another.

I just keep breathing.

Dear Brielle,

You were a good friend to me. You taught me how to be tough. You taught me to stick up for myself. You thought I was pretty, that I deserved a boyfriend and friends and parties and cute clothes. You made me laugh.

But I wasn't a good friend to you. I didn't know how to help you. I didn't know how to stop all the stuff we did to Emma. I should have said it was wrong. It felt wrong, but it felt good, too, to be angry and hateful and mean. But maybe there could've been another way. There must've been another way.

I miss you. I wish we hadn't grown apart. I wish you were at school. But wherever you are, I hope you're happy. I think I might be happy. I'm working on it, anyway.

Stay strong. Love,

Sara

Dear Emma,

I'll spend the rest of my life being sorry. But I'll also be more careful. I won't assume that everyone is strong. I won't assume I know everything about someone just by how they act. I'll try to remember, so that maybe some day I'll feel like I deserve your forgiveness.

Wherever you are, I hope you're happy. And feeling stronger.

Love,

    Sara

Acknowledgments

So many people helped me through the process of writing this book, and I will be forever grateful. Thanks especially to Rebecca Mazur, Erica Jensen, Devi Pillai, and Abby Mcaden for being amazing friends and career counsellors for many, many years. To my fellow writers in PSCWW, thank you for the much-needed deadlines and the excellent notes.

There aren't enough superlatives to describe my agent, Holly Root, and my editor, Donna Bray, so I'll just say: Wow. It is a true honour to work with you. And I am grateful to everyone at Waxman Leavell Literary, HarperCollins Children's Books, and Balzer + Bray for bringing this book to life.

To my mom: It's not an exaggeration when I say you're the best mom in the history of anything, ever, and I love you more than even makes sense.

And to Andy and Calvin, what can I say? You've made my dreams come true.

Author's Note

This book is entirely a work of fiction, but it was inspired, unfortunately, by true stories – and one in particular.

In January 2010, a young student at South Hadley High School tragically took her own life. I went to college in South Hadley, and a dear friend of mine works at the high school, so the event was particularly upsetting – though of course even more so for the families in that small community, who quickly saw their lives turned upside down by a precedent-setting lawsuit against six other students at South Hadley High, accused of bullying and harassing the girl who killed herself.

I couldn't stop thinking about the girls on both sides of this story. And I couldn't stop thinking that, no matter what the accused bullies had done, surely they couldn't have intended for anyone to lose her life – surely no one is that vicious. But we do all have our moments, and our limits. We've each felt deeply hurt by the actions of others; we've said things we regret.

It made me incredibly sad – and still does – that the kids in these stories are kids. As a teenager you're so close to being an adult, and in many ways you have all the responsibilities of one. But you also – or you're supposed to – have your whole life ahead of you too. It's the time we try new things and make mistakes. It's the time we get deeply hurt, say hurtful things, and learn to apologize. It's the incredibly crucial time when we learn that other people are also hurting, are also victims. We learn that life is complicated, and our version of the story isn't the only version.

I wish we had better tools to deal with bullying. I certainly don't know what the answer is, and I know the problem grows more complicated as our methods of communication grow vaster and more unwieldy. But it seems to me that there's always more to the story – at least two sides, if not four or seven or one hundred. And I believe that everyone deserves to be heard.

Other Resources

www.beatbullying.org

www.bulliesout.com

www.bullying.co.uk
Lots of information about bullying, particularly cyber bullying. It includes a 24-hour helpline: help@bullying.co.uk

wouldhavesaid.com
A website that gives young people the chance to express something important to family and friends who have passed away, or with whom they have lost contact.

Childline

Tel: 0800 1111
Calls to Childline are free and don't show up on itemised phone bills from landlines, 3, BT Mobile, Fresh, O2, EE, Virgin and Vodafone.

www.childline.org.uk

Samaritans

Tel: 08457 909090
Calls are charged at local rates.
Email: jo@samaritans.org

The
DUFF

Seventeen-year-old Bianca Piper is smart, cynical, loyal - and well aware that she's not the hot one in her group of friends. But when high-school jock and all round moron Wesley Rush tells her she's a DUFF - a Designated, Ugly Fat Friend - Bianca does not see the funny side.

She may not be a beauty but she'd never stoop so low as to go anywhere near the likes of Wesley ... Or would she? Bianca is about to find out that attraction defies looks and that sometimes your sworn enemies can become your best friends...

Funny, thoughtful and written by the author when she was only 17, this novel will speak to every teenage girl who has ever thought they were a Duff.

April 2012

Also available as an ebook

www.hodderchildrens.co.uk

Hodder Children's Books

LOVE IS A NUMBER

'It's the perfect romance...' Dawn O'Porter

LEE MONROE

When her beloved boyfriend Huck dies, Eloise is wrecked. The ultimate golden couple, she will never find love as perfect ever again. Angry and sad, she texts Huck's phone as if he can receive her messages from beyond the grave.

She never expected to get a reply ...

Dan is travelling to Spain in one last hurrah before uni and real life kick in. One night on his travels, Dan discovers an abandoned phone. He pockets it, then forgets about it.

He never expected it to ring ...